SOUL SIGN

A Zackie Novel

Book 3

Reyna Favis

Dedicated to Bunny Kliman, who may never read this because it's too scary, and Lee Kliman, who may get a mental motion picture when reading the story.

Also by Reyna Favis:

Zackie Story Series

SOUL SEARCH

SOUL SCENT

SOUL SIGN

CHAPTER 1

Any day on this side of the dirt is a good day.

Like other mostly true proverbs, there were exceptions to the rule. For instance, there were those whose remains rested below the dirt, but whose spirits wandered around topside. These souls suffered miserably until they got the help they needed to find their way. After meeting Cam and Zackie, I had gained vast experience in the art of surviving and dealing with these restless spirits.

I clenched my teeth and repeated the mantra about it being a good day as I carried out another moldy box of broken kitchen gadgets from the basement. What had started as an outing to see the restoration of the eighteenth-century Roseberry Homestead had turned into forced volunteer labor. My only consolation was that I had invited Cam to see the house.

Covered in cobwebs and dust, he carried a similar

decaying cardboard box. Cam extended his lower lip and blew upward to dislodge a dust bunny from a shaggy, gray eyebrow. His face flushed with exertion, he glared at me. "Fia, the least you could do when you issue an invitation is to simultaneously issue a warning that there will be work involved. I could have politely declined to become a 911-call-waiting-to-happen."

Shrugging, I walked on to the dump area. "Blame it on Peyton. I didn't know either." I tossed my box with a satisfied sigh, wiped the sweat from my face with a dirty sleeve, and took a break to watch Cam struggle.

Cam was like me, except old and British. He was in his fifties and I was in my twenties, so we had just enough in common to argue about. Besides being search and rescue workers, we shared the ability to communicate with the dead, and we were both dedicated to helping lost spirits move on. The moving on part would not have been possible without Zackie.

Zackie was…complicated. First and foremost, she was a Psychopomp, escorting these lost spirits to the afterlife. Cam and Zackie were an inseparable pair when I first met them. Lately, the Psychopomp had been spending more time with me after someone tried to break in to my place. It was a kind gesture, but Zackie was an insufferable roommate.

Whenever I asked Cam about the Psychopomp's true age, he'd dance around the subject, but he did once mention Anubis, the ancient Egyptian jackal god, patron of lost souls and the helpless. These days, she resembled a Plott Hound—so much so, that a backwoods bear hunter christened her Zackie when he offered to buy her from Cam. Too amused by this *nom de guerre* to establish a better name, Cam just went with it, and so, Zackie she remained. Fortunately, she had a sense of humor, even if she tended to lack empathy for the living. She demonstrated this trait by lazing in the sun while Cam and I labored with the endless boxes.

"Hey, you two. Less chatter, more hauling." Peyton hefted two stacked boxes to the dump zone and deposited them neatly on top of the pile. She was a large, muscled woman, ex-military and resource officer on my search team. Peyton was also training to be a master stonemason, so I was sure she was enjoying seeing how the old stone house was being restored. More important, she was recovering from a spirit haunting and needed something to brighten her outlook.

Cam muttered some dark expletive under his breath and brought his box to the mound of garbage. Eying the top of the pile critically, he shook his head and then opened his arms to let gravity do the work. His box dropped heavily, landing at the foot of Peyton's growing mountain of junk. Unsurprisingly, the cardboard burst open on impact and a cascade of very old, but still colorful, brittle plastic toys tumbled on to the grass.

Peyton blew out a breath. "Now look what you've done." She knelt by the spill and began scooping the debris back into what remained of the box, but then paused in mid action. "Hold on...what's this?" Reaching into the ruined box, she pulled out a stack of sepia photographs, the edges curled and brittle with age.

Cam and I watched over her shoulder as she flipped through the old photos. "What the f-ff..." Her hands stilled and she froze. "They're all dead. These are pictures of dead people."

"Hand them here." Cam reached out his hand and took the stack. I stood at his elbow and looked more carefully at the photographs. There were pictures of children and adults, eyes sunken and their bodies lacking the vitality and animation of the living. Some were on beds

4

or in caskets and surrounded by flower arrangements. Others were propped up by what may have been family members or, even more disturbing, wooden supports that fixed the bodies in standing positions. Hands, unless carefully posed, were frozen in uneasy and unnatural positions that registered in a primal part of my brain and branded the people in these images as empty of life.

Peyton rose to her feet, her face ashen, the toys forgotten. "Do we need to call the police? I realize these are old, but…"

"No." Cam shook his head. "These are *memento mori*." When he saw only confused looks from Peyton and me, he backtracked and tried to explain. "Taking photographs of the recently deceased was a custom in the nineteenth and early twentieth centuries. It was a way for grieving families to memorialize dead loved ones."

"Well, that's a relief. I thought this was some kind of psycho killer thing, posing his victims." Peyton relaxed her stance and the color crept back into her face.

I frowned, fingering the edge of the top photograph, a slumped child held between two siblings, their grief frozen in time. "But why take a picture of the dead? Why not get pictures of them in life, looking happy? Isn't that a better way to remember them?"

"Photography was accessible, but it was still expensive. You're not going to see a lot of poor people in these types of images. For the families, it was usually a matter of getting a picture of someone deceased, or having no picture at all." Cam handed me the stack and I slowly went through each image, trying to get a sense of the people and their time.

I shook my head. "There seem to be an awful lot of pictures. And so many children…"

"It was a different time. Death occurred at home and was a part of life. And remember, childhood mortality was extremely high. There were no vaccinations then. Graveyards are full of children who died from diseases that rarely take lives today." Cam shrugged, helpless to undo the suffering of the past.

"What should we do with them? It seems disrespectful to just throw them in the pile of crap." Peyton gestured toward the heaped trash.

"I suppose we should hand them over to the historical society." Cam's eyes shifted and he rubbed his jaw. "Most families are a little squeamish about having these types of pictures of their ancestors."

Gently, I tried to neaten the pile of photos before handing them back to Cam. "Maybe we should give them to Joel. He can give them to the society." Joel Armstrong was my landlord and friend. He'd also had a frightening experience with a haunting that we'd helped to resolve. I had learned about the Roseberry Homestead because Joel was the contractor working to restore the building, and he thought because I had been a history major, I'd be interested in seeing it.

"Good idea. Let's pass the buck." Cam walked back to the house and we fell in line behind him. We circled the building, dodging scaffolds that supported workers repointing the sturdy limestone of the homestead's exterior. The house was built in the Georgian architectural style with four, equal-sized rooms separated by a center hall running down the middle on both the first and second floors. It had a fearsome symmetry, both literally and figuratively squarely built.

Finding an entrance that led into the kitchen, we stopped to admire the enormous hearth that took up most of one wall. Moving on, we called for Joel, wandering down

7

the hall on the main floor and stepping carefully when the floors swayed subtly underfoot. The walls, stripped of their layers of modern wallpaper and paint, looked tatty and worn, but every now and again, we'd see a glimpse of a fancy stencil from the house's early days and it gave me hope for its future.

We found Joel on the second floor. He was a big man and took up most of the hall. Shaking his graying head in disapproval, he pointed at the twentieth century bathroom fixtures. "We gotta tear all of this out. It's not right for how the house needs to be."

Cam nodded. "Perhaps a privy in the yard would be more amenable to the new look." Waving the stack of photographs, he continued. "So, Joel, we found these photographs in one of the boxes destined for the rubbish heap. We thought you might want to hang on to them and give them to the historical society."

"Whatcha got there?" Joel stretched out his hand to take the stack.

"Er, pictures of the family, most likely. Some would call it *memento mori*—"

Not one to mince words or evade an issue, Peyton

cut in. "It's post-mortem photography."

Joel's eyes widened and he yanked his hand back as if the photos were on fire. "Oh, hell no. I'm not dealing with that shit again." He shook his head with quick, little movements and stepped back abruptly, hitting the wall behind him in his eagerness to put distance between himself and Cam.

"I see." Cam's mouth turned down and he slowly lowered the stack of photos. "I suppose we shall hang on to these then. At least until you're able to notify someone in the society?"

Joel nodded stiffly and then shifted his eyes as he became aware that Peyton was staring at him. "I'm not crazy."

"Didn't say you were." Peyton pushed a strand of bright red hair out of her face. She quirked her lips and then crossed her arms. "Besides, I know all about 'not being crazy.'"

Joel canted his head and looked at her with new appreciation. "Shoulda clicked when you showed up with these two." Edging his way along the wall toward the stairs, he shrugged a shoulder. "You wanna go get some coffee and talk?"

"Sure. I'd like that." Peyton followed him down the stairs, leaving Cam and me to stare at the plumbing.

I sighed. "Probably the best thing for both of them. They can be their own little support group."

Cam grunted and maneuvered past me to follow the others down the rickety stairs. Pausing near the newel at the bottom, he waited until I caught up with him and then forced the photographs into my hands.

Smirking, he called over his shoulder as he trotted toward the exit. "Not 'it.'"

#

I left the photos facedown on my kitchen counter and Zackie did some counter-surfing to give them a good sniff. I thought about finding a more secure place to keep them out of the splash zone, but time was running short. I'd deal with it later. Dinner at Cam's house was at six sharp and I didn't want to be late, possibly missing out on my share of the fried bread. My childhood friend, Ron Falling-Leaf, and his adopted grandmother, Lenora Ottertooth, still occupied Cam's house. This was despite the fact that the Native American spirit we had called Ron and Lenora to help us with had successfully crossed over. Lenora claimed dreams sent by her shaman grandfather told her to extend their visit, that there was more to be done. Worked for me. Lenora cooked wonderful meals and I was frequently invited to partake. It didn't work so well for Cam, who was a bit out of sorts having his space invaded for such a lengthy period.

A bright flash from the bedroom indicated that Zackie had departed through the portal. Being a Psychopomp, she passed with ease between this world and the next, and she took full advantage of this when she tired of keeping an eye on me. I headed to the bathroom to shower and stripped off my dusty, dirty clothes, throwing them on the floor. I took off the work gloves last, revealing the dead hand. The skin was unnaturally pale, mottled blue-gray with burst blood vessels, and the blackened nails looked as if I had applied nail polish. I had learned my lesson about messing with the portal and this corpse-like appendage, something that was of me but no longer really part of me, was a constant reminder to be wary. Only the dead and Zackie could enter the portal with impunity. An insane and poorly thought out impulse had led me to stick

11

my hand through the portal, and my life had never been the same.

No matter how much time I spent with the dead hand, the appearance of decomposition always made me think that it would soon produce an odor of decay. And I'm pretty sure I wasn't completely wrong about that, since the cadaver dogs on the search team gave their trained alerts whenever they caught a whiff of it. I washed the dead hand with soap and water in the bathroom sink, drying it well and then slipping on a neoprene diver's glove before entering the shower. While the dead hand and I have developed something of a détente over time, the thing still freaked me out, and I couldn't stand having it touch me. I soaped up, rinsed off and then just stood there, glorying in the hot water raining down on me. Just as I was starting to relax, the dead hand shot out and turned off the water.

"What the hell!" I screeched. I was about to turn the water back on when a muffled thud impacted one of the exterior walls of the bathroom. I grabbed the towel from its rack and wrapped it around me, determined not to be caught naked and vulnerable by whatever that was. Stepping soundlessly on to the fluffy blue bathmat, I snatched the wooden rod from the towel rack and held my breath, straining for any subtle sounds. After a handful of seconds had passed with no other sounds, I released my grip on the towel. Hurriedly drying off with one hand, I grasped my only weapon with the other, as I dashed to the bedroom.

Zackie had returned and was lying on my bed, her ears perked and her manner alert. She had heard it too, and she flashed me a sly look. Standing up, she made a sound as if she were clearing her throat and then let loose with full-throated hound baying. It was as if the mythical Wild Hunt had scented the intruder, and the pack, filled with bloodlust, was now on his heels.

I shook my head to clear the ringing in my ears and then threw on fresh jeans and a t-shirt. Stumbling into sneakers before rushing out the door with my wooden rod, I hoped I would catch the bastard in the act. Failing this, I wanted to check for signs of an intruder.

Zackie followed me, and together, we inspected the area outside the bathroom. No one was in sight. Bending down, I examined the grass, wishing I had a flashlight and my hiking stick. Search and rescue had taught me the fundamentals of man-tracking, and I carefully checked the grass for light reflection from human footfall damage or compression, otherwise known as shine. Luck was with me, and I didn't need the flashlight. The angle of the setting sun gave a clear view of disturbed areas in the grass, but my eye could only follow the evidence of sequential footfalls— what trackers call the continuity of sign—for a short distance before I lost it. I would need my hiking stick to measure heel to heel impressions, and at my skill level, it would take hours to trace the footfalls over the field.

"Zackie, do you think you could…" I gestured vaguely toward the track. She obligingly put her nose to the ground, sampling the scent left in the bruised grass that was already starting to heal. Extending her neck, she cast around for the next bolus of scent and then followed the trail at a lope to the edge of the woods. Stopping, she picked her head up and gazed at me. "Okay, I get it. He went through the woods to the street." She trotted back as I squatted down to inspect the ground again, this time looking for something to explain the thump. I saw no scuff marks or anything uneven to warrant a trip or a fall.

Giving up, we went back inside. I returned the wooden rod to the towel rack, draping over it my wet towel and neoprene glove, and then put all my dirty clothes in the hamper. As I applied the mortuary makeup to the dead hand, my mind churned with worry. Obsessively blending the tinted creams until I was satisfied it looked like my other hand, I finally called it quits, that it was close enough. I signaled Zackie it was time to go to Cam's. Zackie waited patient as the Sphinx, while I first turned and tested all the locks on my front door and then rummaged through the SAR equipment in my trunk. After I found and pocketed the bear spray, I nodded to her and we clambered into the car.

"Thanks," I said, grateful that she stayed with me, driving to Cam's instead of hopping into the portal and reaching his house by that more expeditious route.

# # #

I climbed up the stairs to Cam's front porch, stopping short as the door silently opened, and Lucas stepped out to greet me. Seeing her chance, Zackie surged forward, squeezing past him into the house. Before closing the door behind him, he turned off the light. It was my turn to surge forward, and I rushed into Lucas's open arms. Hidden by the shadows from the prying eyes of the neighbors, he kissed me like a starved man, like he needed this to keep breathing. It had been days since I'd last seen him, and I returned his embrace with enthusiasm, pressing myself tightly against his body and running my fingers through his long blond hair. Lucas was the lust of my life. It was too early in the relationship for me to be able to say more than that, but I thought we were heading in the right direction and, maybe, eventually, more could be said.

I hadn't seen much of Lucas in the last few weeks. With Halloween just around the corner, the work schedule for his ghost hunter cable TV show was taking almost every free minute. The only upside to this separation was also not being subjected to the spirit of Hannah, Lucas's late wife. They had married right out of college and cancer had taken her only a few years later. I felt for her, I really did, but during our last interaction when I thought we could make peace, she damned near killed me. Since then, we'd been keeping our distance, aided by Lucas's demanding work schedule.

When we finally came up for air, he smiled at me with a roguish twinkle in his eye. "Is that a gun in your pocket, or are you just glad to see me?"

I forced a laugh, since I still felt uneasy. "It's bear spray. I think Rory came calling this afternoon." His face went still, and I quickly added, "I'm all right. Nothing happened."

Lucas moved away, holding me by the shoulders and gave me a penetrating look. Satisfied that I really was all right, he caught my hand and pulled me toward the door. "Let's go inside, so you only have to tell this story once."

We found Cam, Lenora, and Ron at the dining room table, with Zackie lying comfortably below deck. An aroma of cooking food flooded my senses, and the scent of some delectable, savory spice teased me, making my stomach grumble. My friends nibbled companionably on cheese and crackers, while discussing the merits of goat cheese compared to cheese made from cow's milk. Lucas pulled out a chair, waited for me to sit and then announced, "Fia had a visit from Rory today."

Conversation stopped. Ron sat forward, his eyes dark and deadly. He bunched one hand into a fist and the cords from the muscles in his forearm protruded in stark relief. He looked like a bull ready to charge. "Maybe we should pay that *mahtёnu* a visit."

Lucas nodded in agreement, but Lenora shot a worried look at Ron. "No one's goin' anywhere. I got dinner cooking." Shifting her eyes, her sharp gaze fell on me. "What happened?"

"I was in the shower and I heard a thump." I quickly explained the events of the afternoon, leaving out the part about the dead hand. Only Cam knew about it and talking about the dead hand felt like discussing venereal disease. "Anyway, it was just like last time when someone tried to break into my place. The trail disappeared into the woods, probably went to the street, and no one saw anything. We can't be sure it was Rory."

Cam rolled his eyes. "Oh, bullocks, of course it's Rory."

Rory was a spoiled trust fund kid, temporarily slumming it until he came of age and could cash in. After numerous under-the-table payoffs that kept Rory just out of reach of the long arm of the law, his family had had enough of his crap and cut him off. Without any white-collar skills, he ended up cleaning crime scenes to make a living and that was how he came to cross my path. Everyone at the table was well acquainted with how he harassed me on the job. They'd also met Rory in person during a disastrous night out at a bar and, and as a result, thought of him as something lower than the wad of filth you'd scrape off the bottom of your shoe. So far, every time he had come after me, it didn't end well for him. Rory blamed me for his humiliations and hated my guts in a deep and abiding way.

"Maybe I should've followed him into the woods to give the police a positive ID." I leaned an elbow on the table and rested my cheek against my palm. This constant need for vigilance against one thing or another was draining. It would be nice to get something—just anything—off my radar.

"Absolutely not." Lucas leaned forward across the table to make eye contact. "He could have ambushed you out there, and no one would have known. You did the right thing to not pursue him."

"I don't know about that. I would have had Zackie with me. You can't sneak up on a hound. She would have smelled him coming and warned me."

"And what if Zackie had...er, bit him?" Cam arched an eyebrow. "It could have caused no end of trouble with the authorities."

I immediately took his meaning and nodded glumly in agreement. Zackie almost killed a guy who threatened us with a gun. To be honest, I think he would have been better off dead instead of in a persistent vegetative state. The doctors diagnosed it as a brain aneurysm—aneurysm, my ass...

Cam was right. It would have been highly suspicious if two people we had an altercation with were suddenly stricken with a rare medical condition. Better to avoid conflict and avoid notice.

Lenora stood. "Food's ready. Full belly's what you need, girl." She nudged Ron's shoulder. "Help me carry." Lenora returned with a basket of fried bread, but it looked different, white with browned spots from a heated pan instead of the deep fried, uniform golden brown I expected.

"What's this?" I stared pointedly at the basket just as Ron set a huge bowl of steaming, yellow stew on a trivet, and then occupied a second trivet with a hot bowl of rice.

Lenora put a piece of the strange bread on my plate. "This's naan and that's chicken curry. Indian food." When I refused to blink, she continued. "I met an Indian lady in the grocery store. We exchanged recipes." She went back to the kitchen and returned with a creamy spinach dish. "What, you expect frybread every night?"

I took a tentative bite of the naan and wondered what sort of reaction dinner would get at the Indian lady's house. The naan was different from the fried bread I'd become addicted to, but it was hot, chewy, moist, and absolutely delicious. I crammed more bread in my mouth and thought that Lenora could do no wrong in the kitchen.

A canine muzzle popped up from under the table, the rest of the face hidden by the tablecloth. Dutifully, I handed a loaf of naan to the gaping maw and then counted my fingers. Satisfied with the bread offering, Zackie retreated under the table. I turned my attention to heaping naan, rice, curry, and spinach on to a plate, and then tried to be neat about consuming the mountain of food. Consumption worked beautifully—neatness, not so much.

I discreetly dabbed at my face and hands with a napkin and then attempted to clean up the spots of curry on the tablecloth. Cam compressed his lips but said nothing when he noticed the damage. He had long ago purchased a specially treated tablecloth that was stain-resistant.

"Sorry," I said, ducking my head.

Cam exhaled a martyred sigh. "Oh, think nothing of it. I only thought perhaps you'd like a little red wine to go with that."

"How about I brew some coffee instead?" I got up and made for the kitchen. Lenora had set up the coffee maker with fresh grounds and water, so all I had to do was turn it on. While it brewed, I gathered up the sugar bowl, mugs, and teaspoons and brought them to the table. Returning to the kitchen, I hunted through Cam's refrigerator to find the little porcelain creamer. In a quick move, the dead hand snatched up something small from the shelf and held it in front of my face. It wasn't the creamer I was looking for.

Letting the refrigerator door close on its own, I backed up to look at the item under the brighter overhead light. My eyes widened as I realized what I held. Calling out to the dining room, I didn't bother trying to hide the urgency in my voice. "Cam, you better come and see this."

Cam and everyone else crowded into the kitchen. I held up the tiny doll. Tied off with string, the arms, legs, and head emerged as loops made from a braid of black, wiry hair. Spider webs and dust clung to the doll, as did a faint musty odor.

Meeting Cam's eye, I lifted the doll slightly with

the dead hand and looked for an explanation. "Found this in your refrigerator." Cam gave a small nod, that he understood the dead hand's role in the discovery. "I didn't see anything that said it has to be refrigerated after opening, so how'd it get there?"

Lenora and Ron exchanged an uneasy look and backed away from the doll. Cam narrowed his eyes and muttered, "Well, obviously I didn't put it there." He put out his hand. "Give it here."

I placed the braided hair in Cam's outstretched hand, and Lucas pulled out his cell phone. "Hold it still for a second." His mouth drawn down in consternation, he took a picture of the thing lying in Cam's palm. "So, what is it? It looks like it's made from hair."

"An apportation, near as I can tell," Cam said.

Lucas raised an eyebrow. "Explain."

"It's the transference of an object from one place to another by a spirit." Cam shrugged a shoulder. "Someone is trying to get our attention."

"So, it ended up in your refrigerator. But where did it come from?" Lucas's eyebrow persisted in its upright position. It would have been damned sexy had it not been for the circumstances.

Trying for humor, I gave a flippant answer. "Somewhere dusty and dirty?"

Cam cocked his head at me. "Brilliant observation. And where have we been recently that was dusty and dirty?"

My mouth fell open, surprised that I accidentally hit upon something relevant. "The Roseberry Homestead." I reached out and traced a braided leg with my finger. "Do you think it's human hair?"

"Yes, I believe so." Cam nodded and then frowned. "It might be another form of *memento mori*, but a doll would be somewhat unusual. They'd normally make rings or brooches from hair as keepsakes."

Lenora shuddered. "Our people cut our hair in mourning, but we put it in the grave. We don't take hair from the dead and make *fakakta* jewelry."

Ron stared at her bewildered. "*Fakakta*? What the heck does that mean?"

"Wait, you don't know what it means? I thought it

was Lenape." I looked from Ron to Lenora, trying to puzzle this out.

"Means silly, ridiculous." Lenora nodded solemnly. "I also met a Jewish lady at the grocery store."

Cam chuckled. "Welcome to the cultural crossroads that is New Jersey."

Lucas stared at the ceiling and made an exasperated sound. "Can we please just focus, people?" When he was sure he had our attention back, he pointed at the doll. "I could take a small sample and have it analyzed. Then we'd know for sure if the hair was human."

"Good idea, Lucas." Cam went to hand him the doll. "Take this, so you don't run short of sample."

I grabbed the doll before Lucas could take it. "Not 'it' again, Cam?"

"What? It's probably perfectly safe." Cam forced an innocent look. "Besides, he'd never notice it if it weren't."

I rolled my eyes. True enough, Lucas was probably the least sensitive person you'd ever meet. Despite our best efforts, he was completely unaware that the spirit of his wife stayed with him. Still, I did not like the idea of how

25

defenseless he'd be if faced with anything from the unseen world. "Uh-uh, not a chance. I'll keep the doll and just give him a few strands." I turned to Lucas. "That should be enough, shouldn't it?"

Lucas nodded, a corner of his mouth lifting in a skeptical half-smile. He clearly wasn't buying into the idea that the doll could be dangerous to him but wasn't going to argue the point. "The guy I know does forensic analyses for criminal investigations. He doesn't need much."

Cam found some tweezers and an envelope. I carefully pulled three strands of hair from the bundle and teased them into the folded paper. Sealing the flap, I handed the packaged hairs to Lucas. The doll went into a zip-lock bag that I placed in my cargo pocket.

At Lenora's insistence, we next disinfected the refrigerator shelf by spritzing it with kitchen cleanser and wiping it down. In the process of removing everything from the shelf, I found the porcelain creamer.

Returning to the dining room, we drank our belated after-dinner coffee and scrupulously avoided talking about the doll. Still, I was acutely aware of it in my pocket, and I had a hard time sitting still or focusing on the conversation.

When Cam rapped his knuckles on the table to get my attention, I knew I missed something important.

"Anyone home?" Cam raised his eyebrows inquiringly.

"Huh? Sorry, did you just ask me something?"

"I wanted to know if you sent off the paperwork for your passport."

I grimaced. "Yeah, I put it in the mail with the mug shot that makes me look like a serial killer. I should have it back in time for the Scotland trip."

"Serial killer?" Lucas grinned. "Sometimes you can look a little intense, but serial killer? Why didn't you just have them take another picture?"

"The lighting was bad, I was in an evil mood, and I was out of time because I had to get to work." I waved a hand as I made excuses, trying to dismiss the whole thing. Lucas was probably incapable of taking a bad picture, so he just wouldn't understand. "I went with it. Figured the passport wouldn't see the light of day much, since I don't travel a lot."

"True enough," Cam said. "It's only ten years, after

27

all. You can get a new passport when this one expires."

My shoulders slumped as I considered this. "Great. Maybe I should just resign myself to getting special attention from Customs for the next ten years."

"Any new developments on the Scotland case?" Cam asked Lucas.

"Not really. The investigative team is still analyzing the film footage of the jogger who was attacked. For now, it's holding up—no special effects were added, nothing's been tampered with." Lucas paused to sip his coffee. "We're still treating it as unexplained paranormal activity, and we're still scheduled to tape a show on location there next month—and speaking of work, I'd better get going. Early meeting tomorrow."

Lenora declined Lucas's offer to help with the cleanup, and she handed him a bag of leftovers before ushering him to the door. I followed Lucas outside to see him off.

The crisp night air smelled of burning wood from a dozen fireplaces in the neighborhood. I hugged myself, shivering as he opened the car door and placed the bag of food inside. Turning, Lucas wrapped his arms around me, and I leaned into his warmth. I ran my hand along his chest to his shoulders and breathed in his scent before tangling my fingers in his hair and raising my face to find his lips. He took his time, slowly exploring, caressing and tasting. I was breathless when he finished with me.

"You know, you could come and stay with me until this thing with Rory is over." He breathed raggedly as he kissed my neck, whispering his suggestion as he reached my earlobe. My head was swimming, and I almost said yes. It would be so easy to go home with him. But then Lucas suddenly stopped and gazed into my eyes with a look that was both confused and desolate. "I—I'm sorry." He closed his eyes and took a deep breath. I felt his muscles tense. When his eyes opened, a veil had dropped, and his strong emotions had been buried in a place beyond my reach. "I shouldn't pressure you. Maybe now is not the right time." He didn't meet my eyes when he spoke, so I was almost sure it was not what he meant.

Struggling for clarity, I put some physical distance between us and tried to calm my raging hormones. I needed to think and try to understand this. In the space of a heartbeat, he told me he wanted me and then he pushed me away. I shook my head, finding no understanding, and reached for some way to give myself a dignified retreat. "No, you're right. Running away won't solve the Rory problem. I need to catch him in the act and tell the police."

Lucas looked relieved and relaxed his stance as he went along with my redirection. "Or catch him in the act, so you can beat the crap out of him."

"How well you know me." I forced down feelings of vulnerability and gave him a cocky smile.

Having gotten his feet back under him, Lucas winked back. "I remember seeing him squirming on the ground in pain the last time he tried something. I know you can take care of yourself." Touching my cheek, he continued. "I'd just prefer it if you didn't have to."

I put my hand over his and rested my cheek against his palm. He cared about me, wanted to protect me. How was I supposed to reconcile this with his sudden uncharacteristic indecision? Sighing, I thought how nice it would be if things were easier, if there were no confusing twists of emotion. Reluctantly, I released his hand and leaned in for a last kiss, a test of whether things were now weird between us. "You better go." The kiss was sweet. We were back in safe territory.

With a tired smile, Lucas nodded in resignation, stole one more kiss and then got into the car. As he pulled away, I caught a faint whiff of ammonia and saw Hannah sitting in the passenger seat.

I thought about taking a cold shower. Maybe that would dull the hormonal aftershocks inspired by Lucas. Sitting up, I grabbed my phone instead and checked the time—a little after two in the morning. I was tired, but far too restless to sleep. Disgusted with myself, I put the phone back on the nightstand and rubbed my face. In a last-ditch effort to get some rest, I threw myself facedown on the bed and willed my mind and body to be still.

It was no good. Tossing and turning, my thoughts wandered, and I began agonizing over Lucas and Hannah. Maybe I should have bulled my way through the weird vibe and gone home with him. But weird vibe aside, what was I going to do about the dead hand? Thinking about it meandering around during the throes of passion made my stomach turn. And maybe I was over-estimating Lucas's desire for me. What had caused him to pull back so

31

suddenly? Maybe he wasn't as into me as I'd thought. There was also a slim possibility that I read him wrong. Maybe he really did have an old-fashioned sense of gallantry. Or, worst case scenario, he wasn't really over Hannah's passing, and he couldn't bring himself to sleep with someone else. At the end of the night, it was Hannah who went home with him, so maybe I had my answer. It definitely felt like she'd won this round.

I was almost happy when the callout came. My phone erupted with the unmistakable blaring and discordant ringtone that announced a text from the county's emergency dispatch. For once, I did not regret having to get up in the middle of the night to respond.

I snatched up the phone and jumped out of bed, reading the text as I fumbled for the light switch. An elderly woman with dementia had wandered away from the home she shared with her daughter and son-in-law. She was dressed in a pink flannel nightgown that was no match for the cold autumn night. As I sent a quick text to let them know I was available and responding, I noticed that Cam's team had also been called out.

Rushing to the closet, I threw on a base layer for warmth and then tactical pants and a high visibility orange shirt, both made from ripstop material. I sat on the floor to pull on sock liners, followed by wool socks and then shoved my feet into hiking boots that smelled faintly of river mud. Tying the laces securely with double loops like a surgeon's knot—difficult to come loose, but easy to untie—I took a moment to think about whether I had enough food and water in my car.

The phone continued to sound as searchers texted in availability, and county dispatch was able to provide more information on the subject. I took another look at the accumulating texts to find out where to report for staging. Getting to my feet, I made for the front door, snatching the bear spray from my kitchen counter and glancing briefly at the stack of photos and the limp doll in the zip-lock bag. I gave a yell as I pulled the door shut and tested the locks. "Zackie! We have to go."

It was much colder than earlier in the night, and the metal on the car's door handle sucked the heat out of my hand. As I opened the driver's side door, I spied Zackie reclining comfortably in the backseat. Not unexpected, but it still startled me. Settling behind the steering wheel, I turned the key, put the car in gear, and pulled out. In the rearview mirror, I caught a shadowy movement near my front door, and I braked. For a split second, I was undecided whether to continue or to go after the intruder, but then I lost any sign of movement. By the time I pulled out my phone to call the police, I couldn't be sure there had been anything by my door. All was still, so maybe it was just a trick of light. And when I considered that the elderly lady was out there wandering around in the dark, probably confused and very cold, my decision was made for me. She was at-risk for hypothermia and falling injuries, making her the higher priority. I pressed on the accelerator and drove to staging.

# # #

Cam leaned against his truck in the parking lot of the elementary school. The local authorities had selected this site as our staging environment because it was close to the subject's home and had ample parking for first responders. "Did you bring my dog?" Cam said this like it was an inside joke, and I fully expected him to elbow me in the ribs, winking.

I rolled my eyes and ignored him, turning my attention instead to the Psychopomp. "Zackie, your human appears to need direction." Zackie paid us no heed and leaped from my car, her muscles bunching and flowing sinuously beneath her reddish coat. After a full-body stretch and a yawn, she shook off and then jumped on to Cam's lowered tailgate before making herself comfortable inside the truck's cap. I shook my head and went to my trunk to pull out a coat with reflective material sewn on the front and back. "The ride over must have been exhausting."

Cam grunted agreement. He pulled a blanket from the truck's cap and placed it on the tailgate before sitting. "You missed the briefing. The lady's name is Millie and she disappeared about two hours ago. They think she's trying to make her way back to her former home, where she lived before moving in with her daughter. She took her purse."

"Has she walked off before?"

Cam nodded. "They said she was found a few blocks from home, but this was during the summer."

"Is she on any meds?"

"Just blood pressure. She's in pretty good health, aside from the dementia."

That was at least one piece of good news. "How about a cane or walker? How's she on her feet?"

"She's a great walker, according to her daughter. They take walks for exercise every day."

I chewed on my lip. If she was really missing for two hours and she walked well, she could have gone as far as two and half miles in just about any direction. "Anything else I should know?" When Cam shook his head, I slipped into the coat and zipped up. "Okay, I'm going to sign in. I'll be right back."

The trailer housing Incident Command was abuzz with activity, so I made it quick, to get out from under foot. Finding the sign-in sheet, I put down my name, team affiliation and identified myself as a land searcher, then grabbed a map of the area and a printout with a picture of Millie. Before hustling out of the trailer, I jotted down the radio frequency to use and then headed back to the parking lot to wait with Cam for a task to be assigned.

Cam spread out his blanket, so I wouldn't have to sit on cold metal when I joined him on the tailgate. We spent some time studying the map. Millie's home, the Point Last Seen, was marked. We drew a circle around it with the edges set at two and a half miles from the house. It was almost twenty square miles of search area. If we tried to comb the entire region with the resources we had, there was no way Millie would survive long enough in this cold to be found alive. Incident Command would be looking inside the circle for high probability areas to search. There were other family homes, a small strip mall, and a neighborhood park with a pond.

Cam pointed at the pond. "Hope they sent a task to the park." The water could be a huge attractant for people with dementia, and I was worried for Millie.

I shuddered. "She'd either drown or freeze to death if she went in. Let's hope she's not there. Maybe she found a place out of the wind and holed up."

Feeling cold, restless, and uneasy, I jumped off the tailgate and paced around the parked cars. By my third circuit, I had my head down and my hands tucked into my armpits. Steve was moving fast and if it weren't for the high visibility orange he wore, we might have collided. Slight and blond, Steve was Merlin's handler, but I saw no sign of the Belgian Malinois air scent dog as I skidded to a halt. Steve was fully kitted out with pack and eye protection, his radio spitting static in his chest harness. He held a task sheet in his gloved hand, and he looked serious.

"Geez, Fia, you gotta watch where you're going, but glad I found you. Where's Cam?" I pointed, and Steve looked past me to see Cam still seated on the tailgate. Grabbing my arm, he hurried toward Cam. "We're being tasked. They found the purse and they need a trailing dog."

Cam slid from his perch and began rummaging through the truck's bed for equipment. "Where'd they find the purse? Did anyone touch it?"

"Near a little pond in a park. Law enforcement sent a picture to the family for confirmation, but no one has touched it. Waiting for the canine."

I dug through my trunk to find the chest harness that held my GPS and radio, secured it around my torso and then powered up these devices. "Did they call in divers?" I quickly programmed the radio frequency and then yanked out my pack and helmet from under the pile of stuff. My headlamp was on the helmet, so even though the terrain wasn't likely to be rough, I'd wear it to have good light.

"Not yet. She wasn't visible in the water, so she might have gone under, but they're waiting to see what the canine does before they ask divers to suit up." Steve shifted his weight, impatient to get started.

"Just in case, you're an EMT, right?" I clicked on my light and angled it down, so I wouldn't blind anyone.

"Yeah, I am. Are we ready to go?" Steve took a few steps before looking over his shoulder to make sure we were with him. As Cam, Zackie and I followed, he radioed Incident Command. "Task 14 heading out."

It was a short walk to the community park. A small group of searchers and police surrounded the purse, and Cam backed them away to give Zackie room to work.

Cam placed Zackie's harness near the purse and then led her in a large circle around the items. I knew she was familiarizing herself with the scents in the environment as she walked the circle. A thirty-foot lead was clipped to her collar, and Cam reeled the line in and out as Zackie explored the area. Cam kept up a running banter encouraging her to find the subject, mostly for the benefit of the police and searchers who were watching. Coming back to the purse, he slipped the harness over Zackie's head, pulled a strap under her belly and then clicked the end into a heavy snap buckle to secure the harness on her body. After Cam unclipped the long lead from her collar and fixed it to the metal ring on the back of the harness, they were ready to go.

Pointing to the purse, Cam waited for Zackie to dip her nose to the last thing Millie probably touched, and gave a command to take scent. Her head came up and when she pointed her muzzle toward the little pond, my heart sank. Cam gave the final command and told Zackie to get on trail. She lunged toward the water. Steve and I followed behind, while the others watched from a distance. If she went to the water's edge and then jumped on Cam, it meant she'd run out of the scent, and Millie had gone into the water. I braced myself for this outcome.

As Zackie approached the pond, she suddenly veered right and followed the water line toward a pocket of dense growth that formed a barrier on one side of the water. Thickets of briars edged the woods and would have dissuaded the average park visitor from going farther, but subjects with dementia were different. Once people with dementia chose a direction, they would continue, oblivious to any natural hazards and obstacles in their path.

"Millie!" Steve yelled for our subject and we paused to listen before forcing our way through the briars. A thorn caught the cuff of my pants, and I felt something tear. Swearing, I continued to push through and thought about my expensive rip-stop pants. At least the rip wouldn't propagate and maybe I could patch it later. I paused to unhook a thorny branch from my coat and hoped that I wouldn't have to replace the coat.

"Millie!" I called out as loudly as I could. We waited, ears straining for any kind of a response. Hearing nothing, we pushed forward another few steps.

Zackie pulled Cam to the left and he muttered, "Easy." Thorns raked his cheek and snatched at his eye protection. Zackie ceased pulling and waited for him to catch up.

"Everyone up to date on your tetanus shots?" Steve grunted as he pulled free from a taller prickly patch. Then, in a more urgent voice he said, "Full stop. I've found something." Cam and I held our ground and waited. "It's a piece of cloth—looks like pink flannel. She's in here." Steve wrapped flagging tape on a nearby branch and called in the find.

We started moving again, and Cam told us to bear left, that Zackie was continuing to pull him left. After another few torturous steps, we cleared the briars, but the growth was still thick.

"Do you hear that?" Cam looked left, his brow furrowed.

"I hear it." I stopped moving and listened. Sobbing echoed and reverberated through my brain.

"I don't hear anything." Steve shook his head.

The sobbing wasn't Millie. It sounded like a man, but it had the hollow quality of a spectral voice. "Help us!" The plea went out, and Cam and I rushed forward, following Zackie as she tore through the brush toward the voice. Steve probably gave up trying to catch the sound—branches snapped as he hurried after us.

We trusted Zackie to lead us. The sounds of breaking brush and our own heavy breathing obscured the faint but persistent cries. When we at last reached the source of the distressed voice, my eyes were drawn to the spirit of an elderly man dressed in a comfortable, red flannel bathrobe. A nasal cannula, hissing oxygen, was draped beneath his nose.

Wheezing, the spirit pointed to a patch of multiflora rose. "Please, she's in there. You've gotta help her." Zackie stood in front of the man, undecided, her muzzle swinging between the spirit and the thick shrub he indicated. His gaze locked on the Psychopomp, and the gesturing hand lowered as his eyes went wide with recognition.

Cam knelt and peered into the brush. "Steve, Millie's in here. Her eyes are open, and she's conscious."

Steve dove into the brush, heedless of the thorns and did a quick assessment. "Millie, I'm Steve. We're going to help you, okay?" After some rustling as he moved about in the plant, checking her body and limbs, Steve reported back to us. "I don't see anything broken. She has a few cuts and scrapes, and she's shivering." Pulling out a multi tool from his belt, he began cutting away at the thorny stems. "Let's get her out of here and get her warm."

As Cam and Steve worked to free Millie, I accessed my radio and informed Incident Command that we had a find, that she was alive and appeared stable. Grabbing my GPS, I fed them our coordinates, told them about the briars at our entry point, and then left it to search management to plot an evacuation route.

Cam pulled the blanket we used at staging from his pack, and I raised my eyebrows. Our standard kit included a space blanket, significantly smaller and much less weight. Cam shrugged when he caught my expression. "I thought we could use it. I could fit little else in here after the blanket, but I figured you two would be able to compensate if we needed anything else." As he prepared a site to spread the blanket, he jutted his chin toward Zackie and the spirit. "Why don't you pull Zackie back and give us a little room to work."

I nodded, picked up the lead and made eye contact with the spirit, tilting my head toward an open patch away from where Steve would continue his assessment of Millie.

Once we were clear, I turned my attention to the man. His skin had a slightly bluish tinge, as if he were still hypoxic and in need of oxygen. Like the nasal cannula, this was just a memory of his perimortem trauma. Some spirits have a hard time shaking the experience of their last moments, so these visual cues remained. His eyes kept darting uneasily between the ongoing rescue effort and Zackie. I could tell he wanted to go to Millie. I started with introductions, relying on his sense of propriety to keep him out of the fray. "My name is Fia. And you are?"

He looked back at me with a startled expression. "I'm sorry. I'm Ralph, Millie's…um, husband. At least, I

44

think I'm still her husband." He looked down, momentarily confused, his eyebrows knotting and his hands clenching as he shifted uneasily. "Is she going to be all right?"

"I think so." Ralph's face and posture relaxed as he let out a huge sigh and then almost smiled. Brushing back the wispy hairs on his bald head, his face instead grew sad. The sudden shift in emotions made me suspicious. "What happened, Ralph? Did you lure her out and then thought better of it?"

Ralph's head snapped toward me and his mouth gaped open. "What? No! She can barely tell I'm here."

"Why are you still here, Ralph?" I held his eyes, insisting on the truth. Zackie sat at his feet and added her unflinching stare to the interrogation.

"She wanders sometimes. I worry about her." I crossed my arms and continued to stare until he rubbed the back of his neck and grimaced. "Look, I do want her with me, but not like this." He closed his eyes and shook his head, almost like a shudder. Compressing his lips into a thin line, he whispered, "Not like this."

"So, what happened?"

45

"Millie got out of bed and was muttering to herself. She grabbed her purse and went out the door." The spirit paced as he spoke, agitated by having to relive the event. "I followed her and knocked a picture off the wall on my way out, hoping it would wake up Margot and Dennis."

"Then she hit the street."

"Yep, and dressed only in her nightgown and slippers." He rubbed his bald head and took another lap in our small area. "I was able to nudge her toward the strip mall and she stood in a nook out of the wind for a while. There was some heat leaking from the shop, but I couldn't get her to stay."

"You did good. That probably kept her alive. She would have frozen for sure if she spent the entire time outside." I smiled gently, trying to be encouraging.

"Yeah, well, next she headed for that pond." He stopped pacing and gave me a piercing look. "I won't lie— I thought about it. I hate seeing her like this and it mighta been a quick way to go." Ralph sighed and his eyes drifted. "But in the end, I couldn't do it. I nudged her away from the pond. I don't want her to go like that, in the cold water, gasping for breath. I know what that's like." He tapped the nasal cannula and a single tear trickled down his cheek. Getting down on one knee in front of Zackie, he pleaded with her. "Can you make it easy for her? Please? I'll do anything."

Zackie placed a paw on his knee, silently communicating. Ralph released a stuttering breath, bowing his head. "Thank you, just…thank you."

"Do you want the Psychopomp to take you over?" I asked.

Ralph shook his head. "Okay if I stay with Millie? I'll go when she goes, all right?"

We couldn't force him, even though I was pretty sure if I had enough time, I could wear him down. But at that moment, we had to do what was best for Ralph. I looked to Zackie for agreement with Ralph's plan. "Okay. Zackie will take you both when it's time."

Glancing away, I wiped a tear from my own eye and thought about Hannah and Lucas and the uncomfortable parallels to Ralph and Millie's story. Marriage doesn't end just because the body fails. Just like Ralph doted on Millie, Hannah was devoted to Lucas. I was convinced she was committed to his well-being and protection. But was there a limit? Was there a scenario where her need to be with Lucas would exceed her desire for his safety? Did she also sometimes feel a dark pull that was in opposition to his continued life on this side of the divide?

These new and disturbing thoughts were interrupted by the crackle of the radio. "Task 14, Incident Command."

I depressed the talk button and replied, speaking slowly and clearly before releasing the button. "Go for Task 14."

"A team has been dispatched to clear brush and carry out the subject. What are her vitals?"

"Stand by." I released the talk button and called to Steve. "IC needs her vitals. Relay? Or do you want to talk to them directly?"

"I got it." Steve pinched the mike clipped to his shoulder and began reciting the numbers associated with Millie's pulse, respiration and blood pressure. She lay on the ground wrapped in Cam's blanket. A flash of metallic fabric peeking through the folds showed a space blanket, used as the first layer to reflect back her body heat. Incident Command read back Steve's report on her vitals and told us to hold tight, that the rescue team would be there soon.

Things went quickly after that. A team of searchers and firefighters cut a path through the briars with a chainsaw and carried in a Stokes basket for Millie. We helped the team to package our subject into the basket using tubular webbing to hold her securely, and in minutes, she was loaded into the waiting ambulance. Unknown to the ambulance crew, they also transported a stowaway. Ralph stayed by Millie's side as they sped off, uttering words of comfort she could not hear.

# # #

I pulled into my parking space, killed the engine, and then glanced at my phone to check the hour. It was still dark but almost time for my morning alarm to go off. I sat in the car and chugged the remainder of my coconut water. Maybe it wasn't the breakfast of champions, but it would have to do. Spirit work tended to screw up my electrolyte levels, and this stuff was the elixir of life when I needed to restore balance. Yawning and rubbing my eyes, I focused on mustering the energy to walk to my door. Despite the fatigue, I felt a prick of anxiety. Someone had maybe been messing around my place when I pulled out. While it was unlikely that someone was still there—if they had even really been there—just in case, I grabbed the bear spray out of my pocket. A look around the area for signs of trespassing showed nothing obvious from my vantage point, so I tumbled out of the car and headed for the door on cold, stiff joints. Zackie followed me, her tags jingling and nails clicking on the asphalt.

My key was ready in one hand, poised to enter the lock, and the bear spray was locked and loaded in the other. I started to feel a little foolish. Zackie would have scented anyone in the vicinity, and I could trust her to have my back. I blew out a breath and relaxed my guard, ruefully shaking my head at my creeping paranoia. As I inserted the key into the lock, Zackie stood up on her hind legs and planted her front paws on the door. Her nose stretched toward a smudge of reddish brown that I had to look up slightly to see. It was easy to miss because the dark brown color of the door camouflaged the stain, but there was a definite smear of something. Letting the key chain dangle from the lock, I grabbed a tissue from my coat pocket and then reached up to dab at the stain. The tissue came away clean but left a little behind because the stuff was tacky after having frozen to the door.

"Is that blood?" When I looked at Zackie to get her opinion, she licked her chops. Bingo. I scrunched my eyes closed for a moment. "Damn it."

Zackie jumped down and I hesitated, not really wanting to know what might be waiting for me inside. The Pyschopomp and I don't always agree on what constitutes danger, so I took a moment to scan the area for additional blood or anything else that would warrant more worry. The stuff on the door was the only weird thing I could find. I folded the tissue to cover the contaminated area and put it in my pocket, out of the way.

Squaring my shoulders, I grabbed the key again, twisting it in the lock and then repeated the action for the rest of the locks. I held my breath and listened hard as I inched the door open, bear spray at the ready. Just as dim light spilled through the cracked door, the alarm to rise and shine went off on my phone. The sudden sound triggered my PTSD and adrenaline surged through my body. My heart raced like a thoroughbred in the Kentucky Derby and the swearing started in earnest. Clamping a hand around the phone, I jabbed at the screen until the noise stopped.

The Psychopomp was unperturbed and made a beeline through the door for my unmade bed, but the PTSD wasn't through with me. I felt compelled to find the source of danger. I spun to look behind me with bulging eyes, and then quickly twisted back to scan the suddenly bright interior. My damned pupils were dilated and every detail of every shadow in the room commanded my attention. My heart continued to hammer even though everything was as I had left it: the window blinds were tightly blinkered; the door to the bedroom was open; the room lights were on; and the photographs and zip-lock bag with the disturbing hair-doll sat on the kitchen counter. I would have been reassured if it hadn't been for the blood on the door and the warning sirens going off in my head.

Logically, because Zackie wasn't reacting, I knew this situation was not DEFCON 1. But I needed to convince my body of that. I shut the door and leaned my back against it while I did a breathing exercise Cam taught me to calm down. Inhaling a long, slow breath through my nose, I held it for a count of three and then slowly released the breath through my mouth, concentrating on relaxing the muscles in my face, shoulders, and stomach. Three repetitions later and I felt more in control. I moved on to directing my mind away from feelings of fight or flight and on to something more rational and concrete. Nodding to myself, I decided my next order of business would be to clean the blood off the door.

For once, it paid to work for a crime scene cleanup company. I went to the cabinet below the kitchen sink and dug out a bottle of Microban, an enzyme cleaner we used for small blood spills. I liked the way this agent chewed through stains, so I had gotten a small bottle and some latex gloves for home use. I slipped a pair of gloves over my shaky hands and then grabbed a small container that I filled with hot water, adding a few drops of Microban. Replacing the enzyme cleaner under the sink, I next took out the spray bottle of regular kitchen cleaner. Armed with the container, some paper towels, and the spray cleaner, I opened the door and went to work. After wiping the warm liquid cleanser on the bloodstain to melt and dissolve it, I concentrated on drawing the moistened towel from the outside edge to the center of the stain. I'd used up all the liquid in the container and nearly all the paper towels before I was satisfied that I got most of it. I treated the area with the kitchen cleanser and wiped and wiped some more. If I had been at work, I would have finished up with a deodorizer and thrown out all the crumpled paper towels into a biohazard bag. Since I was doing the home version of a cleanup, I called it quits after using the kitchen spray and threw out the paper towels, contaminated tissue, and gloves in my trash can.

The mechanical, repetitive actions of scrubbing the door clean had been therapeutic—my breathing was even, my hands had stopped shaking, and my brain was no longer buzzing. I peeled off my coat and after thoroughly washing my hands, I was ready to eat something. I set up the coffeemaker and then went to the fridge to figure out breakfast. The shelves were stocked with a delightful assortment of food from a recent shopping trip, and I decided to feast on an omelet stuffed with cheddar, ham, diced onion, tomato, and green pepper.

Once my belly was full, I sipped my coffee and thought about the significance of the blood on the door. I seriously doubted that it was lamb's blood like in the Bible, and now a deadly disease would pass over and spare my firstborn. But was this some kind of threat or warning to me? Maybe the person skulking about my place last night decided to leave me a message. Belatedly, it occurred to me that I should have left the blood on the door and called the cops. I reached for my phone and dialed the number for the officer who responded when my landlord and his dogs had chased off an intruder trying to break in. The officer's voicemail picked up, and I left an apologetic message that I found blood smeared on my door, but I had cleaned it off without thinking.

I sighed and rubbed my face. The sleepless night was catching up with me despite the infusion of caffeine. I gathered my dirty dishes and brought them to the sink to wash, mulling over my incompetence as I cleaned up. While I would have liked to blame either the PTSD or sleep deprivation for stupidly removing evidence, I knew these were near constants in my life, and I would need to up my game in the future. If Lucas or Cam had been there, they would have stopped me, but they hadn't been there and likely wouldn't be there in the future when some other threat would loom on the horizon. I needed to rely on myself to be smarter, to think before reacting. And wasn't that what Cam had said about me? That I was the most impulsive person he knew? Things had to change or something bad would happen.

I left the dishes in the drain to dry and then found my coat where I had dropped it on the floor. Bringing it to the bedroom, I surveyed the fabric for damage. The thorns had not destroyed the coat, and I could only find one tear that I would need to stitch up. Checking my pants leg where I had felt something give during the push through the brambles, I saw a rip, but thought I could best repair that with an iron-on patch. Both pants and coat should still be serviceable, which was good news, since SAR volunteers were responsible for their personal equipment. Unlike EMTs, no one would offer us uniforms or radios, GPS or anything else we needed in the woods. Team insurance was provided by the sweat of our brows, doing roadside cleanups to raise funds. The roads were free of garbage thanks to us and the inmates, who coincidentally also wore orange. The thought might have been funny if I hadn't been so tired.

Stripping off my SAR clothes, I made a pile of laundry that I would take care of later and took a quick shower before slipping on my PJs. A cotton glove to cover the dead hand completed my outfit.

"Zackie, move over." I pushed on the hound, who was stretched out to take up maximum space on my bed. She made groaning sounds as she allowed me to inch her body over just enough to let me squeeze in next to her. With a few hearty tugs, I was able to release the comforter and sheets from under Zackie's bulk and cover myself. Sleep took me almost as soon as my head hit the pillow.

# # #

I pried open a crusty eyelid and brilliant sunlight

streamed around the slats of the closed blinds, stabbing my pupil until it constricted. It didn't feel like morning, and this wasn't the tentative glow of a sunrise playing on the blinds. I probably hadn't missed an encore performance of my phone's morning alarm by sleeping straight through to the next day. With a grunt, I sat up, noticed that Zackie had abandoned me and then reached for my phone to check the time and date—same day and I was just in time for lunch. Yay me.

Plodding groggily to the kitchen, I nearly tripped over the hair-doll lying on the floor outside of my bedroom. My eyes shot to the kitchen counter where the empty zip-lock bag sat next to the stack of photos. The stack was neatly arranged with one picture separated from the rest. I looked back at the doll and then accusingly at the dead hand. "Bastard," I muttered.

I picked up the doll, carried it to the counter and placed it carefully back in the zip-lock before examining the lone photograph. It was the picture of the dead child held upright by its siblings. The children's eyes haunted me. Their features were drawn down by the weight of grief, but there was also a dazed quality to their expressions, the shock of a young life's first brutal loss. I tore my gaze away from their naked pain, forcing my mind back on task and scanned the picture for the doll. There had to be a connection between the doll and this photograph, otherwise why position these two objects so blatantly? It seemed likely that one of the children might be holding this toy, or perhaps the doll sat propped in the background somewhere. No dice. The children's hands were empty, and no doll posed with them to soften the tableau. Also, the room was not a child's room, but a formal parlor. The only decoration on the mirrored mantel in the background was a clock flanked by two fluted vases. Could the doll be a *memento mori* made from the dead child's hair? Again, no joy. All the children were fair, and the doll was made from unmistakably dark, almost black hair.

I was so focused on finding the doll in the picture that I almost missed it. There's a phenomenon called inattentional blindness that I had learned about in a psychology class, and at the time, it made me think that this might account for why so few people saw the spirits walking among us. In the seminal experiment demonstrating inattentional blindness, subjects were asked to count the number of times a basketball was passed between players. They became so intent on their counting task that they completely missed a woman wearing a gorilla suit entering the scene and thumping her chest before walking away.

For me, the gorilla appeared in the form of a forlorn image in the mantel's mirror. A pale, translucent silhouette of a slender woman in a full skirt stood with her head and shoulders bowed, arms hanging listlessly at her sides. She had been captured by the postmortem photographer, probably so intent on the children that he missed the reflected image of a specter standing along the far wall.

This image of the siblings was not simply a *memento mori* for a dead child—it was legitimate spirit photography. The Victorians had produced a slew of fraudulent spirit photographs. Double exposures of models draped in gauzy veils were superimposed to hover near images of standard issue living people. These doctored photographs appeared hopelessly hokey by modern standards. The spirit caught in the mirror was no double exposure, and it was too precisely shaped to be explained away as a play of light from a nearby window. I grinned as I thought of non-believer Lucas and what he might have to say about it.

My empty stomach growled like a cornered badger, reminding me that I needed to move lunch up on my list of priorities. I stacked the photographs on the counter, placing the bagged doll on top, and then turned to rummage through the refrigerator for something to eat. Pulling out the ingredients to make a ham and cheese sandwich, I mechanically went through the motions of preparing and eating lunch. My mind was elsewhere, still picking apart the mystery of what the doll had to do with the *memento mori* pictures. My instinct told me that just because I had found the ghostly image in the mirror didn't mean I was done. Both the doll and the one photograph had been situated to catch my attention, ergo there had to be a link I was still missing.

I brushed the sandwich crumbs from my face and pajama top on to the empty plate and considered using a licked finger to bring these back to my mouth. Cam would not approve. He had been on me lately about cleaning up my act. Besides his promptings, I also worried that if I didn't start reining in my bad habits, I might accidentally do something like this in front of Lucas someday. Sighing, I brought the plate to the sink and washed it while I planned how I'd use the remainder of the day.

The first order of business was a shower. After that, I would visit Cam and get him up to speed with my recent activities. If I could drag that out long enough, I'd get invited to dinner. I resolved to speak slowly.

# # #

Lucas was tied up at work, so only the four of us sat around the dining table after the meal, sipping coffee and scrutinizing our assigned *memento mori* pictures. Ron thought that if we divided up the images, each one would get a more thorough going-over. We'd be more likely to find something, provided there was something to find. Many of the pictures used the same formal parlor as the sibling photo to pose the survivors and their dearly departed, albeit from different angles. These proved the most fruitful, giving us suggestive shadows or unexplained vague, luminous shapes along the wall where the image of the specter had originally been captured. If we hadn't been primed by the clear and compelling image of a woman in skirts that had been caught in the mirror, we would have missed these subtle clues.

"Someone is definitely attached to that room." Cam set down his photographs next to a half-full mug of coffee and stretched wearily, joints cracking, the after-effect of the early morning callout. "We'll need your landlord to let us back into the Roseberry House when it's not crawling with workers." He yawned, covering his mouth with the back of his hand. "Sorry, I'm knackered."

The yawn was contagious, and I soon followed suit, rubbing my face to try to wake up. "Yeah, I'll talk to Joel," I mumbled through my fingers.

Ron's eyes were soft with concern. "You're too tired to drive. Why don't you stay here tonight?"

I looked at him through my splayed fingers. "This is about the blood on the door, isn't it?"

Nodding, he crossed his arms. "Did that cop ever get back to you?"

"We're playing phone tag. He left a message that I shouldn't worry about cleaning up the evidence." I yawned again and put my head down on the table, cradling my cheek on my forearms to keep Ron in view. "There's a backlog of rape kits from active cases that haven't been analyzed. My stuff would have been real low priority."

Ron grunted his acceptance of the situation. "And you're sure this isn't anything dead coming by your place?"

I didn't want to get into all the weird sensory cues I have when spirits are involved. Depending on the particulars of the deceased's story, colors either muted or intensified, sounds might become distorted, and I could even get tastes or smells that have nothing to do with the environment. I kept my answer simple. "No, Ron. My spidey senses aren't tingling."

"Okay then, how 'bout we switch places tonight? You sleep here, and I'll stay at your place." He stretched out his hand to me. "Gimme your keys. Maybe I can catch the bastard in the act and give him the surprise of his life."

Shrugging and not bothering to lift my head, I fished around blindly in my pocket until my fingers tangled with the key chain. I handed the jangly metal to Ron and then issued my demands. "Just don't eat all my food and no wearing my bathrobe."

Ron flashed a grin as he pushed back his chair to stand. "Will do for the bathrobe, but no promises about your food if I wake up in the middle of the night."

I shot Lenora a desperate look. "Can you maybe give him a doggie bag, something to go, so my fridge won't be empty?"

Rolling her eyes and muttering, Lenora shuffled to the kitchen. After a few minutes of scraping and pot-banging, she emerged carrying a bulging grocery bag that she placed on the table. Hands on her hips, she eyed Ron. "First you clean, then you go." Her eyes next settled on me. "Put this in your car, so it stays cold and then you help him."

We did as we were told, while Lenora and Cam bid us a good night and headed to their rooms. Once the pots were scrubbed and the rush of water could be heard from the dishwasher, I followed Ron to the door.

"You can find clean sheets in the linen closet next to the bathroom." Biting my lip, I touched his arm as he reached for the doorknob. "And thanks for doing this. Just…just be careful, okay?"

Ron looked over his shoulder and a half-smile played on his lips. He cracked his knuckles, and I felt the muscle on his arm balloon with this small action. "Oh, I'll be real careful with him."

I locked the door as I heard my car's engine start, foraged through the pockets of my coat in the hall closet to find one of my winter gloves and then grabbed the comforter from Ron's bed before settling on the couch. It was too much effort to change the sheets. I managed to pull the glove over the dead hand before burrowing into the couch cushions, immediately drifting into a deep sleep, cocooned in the soft folds of the comforter.

# # #

The front door banged open, waking me. I sat up, sleepily rubbing my eyes until something suddenly dropped into my lap, causing me to shoot out of my bed.

Clutching my chest, I bared my teeth at Ron. "What the hell!"

"Lucas sends his regards." A slightly rumpled Ron pointed to the floor where a bouquet of wilting roses wrapped in a decorative red foil lay next to the discarded comforter.

That stopped me cold. "You saw Lucas?"

"Showed up at your door late last night. Seemed kinda surprised to see me there." Ron grinned, his eyes crinkling with amusement.

"Damn it!" I picked up the bouquet, cradling it to my chest and deeply regretted the impulsive decision to switch places with Ron. If only I had been in my own bed last night…I let the thought trail off as I felt a blush color my cheeks. Ducking my head, I pretended to smell the roses as I hid my flaming cheeks from Ron.

"And no sign of Rory. Wasted effort, I guess." Ron handed me my keys, picked up his comforter and then entered the hall. Pausing, his head turned to follow his nose, inhaling the aroma that wafted from the kitchen. "I'm going to take a quick shower. Save me some pancakes."

"Lenora's making pancakes?" I pushed past Ron and followed the scent of breakfast.

I found Lenora feeding a freshly cooked pancake to Zackie and wished them both a good morning. Lenora mumbled her greeting, concentrating on pouring more batter on to the griddle before glancing up and noticing the bouquet. Reaching into a cabinet, she pulled out a glass pitcher. "Put those in water before they die."

I took the pitcher to the sink and then unwrapped the flowers to find a little packet of preservative nestled among the stems. It had clear instructions that told me exactly what to do. Eager for breakfast, I rushed to arrange the roses in the improvised vase, and a thorn slashed the dead hand, tearing a sizeable gash in the skin. If I'd done this to my good hand, I'd be dripping blood on the floor and wondering if I needed stitches. On the dead hand, I didn't feel it, and though I expected some pustular discharge to leak from the laceration, nothing foul oozed out. The wound did draw my attention to the fact that the winter glove I had put on the night before was missing. I also needed to do a quick touch up on the mortuary makeup before breakfast.

Before Lenora could get a good look at me, I grabbed the flowers and took off for the dining room. "These will look pretty on the table," I said as an excuse as I ran off. From there, I dashed to the hall closet and searched the pocket of my coat for the little makeup kit I carried for just such an occasion.

Trotting down the hall, kit in hand, I arrived at the bathroom to find it still occupied by Ron. I politely pounded on the door with my fist to let him know a line was forming outside. The off-key singing from the shower went on unabated, maybe even a little louder. Huffing, I went to Ron's room and shut the door. The light in the bathroom was better for this, but I didn't want anyone to see the dead hand looking dodgy.

The makeup only needed a little bit of fussing to get it back up to snuff. As I dabbed foundation here and there and then blended the colors, I paused in my efforts as it registered that the gash was gone. The dead hand looked like nothing ever happened. Shaking my head, I wondered why I even bothered being surprised. This thing had its own rules and its own logic, and really, who was I to say what was normal? I sucked in my lips to keep my thoughts from leaking out and finished applying the makeup.

When I was satisfied with the touchup, I sent a quick text to Lucas to thank him for the flowers. He didn't text me back immediately, so maybe he was still asleep or, more likely, he was already back at work and busy with something. Shrugging, I tucked the makeup kit in the left leg pocket of my cargo pants with the bear spray, keeping my stuff out of reach of the dead hand. And since you can't live a full life on an empty stomach, I went to claim my share of the pancakes.

"Did you lose this?" Cam, sitting alone at the table, held out the winter glove to me as I took my seat.

"Yeah, where'd you find it?"

"In the fireplace." He handed me a zip-lock bag. "With this."

I was literally left holding the bag, staring at the hair-doll, my jaw slack. The only sounds came from Lenora in the kitchen, telling Zackie she'd eaten enough pancakes. "I swear I didn't bring this with me, Cam."

"Mmm… right. Didn't think it was you that left these in the fireplace for me to find, either." Cam dug a fork under a stack of pancakes and maneuvered them onto his waiting plate. "Likely another apportation. Maybe aided by your dead appendage."

I put the bag in my leg pocket with the makeup kit and bear spray. "Must be urgent. They're really trying to get our attention." I filled my mug with coffee and then speared two pancakes at a time with the fork until I acquired a sizable stack on my plate. The heat rising from the stack carried the heavenly scents of vanilla, egg, and butter. My mouth watered and I hurried to apply a thick coating of gooey maple syrup.

When I finally looked up, Lenora was setting down another platter of pancakes in front of Ron, who had finally emerged from the shower, his long hair still damp. He ate slowly, relishing the pancakes with precise, zen-like actions of his fork, yet he still managed to dash my hopes of getting second helpings.

As I stared longingly at the rapidly diminishing pancakes, Cam cleared his throat, a sure sign he wanted to return to discussing the urgency of our unknown spirit. "You need to talk to Joel today about getting into the Roseberry House. This spirit may escalate things if she doesn't soon get the attention she seems to need from us."

Pausing his fork, Ron exchanged a glance with Lenora. "You want us to come for this?"

Cam shook his head. "Not just yet. Let us assess the situation first."

I sighed and glanced at the time display on my phone. "It's still early. I might be able to catch Joel before he leaves for work." I drained my coffee, wiped the sticky bits off my face with a napkin, and then stood up to leave. "Thanks for breakfast, Lenora."

"Not taking your flowers?" Lenora gestured at the table's centerpiece.

"Nah, you enjoy them. I'm here more than I'm home. They won't last if I take them." Secretly, I was hoping that Lucas would make another attempt at a nighttime visit and I would need my tiny card table for a new bouquet.

As Cam saw me out, I heard Lenora offer Ron seconds, saying she could make some more batter. I shut the door and deeply envied Ron's status as the cherished grandson. Heading to my car with Zackie trotting behind me, a fine drizzle beaded on my unwashed, greasy hair. I wondered if I could get any perks for being a servant of the Psychopomp. But being that Zackie received the first pancake, that probably told me all I needed to know about the pecking order and what I could hope for.

When I pulled into my parking space and spotted Joel's red pickup truck, I knew I hadn't missed him. But he would be leaving soon, so I hustled to his door and knocked, figuring Zackie would find her own way into my place. Dogs barked and snuffled behind the door as footsteps approached, and the deadbolt was drawn back with a solid clunk. The door opened to reveal Peyton, dressed in Joel's navy, terry cloth bathrobe.

"Oh, um, hi Peyton. I, er, didn't expect to see you

here."

Peyton wore a lopsided grin. "Came as a surprise to me too, but here we are. I expect you wanted to see Joel." She stepped aside and motioned for me to come in out of the rain. I pushed past the eager dog noses and counted three dogs instead of the expected two. Peyton's Simber had joined Heckle and Jeckle, the resident black and yellow Labradors. As I gave their ears a quick rub in greeting, Peyton called up the stairs. "Joel! Fia wants to talk to you."

Joel came down the stairs with a spring in his step and that same lopsided grin. "Morning, Fia. Watcha need?"

For the second time that day, I felt a stab of envy. Rather than dwell on how easy and natural simple human acts were for other people, I forced my thoughts to the business at hand. "The Roseberry House—when can we get into the place? Like, when no workers are around?"

Joel lost a little of his good humor. "By 'we,' I'm thinkin' you mean you and Cam. Am I right?" When I nodded, he continued. "Good, 'cause you know how I feel about that stuff. And I don't want this little lady here to have to mess around with it either. She's had a lifetime of that stuff from what I've heard." He put a protective arm around Peyton, and she leaned into him, like they'd been together for years.

With an effort, I kept my expression neutral, so they wouldn't see how badly I wanted what they had. "It'll be just me and Cam. Oh, and Zackie. And maybe Lucas, if he needs material for his show. Will that be all right?"

Joel grunted an agreement and then reached around to a collection of keys hanging from his belt loop. Selecting an old-fashioned skeleton key, he detached it from the ring and handed it to me. "The old lock still works good. You can have this 'til you're done—I got a copy. The crew knocks off at four every day, when we start losin' the light."

The key was heavier than it looked. I put it in my leg pocket with the growing collection of stuff and wondered if I was going to start walking funny, the weight of everything crammed in that pocket dragging me to one side. Hitching up my pants, I thanked Joel and then left him and Peyton in their cozy nest. I returned to my almost-empty place. Zackie was once again stretched out on my bed, now stripped of sheets after Ron's visit. Lenora had trained him well in the art of being a house guest.

I looked at the neatly folded sheets next to my rumpled pile of SAR clothes on the floor and decided that if I was going to feel crappy about my life, I might as well get some laundry done. But first, I called Cam to let him know I had the key.

CHAPTER 2

"Stop pushing. I almost have it." Cam removed his hand from the small of my back, and I twisted the key another millimeter in the stubborn lock. Zackie slapped the door impatiently with her paw and shot me a dirty look. Glaring down at her, I returned the look with compound interest. "Find your own way in."

"Would you hurry up? The storm's about to break." Cam aimed his flashlight at the lock and glanced uneasily upward as a finger of light flickered and stretched across the forbidding sky. The wind chose that moment to gust, throwing a splatter of water from the slanted roof down on our heads. Zackie had already taken herself to the far side of the house and produced her own flash of light as she entered the portal. Her exit was well-timed to miss this particular bit of misery.

I pushed sodden hair out of my eyes and continued

working on the lock with cold, stiff fingers, jiggling the key a smidgen clockwise before forcing it again in the opposite direction. The mechanism at last clicked into place, allowing the bolt to slide out of the slot in the door jamb. "We're in."

Instead of a modern doorknob, I tugged on a wrought iron ring pull and nearly lost my grip when the door opened broadside to a sudden gust of wind. We secured the door behind us to prevent it from smashing against the stone of the outer wall, and we felt our way through the dark. The beam of the flashlight bounced erratically as we negotiated the two steep and uneven steps down into the kitchen. A pungent, musty odor surrounded us, evidence of the mold and mildew that had infected the floors and walls during the years the house had stood derelict.

Standing before a wall dominated by the enormous kitchen hearth, I flinched as lightning flashed and thunder cracked somewhere close overhead. Cam angled the flashlight catty-corner toward steps leading up into the main house. Zackie peered at us from this opening, but then turned and walked away, her attention diverted by some smell, sight or sound we could not detect. As we prepared to move, heat baked the back of my legs, and the sound of food sizzling on a griddle made me turn to check the hearth. Also sensing these things, Cam turned to examine the hearth.

Sniffing at the sudden scent of cooking food, he raised his eyebrows. "Smells like bacon and cornbread."

"Johnnycakes maybe? They used to—"

Faint and far away, we heard an old woman's voice. *"Mary, turn those cakes afore they burn and…"* The voice faded along with the heat and smell of food cooking, and the room returned to feeling cold and smelling of rot.

I shook my head, trying to clear the odd sensations that still swayed gently inside me. "Weird. It's gone now. What the heck was that, Cam?" It had not felt like a presence, lacking the immediacy and strength of a spirit seeking us out, and it was so very distant.

Cam spoke softly, almost reverently. "It's not common, but some places—very special places—absorb the history of what went on. Think of it like a recording that plays back under the right circumstances." Cocking his head as some new sound drew his attention, he stepped toward a low, narrow door separated from the hearth by a short expanse of wall. Cracking open the door revealed a low ceiling with a twisting flight of narrow Jersey winder stairs leading up into the darkness.

Cam smiled, his eyes wide with wonder, and cupped an ear upward to listen. I tiptoed behind him to also hear the soft strains of the past. Childish giggles echoed down the stairs from some time long ago. I gasped, enchanted by the sound. *"Look Joseph! I have a new dolly! Mamma said..."*

Still smiling as the little girl's voice faded, he sighed and closed the door. "Sweet as these memories are, we should keep going."

The wide planks of the floor felt spongy beneath our feet as we stepped carefully through the kitchen and up the steps into the next room. A sweep of the flashlight revealed a fireplace tucked in one corner. We stood for a moment getting our bearings, and I soon shook my head. This was not the room in the picture.

"It's smaller, isn't it?" Cam offered.

"Yeah, and the window isn't right, either." As I spoke, lightning flickered through the panes, followed by the low rumble of thunder.

"The dress is pretty, but the stitching…"

"Merry Christmas! I am so pleased…"

"She is never happy, that one. I try to be a good husband, but…"

Cam found a doorway that led into a short hall, and we left the snatches of conversation in that room to go on without us. Passing the stairs leading to the second floor, we decided against entering a room on our right that held no resemblance to the room in the photo. The hallway turned and brought us to another door and another room. A warm, summer breeze blew softly from the closed window, bringing the scent of honey locust and the sound of bees, meandering lazily in a lush garden.

"That pie was delicious! May I have another…"

"…threw a shoe and came up lame this morning…"

This room felt right, sort of. The window and the fireplace were located where I expected, but the size of the room was all wrong. The photos gave me the impression of something smaller, not this long, rectangular room that spanned the house from end to end.

Cam cast his gaze up and down the long room,

brows bunched in consternation. "We're about out of rooms."

"Yeah, there's no way they'd lay out a body upstairs and this room's too big." I backed away from the mantle and looked at it through a frame I created with my hands. "This is the shot, though."

"And where would you place the wall?"

I backed up some more until it felt right. "About here, maybe?"

Cam walked over and stood next to me, and then looked up. Pointing upwards, he grinned. "They took out the wall at some point."

Craning my neck, I looked up to see what had him so excited. "I'll be damned. That would explain it." The ceiling showed a shadowed, depressed area in the crumbling plaster that was vaguely the width of the walls in the house. While we stared at the ceiling, Zackie wandered into the room, sat next to Cam and pointed her muzzle upward, trying to see the thing that had caught our attention. In another minute, maybe the spirit would join our small group of rubbernecking tourists, also wanting to know what we were looking at.

Starting to feel a bit silly, I cleared my throat and brought my eyes back down to the fireplace mantle. Imagining a mirror centered over the mantle, I sighted a line to what would have been the source of the spirit reflection. The line extended to an area on the non-existent wall near where it would have met the wall shared with the hallway. Standing at the site where the spirit had manifested in the photo, I cast my senses outwards, mentally calling to her.

Something… was…there. But it was so weak, I could barely make it out above the clamor of the past that seeped from every corner of the house. Taking a breath, I went deeper and was rewarded when the flickering presence of a young girl materialized. Her pale-yellow skirts flared as she turned to run, having second thoughts about responding to my call.

I reached out my hand. "Wait, don't go. I just want to talk to you." Her eyes, dark and ringed with sleepless circles, were large and frightened. Framed in a dusky face with high cheekbones, she looked fragile and helpless. "It's all right. I won't hurt you, I promise."

Cam took a step toward us and the whites of her eyes showed panic as her nostrils flared. Her hands were clutched tightly at her abdomen, and she made a strangled noise as she moved her weight from foot to foot. She was desperate to go but fighting her fear to stay.

Without turning, I held up a hand for Cam to stop where he was. This spirit was terrified of him and if he came one step closer, she was going to flee back into the ether. Given her stark fear, I was surprised that she had come forth at all.

"I know you have something you want to tell me, or you wouldn't have come." I nodded encouragement, all the while trying to understand her. She was a young Black woman, bird-like and small in stature. She was probably in her late teens, but her petite frame made her appear younger. She wore a plain, white cap over her hair and her clothing was made of a coarse, homespun fabric, with only a hint of yellow coloring. A longish shirt fell past her hips, partially covering a skirt of the same pale yellow. Her clothing suggested the Colonial era.

She said nothing but swallowed convulsively as she wrung her hands and pressed them to her stomach. I wondered if a spirit could throw up. "My name is Fia. That man over there, his name is Cam. And Zackie, you probably already know." Her eyes flicked to Zackie and a look of intense longing transformed her face. I took this cue and kept going. "The Psychopomp would never let anything harm you. You know that. You can trust her."

Zackie walked to the frightened spirit and then turned to face me, pressing her flank against the young woman's leg. Reaching down with a shaking hand, the spirit buried her fingers into the soft fur and sighed as she leaned her weight on Zackie's shoulders.

Maybe taking strength from this contact, the young woman finally spoke, her voice quavering and barely above a whisper. "Phebe. My name is Phebe." Her eyes were downcast, and her shoulders slumped from this effort.

"Tell us your story, Phebe." Cam spoke softly from across the room, but still the spirit flinched as if she'd been struck.

I exchanged a worried look with Cam. "Did someone beat you, Phebe?"

Her lips quivered as she strove to stop the misery from escaping, and her shoulders shook with silent weeping. She stared at the floor and used the back of her hand to wipe away the tears that streamed from her eyes like blood from a fresh wound.

Recalling the delight in the voice of the little girl from long ago, on impulse, I grabbed the hair-doll from my pocket and offered it to Phebe. She seemed so young and vulnerable, a doll seemed the right thing to comfort her. Phebe's eyes, still shiny with tears, lit up as she took it.

"I thought I'd lost it." Cradling the doll in her hands, she pressed it tenderly to her cheek. "Oh, Phillis, how I miss you."

Pleased that I'd done the right thing, I smiled gently at the spirit. "I'm glad we could return Phillis to you."

Phebe wrinkled her brow, confused. "I did not name my doll Phillis. Phillis gave me this doll." Her face crumpled and the tears flowed in great drops down her cheeks. "She gave me this doll on the last day of her life, when she had nothing left to give." Wracked by sobs, her legs gave way like a marionette that had its strings cut. She came down hard on her knees, hunching over the doll that she clutched to her chest. Zackie placed her head on Phebe's back and made soft, comforting sounds to soothe her.

I got down on the floor next to Phebe. "Who was Phillis? What happened to her?" Getting no response, I bent until my cheek scraped the floor, trying to get her to look at me. "Phebe, how can we help if we don't understand what happened?"

After some moments, the spirit straightened and took a steadying breath, knuckling her eyes to wipe away the tears. Zackie touched her nose to Phebe's face to offer reassurance and then settled next to the spirit, the warmth of her flank a firm support. Waiting for the spirit to respond, I sat back on my haunches, but started, almost jumping to my feet as the storm threw gouts of water against the window. The slap of rain against the glass was almost deafening in the silence.

"You can help Phillis?" She spoke in a small voice, her eyes on the doll as a finger caressed the toy.

"We can try." I didn't want to make any promises, not understanding the full story, but her eyes shot up and locked on me. They were deep wells of distrust.

Cam, sensing the tension, spoke soothingly. "We've helped others. But it's not always easy. We won't lie to you and tell you that what we'll do will work for Phillis. We have no way of knowing until we try."

Her breathing grew agitated at his words, but she

85

gave a jerky nod. Forcing the words out between stiff lips, the pain seared her face. "They burned Phillis. They did worse to Mark."

I leaned toward her, struggling to understand. "Do you mean they burned her body? And you wanted her remains buried?"

"No!" Phebe clenched her teeth and began rocking. Her voice was thick with emotion, but she enunciated every syllable, stopping between each word as she struggled to make us understand her horror. "They...burned...her... alive."

I sat back, shaken and repulsed. That anyone should have to die so horribly...My eyes lit on Zackie, begging her for comfort and some way to shield me from the certain knowledge of the extremes of human cruelty. Holding my gaze, she drew me in, as if I were inside the event horizon of a black hole, helpless and spiraling down. The weight of millennia crushed me, and I breathed with difficulty, the air growing rank and heavy like a sealed tomb. It was useless to resist. I was paralyzed, mind wide open, as I was forced to witness countless eons of human depravity— a little girl with empty eyes, her face bruised and lip bleeding, is shoved into a gas chamber by a bored guard; a man's hands jerk against restraints—his ruined fingers look like hamburger—as a crude, wooden mallet comes down again, he shrieks, his eyes rolling wildly; the wheel of the rack turns until the ropes squeal, stretched to their limit, and the sharp crack of the woman's bones separating from her body interrupts her frantic moans...

It went on and on, wave after wave pounding my psyche. I was left emotionally flayed. The point was clear— Phillis was just one death among so many heartless acts perpetrated by my kind. At last, Zackie released me and I filled my lungs with the cool, wet air from my time. I was drained, my blood pumping sluggishly and my limbs too weak to stand. Her eyes, like pools of whiskey, were soft with emotion, but where I had sought compassion, she gave me only pity.

I cast my eyes to the heaving floor, the vertigo making it rise and fall like the deck of a storm-tossed ship. Gasping for breath and swaying, I heard Cam from a long way off. "Fia, close your eyes and breathe." His voice, calm and authoritative, steadied me. After several breaths, eyes closed against an uncertain landscape, his next words were sudden, gruff and demanding. "Now, get off your arse and help this spirit."

Color flamed my cheeks and I stared at him, open-mouthed and frozen. "Cam, you have to give me a moment. It was awful and—"

Cam rolled his eyes, hands on his hips. "Oh, none of your excuses. You've had your moment. Get to work."

Baring my teeth, tears in my eyes, I snarled at him. "Screw you!" It was like returning to an alternate universe where the people you thought you knew were every bit as evil as in Zackie's vision. I couldn't make sense of it.

The spirit pressed her hands to her mouth and backed away from us, terrified by this exchange. Cam waved his hands with impatience. "Hurry up. You're losing her."

Ignoring him and the gnawing pain in my psyche, I pulled myself together for the sake of poor, frightened Phebe. With a hoarse voice, I pleaded with her and reached out a trembling hand to stay her progress. "Please, don't go. It's all right. Talk to us about Phillis."

Phebe's image flickered as she backed away, shaking her head. In a last-ditch effort, I threw out questions to get her to stay. "Why did they burn Phillis? Did they think she was a witch?"

Phebe froze, her face drew down with anguish and her mouth worked soundlessly. Finally, she forced the words out. "She killed John Russell." Her color drained until she was nothing more than a pale shade of gray. Turning her back on us, she faded into the darkness.

# # #

Pushed along by the wind, clouds released rain in spurts that drummed like a funeral dirge on the roof of the parked truck. We stared out through the windshield to avoid looking at each other. Zackie lay on a blanket inside the truck's cap, ignoring both of us.

"You know why I had to do that, right?" Cam unscrewed the cap and handed me a bottle of coconut water. "Drink."

Not trusting my voice, I swallowed some liquid and then shook my head, my eyes still damp with hurt from how he had treated me. And everything ached. I have a long history of damage from my years of solitary struggle, and I had never felt so bruised and battered after doing spirit work.

Cam sighed. "Zackie was giving you the 'Savagery of Humans' lecture. You don't just bounce back from that." He forced damp, gray locks from his forehead with a rough swipe of his fingers and then crossed his arms. "When it happened to me, Lummie slapped me hard across the face to shock me out of it... You can die of grief, you know."

I turned in my seat and faced him fully. "Why'd Zackie do it if it's so dangerous? And why just then? We were making progress with Phebe. That was really bad timing."

"Because you asked her for the lesson. Don't shake your head at me—you essentially asked her to protect you from the suffering. I felt it." Cam's eyes softened with sympathy. "If you're going to keep going in this work, you need this perspective."

"Or what?"

"Or you'll become so hardened, you won't be you anymore. That's assuming you don't die from the grief." He nodded his head, his brow furrowed with concern. "I can't emphasize this enough. Broken heart syndrome is a real, physiological cause of death."

"Okay, I believe you. But how does it help me to

know the entire history of human carnage?" I pressed my knuckles against my temples, trying not to lose it. "I feel...I feel—"

"It's a loss of innocence, Fia. And for that, I am truly sorry." Cam reached out and took my hands in both of his. "But this is also a process. Right now, you are overwhelmed with the violence and the pain. When that cacophony dies down, you'll be able to trace back to the root cause. How almost all these horrifying acts came to be and continue to be."

A tear trickled down my cheek. I tried to smile, tried to summon up a bit of bravado to show him that I'd get through this. "How 'bout you just give me the cliff notes on this one?"

His eyes dropped and then he closed them. "It's painfully simple, actually. You'll laugh." But nothing in his tone made me believe anything about this was amusing. Looking back up to meet my gaze, he laid out his hard-earned wisdom. "Hurt people...hurt people."

I would have liked to say 'Eureka!' or, if I were smarter, something a little more profound. But the arrow hit the bull's-eye with these words, and I felt the truth of it. My heart ached that so much had gone so wrong in this self-perpetuating cycle of human cruelty. The tears flowed freely down my face and I choked out a tortured laugh at the absurdity of it all.

Cam smiled sadly. "That's my girl."

#

The knock on my door came just before midnight. I sat at the little table, staring at nothing and unable to motivate myself to get up to go to bed. Sleep would avail me nothing. The soft sound of Zackie snoring drifted from my bedroom, but I knew if I joined her, I would wake up feeling just as spent and just as hopeless. What was the point?

The knock came again, and I trudged to the door, if only to make it stop. Standing on my doorstep with a bouquet of white roses in his arms, Lucas's smile faltered when the dim light caught my features. Drops of rain glistened in his hair and darkened the royal blue tissue paper protecting the roses.

"What's happened?" Fine lines formed around his

eyes, and I thought how young he was, too young for these worry lines to be etched in his face. My only solace was that Hannah had started this change in him from carefree youth, and I was just reinforcing a well-worn path.

Stepping inside and closing the door, he tried again. "Something's happened. You look…shattered." He shook his head, bewildered, the concern growing in his eyes. Lucas placed the flowers on the kitchen counter and then drew me to sit in the chair I had left askew near the table. Kneeling beside me, he studied my face and touched my cheek with his fingertips. He said nothing, waiting for me to speak, all the while holding my eyes with his. It was as if he were willing me back to the person I had been a scant few hours ago.

He didn't deserve my silence. It wasn't his fault that the world not only harbored but actively nurtured cruelty and injustice. I forced myself to speak and my voice sounded rough, as if dust coated my throat. "I'm sorry. Sometimes this work takes its toll."

It was the best I could do, since there was nothing I could say that would help him understand. Parts of my reality would always be beyond his ability to comprehend and internalize.

Lucas looked down and he sighed softly, realizing that this was all he was going to get out of me. Shifting gears to practical action, he pulled me to my feet. "C'mon, let's get something to eat." He helped me into my coat, ushered me out the door and to his car. A listless rain fell as we took a short drive to an all-night diner. The clientele, a tired group of long-haul truckers and a few night owls coming off second shift, barely glanced our way as we entered. The mood was subdued, and the conversation muted.

We grabbed seats in an out-of-the-way booth. When I told him I wasn't hungry, his eyebrows shot up in disbelief. The lines around his eyes returned as he picked up the menu. "Unacceptable. You'll feel better after you've eaten."

Lucas ordered a half dozen desserts and mugs of hot chocolate with whipped cream. To please him, I sipped from my cocoa as we waited for the sugar bonanza to arrive. He toyed with his fork, balancing it on its edge and then tipping it over, eyebrows drawn together and deep in thought.

Frowning, he raised his eyes until they locked with mine. "When Hannah died, I was sure I'd lost everything, and nothing would ever be the same."

"And you were wrong about that?"

"No. I was one hundred percent right." The corner of his mouth lifted in a sardonic half smile. "Sucks to be right sometimes."

The waitress appeared with a tray full of desserts, and we both sat quietly as she filled our table with small dishes of apple pie, rice pudding, brownies, cheesecake, black and white cookies, and chocolate pudding. She gave each of us a plate and told us to enjoy. Lucas reached for a cookie and raised an eyebrow at me, so I took the other cookie and nibbled.

Wary because we were discussing Hannah, I felt my way with care. "I knew you were depressed—"

He shook his head. "Depressed isn't the right word for it." Lucas chewed thoughtfully for a moment. "This was a life-changing event. It marked me. I define my life as the time before and after Hannah died."

The cookie was gone, so I spooned some rice pudding on my plate. When I next looked up, the smell of ammonia was palpable, and Hannah sat next to Lucas in the booth. I stared dully at her, too spent for any games. "I can understand that. Death and marriage are seismic shifts in anyone's life." I filled my mouth with rice pudding, so I wouldn't have to say anything else. The overhead fluorescent lights flickered and dimmed as Hannah solidified and became more vivid. Speaking to a customer at the counter, the waitress gazed up and then shrugged her shoulders, going on with her conversation.

"It was harder because it completely defied expectations. This wasn't supposed to happen to someone in her twenties. We hadn't been married that long." Lucas put the cookie down on his plate, having lost interest in it. "We had our whole life together planned out…I'd publish a few more papers and then my postdoc adviser was going to help me get a job in pharma. Hannah had her doctorate but wanted to go to law school and become a patent attorney. Money was tight, but we were saving for a house. We both wanted kids…"

Hannah sat back with a sigh and looked at Lucas, her eyes wistful with thoughts of what might have been.

"Our entire future floated away like smoke when she died. It was like waking from a dream into… something else." Lucas paused, his eyes drifting to watch the rain drip down a window. When he swung his attention back to me, his gaze was penetrating. "Reality was suddenly different."

I looked at him sharply. How could he know that was how I felt? When I tried to speak, I had no idea what I was going to say, and he held up a hand to stop me.

"Something happened to you and it's not something you really want to discuss with me." He shook his head as I tried to say something to smooth this over. "I know. It's okay. You don't have to tell me everything."

"Lucas…" I reached out to touch his hand. Hannah clutched his arm and leaned against his shoulder, spitting venom at me with her eyes.

"Look, I can tell whatever's happened, it changed your world." He grasped my fingers. "You now have this event that forever breaks your life into two pieces. I understand that, and I understand why you can't talk about it." He shrugged and gave a rueful shake of his head. "It's taken me this long to be able to talk about Hannah."

I nodded back, uncertain what to say. This went beyond a simple inability to process the magnitude of the situation. This was something that formed a great divide between us. I squeezed his fingers, but found myself looking to Hannah, my eyes pleading for connection and understanding. To me, she was the embodiment of inexplicable suffering caused by an indifferent universe. The quality of her suffering was different from what I had experienced with Zackie, and as I struggled to differentiate these experiences, something inside me shifted.

As my feelings of pity for Hannah fell away, an illuminating new sense of compassion replaced it. Pity had been passive and accepting of what was perceived as unchangeable; it held anything unpleasant at arm's length and provoked compulsive thoughts of *Please God, let this not happen to me.* Compassion was engaged; it was curious, thoughtful and actively sought connection and solutions to the misery felt by another. It was a hard-won epiphany, but I understood now why Cam said this was a lesson I had to have.

Hannah's eyes narrowed with suspicion, and she cringed back and away from me. After a moment, she blinked and her brow wrinkled, maybe confused at what was happening. Her posture relaxed, and she gazed back at me. Cancer treatment had taken all her hair, including her eyebrows and lashes, and I found her expression hard to read. In another moment, the lights flickered again, glowed brightly and then she was gone.

I couldn't put my finger on why this realization had freed me from the pull of the abyss, but I felt infinitesimally better. And was it possible that Hannah and I just had a moment, bonding through our separate suffering?

When Lucas released my hand and then slid the apple pie in front of me, I dug a fork into it. "I'm starting to think you're enabling me."

He grinned and the worry lines smoothed as relief spread to his eyes. "I like to think that I keep you breathing, despite your best efforts."

"It's a lot of work, isn't it?" I pushed the pie toward Lucas, so he would take a bite. "I'm guessing going out for a midnight snack was not what you had in mind tonight."

Lucas took a forkful of the pie and raised an eyebrow at me. "Well, I'm enjoying it more than the midnight snack I had with Ron. Imagine my surprise when he greeted me at your door, wearing nothing but a pink robe that barely concealed his considerable charms."

"Seriously? He wore my robe? Bastard… I asked him not to do that." It felt good slipping into our regular banter. The conversation was still a little forced, but I felt relaxed enough to reach for the pudding.

"Ron told me what happened. I take it he didn't catch the guy who bloodied your door?"

I shook my head as I swallowed a mouthful of pudding. "I think the video would have gone viral by now if some massive dude in a pink robe beat the crap out of an intruder." Lucas chuckled and then reached over with a napkin to wipe away a smudge of chocolate near my lip. "Thanks. Maybe the guy's given up."

Lucas's grin faded. "I wouldn't count on it. You should keep that bear spray with you."

"Mmm…" I grunted a reply, not wanting to think about this problem. After draining my cocoa, I suggested we take the rest of the food home and call it a night.

# # #

I awoke to an unfamiliar pressure on my abdomen. Lucas's arm draped across my stomach and added to the discomfort of a full bladder. I had a quicksilver flash of disappointment, that I'd somehow missed what must have been the best night of my life. But memory flooded back when I realized we were both fully clothed and lying on top of the covers. The late night of emotional turmoil and a sugar coma had contrived to reduce us to platonic sleeping buddies. So much for the hot, wild night of unbridled lust Lucas must have hoped for.

"Lucas?" I nudged his shoulder and tried to sit up.

"Mmmph...What time is it?"

"I don't know, but I really need to get up."

He lifted his arm and then rolled to a sitting position. Rubbing his face and swearing under his breath, his long legs dangled over the mattress edge. I scooted over and planted my feet on the cold floor. The dull, gray pre-dawn light of the room did little to help me navigate, but I managed to make it to the bathroom without tripping over anything.

Mission accomplished, I went to the refrigerator to make us a hearty breakfast. "Damn it! Midnight snack, my ass, Lucas. You guys cleaned me out."

Lucas emerged from the bathroom, his hair standing up in an appealing cowlick. "Don't worry about breakfast. I have an early meeting and need to get going."

From the almost empty refrigerator, I pulled out the leftover cheesecake and brownies. Judging the brownies to be the safer thing to eat while driving, I offered the little plate to Lucas. "Take these."

He slipped on his coat, accepted from me what passed for breakfast in my home and then gave me a soft, lingering kiss. No hard feelings from him for missed opportunities, but I had my regrets. Just before stepping through the door, he stopped and scanned the room. "Wait, where's Zackie?"

I sensed a flash of light from the corner of my eye and then heard the jingling of tags just before she stuck her head out of the bedroom door. Relieved that I wouldn't have to come up with a story, I gave a nonchalant shrug. "She must have been under the bed."

Lucas hesitated at the door. "You want me to take her out before I go?"

Zackie ducked her head and raised the whiskers protruding above her eyes, the dog equivalent of eyebrows.

Her mouth opened slightly, revealing the tips of her canines in a toothy grin. She took two steps forward, amused by Lucas's offer and willing to see where it might go. It amazed me. Zackie could still find a way to be carefree and light-hearted, even after living through everything she had shown me the previous night. Maybe that was the key to it, to be able to survive and not go mad with the pain.

Positioning myself in front of Zackie, I blocked her progress. She was going to make Lucas late for work with her shenanigans. "No, it's okay. You should take off. I'll feed her breakfast first and take her out after."

Lucas leaned in for a final kiss and then closed the door behind him. Sliding past my block, Zackie positioned herself in front of me and sat down. She pointed her muzzle at the cheesecake and then gave me a meaningful stare. I had, after all, offered to give her breakfast.

Cursing my fate, I unwrapped the dessert and put it on the floor for her before returning to the refrigerator. A second look through the shelves didn't improve matters, so I sent a desperate text to Cam and invited myself to breakfast at his place.

After a quick shower, I chugged down the last of

my orange juice and used the washed-out plastic container as a makeshift vase for Lucas's flowers. I did a crappy job with the arrangement, but I'd live with it. By the time I finished the door-locking ritual and got to my car, Zackie was lounging in the backseat. She wore the self-satisfied look of a dog who had just eaten cheesecake.

My empty stomach growled, and I muttered to her as I slid into the driver's seat. "You suck."

# # #

"Would you quit staring?" I glared back at Cam.

We had eaten cheese blintzes drowned in blueberry syrup for breakfast, the recipe courtesy of the Jewish lady from the supermarket. While Ron and Lenora cleared and washed the breakfast dishes, Cam took the opportunity to sneak concerned looks at me over his coffee mug.

"I shouldn't have just let you go home. Being alone after that experience is not healthy." Cam put the mug down and leaned forward to give me a frank evaluation.

"I wasn't alone. If you must know, Lucas came over."

Cam's eyebrows shot into his hairline. "Oh. I see." He sat back, actively suppressing questions about my night. "After what you went through, it's natural that some people—"

I thumped down my empty mug, aggravated that I felt compelled to prove to him that everything was normal with me. "No, you don't see. There was nothing to see. Nothing happened." I gazed at the ceiling. "Why am I even telling you this?"

"What you tell him?" Lenora appeared and gathered up the final dishes, seizing our mugs, whether they were empty or not.

"That Lucas showed up at her door again last night, but nothing happened." Cam reached for his mug, but Lenora backed away, unwilling to delay the breakfast cleanup.

Lenora nodded approval to me and shifted the mugs to one hand, so she could grab the used napkins. "Good girl. He bring you flowers? You invite him in for a little snuggling?"

"Oh my God! Do you people have no boundaries?" I got up from the table, red-faced with a mix of outrage and embarrassment.

"Just a question. You don't have to get all huffy." Lenora tsked and gave Cam a look of bewilderment before returning to the kitchen.

Cam shook his head and chuckled as he regarded me. "You'll do, I suppose. Definitely not withdrawn or trapped in depression."

"I'm fine. Really. We should keep going with Phebe and Phillis."

"And Mark. I discovered some things about the case last night." Cam stood and motioned toward the doorway leading to the hall. "Let me show you the files."

He took me to his study and turned on the computer. While it booted, he positioned a folding chair for me next to his office chair. "No one has ever been burned at the stake for murder in New Jersey. Only arson—and only if you were an African and a slave."

I felt a fluttering unease in my gut, like cold fingers pinching and twisting. I swallowed hard to keep my breakfast down and took some deep breaths. Cam looked concerned and paused his explanations. "Here, sit. All right, then? Not too soon?"

"Yeah, kind of creeps up on you…" I swallowed again. "S'okay now… You said something about slavery in New Jersey…" I forced myself to think, to focus on facts.

Cam perched in his chair, leaning forward as he clicked through folders on the desktop. "You're not surprised. Most people think slavery's only a Southern abomination."

I shook my head. "Learned all about it in college. Part of regional history I had to know for the major."

"Ah, yes…right. History major." Distracted, Cam found what he was looking for and clicked open the document. "Take a look at this."

It looked like the transcript from a trial. Leaning forward, I began to read out loud. " 'The examination of Phebe, a negro servant of John Russell, late of Charlestown, deceased— ' " My voice trailed off as my eyes began skimming the document. The year listed was 1755. "Holy crap, Cam! Where did you find this?"

Cam attempted to look modest, but he couldn't pull it off. "Oh, it wasn't too hard."

"You must have spent all night going through your genealogy databases to finally get to this document." I stared at him in awe. "How were you able to trace Phebe? I didn't think they kept good records for the people they enslaved."

Cam fidgeted and rubbed the back of his neck, his color rising. "Well, actually, you can find a good deal of information by checking wills and receipts for the sale of goods. But it never came down to that."

"Then how'd you do it?" I made a pinching motion with my thumb and index finger. "I am this close to bowing down before your greatness and telling you I'm not worthy to be in your awesome presence."

Cam pressed his lips together and his face flushed red. "I did a Google search on the names, all right? I typed in Phebe, Phillis and Mark and this document came right up. That's it." His expression became sheepish and he muttered the last bit of the confession. "That is, after I wasted half the night combing through the genealogy databases and deeds records for the Roseberry Homestead."

"That, um, really stinks." I tried to keep a straight face and be sympathetic but couldn't help cracking a grin.

"Right." Cam swiveled his chair to look at the screen. "If I can get you to focus on the document, you'll see that our Phebe isn't blameless in what transpired."

"What do you mean?"

"She turned State's evidence and threw Mark and Phillis under the bus. Said they poisoned John Russell." Pointing to the screen, he made his case. "Right here, the prosecutors ask about poisoned water and who had put the white powder into the water. Phebe answers that it was Mark." Scrolling down, Cam pointed to another exchange between Phebe and the prosecutors. "When they ask how many times the poisoned water was added to her 'master's victuals,' she says Phillis gave her the powder and it was added to his chocolate. Phebe then goes on to give a schedule of exactly when Phillis added the poison to John Russell's food."

"That lying bitch!" I pounded a fist on my thigh. When that proved ineffective in getting the anger out, I got up and paced around the small room. "She totally took us in with her 'Oh, Phillis, how I miss you' crap." I was thinking about how I was going to kick her lying ass back to Charlestown when something in my heart twisted. I had to sit down. Glassy-eyed, I turned to Cam. "But it wasn't all an act, was it?"

Cam had sat quietly through my short-lived tirade. In response to my question, he slowly shook his head. "No. She was genuinely wounded by their deaths and she was sincere in her desire for us to help Phillis."

"And someone hurt her. She showed all the signs of abuse." The words came whispering back to me—*Hurt people...hurt people.*

Cam cocked an eyebrow. "True enough. But don't be too taken in. Phebe is still doing what she can to manipulate the situation."

"And we don't know enough yet to figure out her motivations." A sharp edge of frustration began to fray my patience with this spirit. Weren't things complicated enough, teasing out the stories from the past, without the dead playing games with us?

Cam gave me an appraising look and then nodded, a look of satisfaction spreading on his features. "Yes, very good. Motivations are key to discerning what is real and what is manipulation. Keep that in mind as we move forward with this case."

#

Only one thing has ever gone bad in my refrigerator. Milk once went sour when I almost died and I needed to convalesce at Cam's house. Other than that, everything else has been eaten long before the sell-by date. Empty refrigerator shelves may be a way of life for me, but it still steamed my dumplings when the cupboards were bare because someone else raided my supplies.

I went to the grocery store bearing a grudge against Ron and ended up throwing a frightening amount of food in the cart because my sense of food security had been shattered. It was probably a good thing when I received a text from Gander, my boss, to tell me we had a job. The cashier had only scanned about half my groceries, and I knew the total cost to refill my cupboards was going to be alarming.

Gander's text gave me the bare bones of the "where" and "when" for the job. The "what" would have to wait until his onsite briefing. If traffic cooperated, I'd have just enough time to drop off my groceries before heading to the site. I tapped out a quick message to let him know I'd be there, threw my purchases into bags, helter-skelter, and then pushed the heaping cart through the parking lot at a brisk trot.

Working for a crime scene cleanup company was just as unpredictable as volunteering for SAR—you never knew when you'd be called out. The two jobs had a lot in common: both were physically demanding and required workers to be able to withstand minor and major discomforts. The key difference was that cleaning up biohazardous waste paid the bills, including bills for new SAR equipment after something inevitably broke or tore.

After dropping off the groceries and driving just a little faster than the speed limit, I arrived with a few minutes to spare at a two-story family home on a corner lot in Lopatcong Township. A white truck parked in the driveway bore the ambiguous company name, BioSolutions. Most homeowners were happy if we didn't make ourselves an attraction for nosy neighbors, so we tried to keep things low-key, including the company name.

I parked on the street and went directly to the truck. Goose, already dressed for work in a white hazmat suit, held the truck door open for me. His white blond hair danced in the cold breeze as he greeted me with a lazy smile. "Fia! Howzit, brah?"

"How's it going, Goose?" I gave him the fist bump he was looking for and then stepped up into the truck. Goose was a transplanted West Coast surfer with slightly different customs than his Northeast brethren and a distinctive way of expressing himself. To Gander, the dialect was frequently impenetrable, and I would be called upon to translate. It was weird, but my ability to comprehend a spirit, regardless of the language it used in life, helped me to understand Goose.

Inside the truck, I put all my clothes and personal items in a large, plastic container and stacked it on top of the one holding Goose's stuff. After slipping on disposable underwear and socks, I zipped myself into a Tyvek hazmat suit and then pulled on a pair of boots, followed by the disposable boot covers. Next came the duct tape: around my ankles to seal the boots to the hazmat suit, and then around the boot covers to secure them to the boots. Before heading out, I grabbed a spray sock to protect my head, and then goggles, a respirator, two pairs of nitrile gloves, and a roll of duct tape. I'd finish dressing outside, since I'd need help with the final bits of taping.

Gander stood near the truck's door, his dark face

somber and his hands clasped before him. The tight curls at his temples were just beginning to gray and his face was lined with life's experiences. All he needed was a Bible in those hands and he could be a preacher, dignified and full of gravitas. He greeted me in a soft, Southern drawl. "Afternoon, Fia. Step down and I'll start the briefing."

I stood next to Goose. "Is this all of us for this job?"

Gander nodded. "It's a small, contained site in the basement. Three people should be able to get this done in a few hours. JoJo will be here shortly." JoJo Kennelly was our equipment guy. He made sure we were suited up properly before entering a site and hauled away the biohazards after the job was done. With a fringe of gray hair that tended to flop in his eyes, he bore a striking resemblance to an Old English Sheepdog.

"JoJo with the late takeoff." Goose waved a shaka in greeting as a white van with the BioSolutions logo backed into the bottom of the driveway. JoJo emerged from the vehicle and jogged up to join the group.

Gander nodded to him and continued. "As I was saying, the site is in a small area in the basement. There is human biohazardous material, the consequence of a suicide by gun. We will need to decontaminate the floor and walls. Failing this, tile and dry wall may have to be removed."

Sadness swept through me like a desert wind. I thought about Maggie and her desperation before she took her own life with a gun. She died alone in the woods, the spirit of a long-dead Native American her only witness. I could seriously do without dealing with another lost soul from a suicide, but it wasn't like I had a choice in my clientele.

Sighing, I pulled the spray sock over my head and made sure it covered my neck before running some duct tape down the zipper front of the hazmat suit. Handing the tape roll to JoJo, I slipped on both pairs of nitrile gloves and then presented my hands. JoJo snugged the sleeves around the wrists of my gloves with a wrap of tape and then taped my hood to the suit. As I slipped on the respirator and goggles, JoJo helped Goose and Gander finish suiting up. We walked down to the van together and JoJo gave us terry-cloth rags, two buckets containing various plastic bottles of cleansers, hazardous waste bags, and needle nose pliers.

I held up my pliers and gave Gander a questioning look. "What's up with these?"

"It's for the skull fragments, Fia. The man shot himself in the head and some of the bone is lodged in the walls." Gander turned and headed to the house. I followed behind Goose, so I would be in the back. If the spirit of the deceased decided to make an appearance, it would be better for everyone if I kept my interactions to myself.

The front of the house had a faux brick exterior with white trim and a contrasting black door with matching shutters. It made me think of an English manor house until I saw that the side of the structure was covered with white vinyl siding. We let ourselves in through a side door that led to a mud room with a washer and dryer and the clean smell of laundry detergent. Passing through this small room into the kitchen, we found one wall decorated with a beautiful display of family pictures, and we stopped to admire it.

Most of the recent photos showed an older couple posing with what must have been their children and grandchildren. There were pictures of holiday get-togethers—a Christmas tree in the background of one photo with a half dozen people gathered around, a child in a Halloween costume in another. There were also older pictures of the couple on their wedding day—the bride, a vision in white and the groom so handsome in his military uniform. There were some photos of the family on camping trips when the kids were young and others with the man building a treehouse, go-carts, and toy boats with the kids. The most recent pictures with the kids and grandkids featured only the older man. Tacked up near the family pictures was a calendar that was now forever frozen in the month of October.

We continued past the white Formica kitchen counters where the dish drain held a mug and a plate, waiting to be returned to their place on a cabinet shelf. Just before the family room, an open door on our right led down into a half-finished basement. A comfortable-looking couch sat in the near corner surrounded by bookshelves. In the far corner of the room, just as Gander had warned us, was a pool of congealed blood on the beige, tiled floor. The wall opposite this grisly puddle was pockmarked with small indentations and painted with an ugly reddish-brown splatter.

As expected, a mushroomy taste welled up in my sinuses and the room's colors existed only as shades of gray. This was how suicides presented to me. All sensations were muted and sounds especially came across as flattened, like I was hearing everything underwater. I would have to listen extra hard if Gander or Goose said anything to me or maybe try to read their lips.

We put our stuff down and did a more thorough survey of the floor and wall. Gander noted that the odor wasn't bad—just a slightly funky scent of old blood—so the body must have been discovered quickly. To prevent us from tracking the mess around the rest of the room, we'd set to work on the floor first. Afterwards, we'd deal with the wall.

"I'll go get water from the kitchen." I grabbed a bucket and removed the cleansers before heading back upstairs. As I filled it with water from the sink, someone tapped me on the shoulder. I wasn't surprised to see the older man from the family pictures standing behind me, his white hair styled in the military crewcut of his youth and the thumbs of his strong, workman's hands tucked in his belt.

"I was wondering when I'd see you." I stuck out my hand. "Fia. Pleased to meet you."

The spirit appeared amused by the formality, but shook my hand, giving me the feeling of static electricity where we made contact. "The name's Robert, Robert Minarelli. Thanks for doing the cleanup. Not something I'd want my family to see."

"Hey, not a problem." I watched a drop of blood drip on to his shoulder and then looked closely at his face. Affable expression, held my gaze with no furtiveness, and showed no signs of distress. "You don't seem particularly traumatized by all this."

Robert shrugged. "I'm not. Had to be done."

I tilted my head, intrigued. He showed no indications of guilt, so his suicide wasn't to make up for something bad he'd done. "Why's that, Robert? Why did you have to do it?"

The corners of his mouth came down a little and his shoulders sagged until he cleared his throat and forced himself to square them. "Got a bad diagnosis from a doctor and then several more when I went for second and third opinions. No cure and nothing to help. It was going to be slow, and it was going to be bad."

"But your kids would have helped you through it, wouldn't they?" The pictures showed a tight-knit family and I felt sure they would have been with him every step of the way.

He stuck his hands in his pockets and rocked a little on his heels. "That's just it. I didn't want them to have to suffer, watching me go. I also didn't want being sick to use up all my savings. I'd have nothing left to leave to my family." He nodded, half to himself, and his lips compressed to a tight line. "Had to do it. Best thing for everyone."

"I'm really sorry about this." I wasn't sure it was the best thing for his family, but things were bad enough for him without me judging. "Anything I can do to help you move on?"

His face lit up. "I was hoping you'd say that. There's just one thing I need squared before I go. Let me show you."

Robert turned and went down the stairs to the basement. The back of his head was a bloody hole, and it hurt my heart to look at it. Picking up my bucket of water, I followed him until he stopped at a toolbox left near the wall by the couch. I put my bucket down next to the congealed pool of blood on the floor, which appeared puckered and less solid. Gander and Goose had already treated the blood puddle and the wall with Liquid Alive enzyme and, they stood gossiping as they waited for the enzyme to break down the clots.

Robert pointed to the toolbox. "I put letters to my son and daughter in there. I had this all planned out—" he jerked a thumb at the wall covered in gore "—and didn't want to spoil our last weeks together...I never told them about the diagnoses." Robert's forehead creased with worry and his eyes clouded. "It's all personal stuff I wrote for them, and I didn't want the cops to find it first, so I hid the letters in the toolbox. I figured the kids would find 'em eventually, but the longer it takes, the worse it is for them. They'll blame themselves." Robert looked up at me, eyes pleading. "Think you can help them get the letters? So they'll understand?"

I nodded, not wanting to talk to him in front of Goose and Gander, even though they were engaged in their conversation and not paying any attention to me. I took a good look at the toolbox and noticed that it was unlatched.

I walked back to the blood puddle and picked up the second bucket, ostensibly to get more water, but this time I went by the toolbox, planted my foot against the box and heaved it on to its side before deliberately tripping over it.

It was heavy with tools, but the box upended and out came the letters and a few screwdrivers. I sprawled convincingly over the mess and waited for a reaction.

"Whoa, Fia! Serious wipeout. You all right?" Goose came over and helped me up.

Gander inspected my suit for tears as soon as I was on my feet. "No breach. You're okay to continue work, if you're not hurt." He raised his eyebrows in question.

"No, I'm all right. Just a little embarrassed." I faked testing my ankle and then bent down and picked up the letters. "Hey, what's this?" The envelopes bore the names of Robert's children: Scott Minarelli and Jennifer Minarelli Tyson.

"Let me see." Gander reached out his hand and took the letters. "Minarelli is the name of the man who shot himself. These must be his kids—wasn't there a boy and a girl in those old family pictures?" Gander squinted as he tapped the envelopes against his fingers. "In fact, I think Scott's name was on the work order."

"We could have JoJo call Scott to let him know we found these." I stretched out my hand. "Want me to take these up to JoJo?"

Gander handed the letters back to me. "Sure. Just tell him to urge Scott to share the info with the police and also, don't let Scott down here. If for some reason he insists, JoJo can tell him it's for safety reasons. The son shouldn't have to see this place before we clean it."

# # #

Robert was gone, the letters delivered, and I was freshly showered and ready to go home. We had finished with the basement, and JoJo had taken off with the bags of waste we generated. Goose and Gander were in the truck decontaminating, so I pounded on the door a few times and told them I was leaving.

The soft shadows of the autumn dusk surrounded me like a familiar melody as I walked down the driveway to my car. I mentally inventoried my grocery purchases, deciding what would be easiest to cook so I could have an early night. As I raised a hand to stifle a yawn, something heavy rushed past me and sent me skittering for balance.

"What the f-ff—" I caught myself, planting my feet so I could spin around to see if it was coming back at me. A dark blur rounded the corner and moved quickly out of sight. My heart thundered and I took a few gulping breaths, no longer tired and muzzy. Blood danced beneath my skin, and everything around me came into sharp focus. Whatever it was would have no chance of sneaking up on me now that the PTSD had kicked in.

My body was in DEFCON 1 and for once, I was grateful for this hyper-alert state and did nothing to impede the flow of adrenaline. I pulled the bear spray from my pocket and made a slow rotation to check every direction for any threats. My ears picked up the faint sounds of rushing water from the shower in the BioSolutions truck, but no furtive, more concerning sounds were evident.

I approached my car and took the bear spray in my other hand, so I could fish out my keychain with the tiny LED flashlight. The powerful little light illuminated the interior of my car and reassured me that no one was in there waiting for me. Still, I checked under my car with the flashlight and then did a circuit, walking all around the vehicle to prevent an ambush.

After working the basement cleanup, the smudge on the driver's side door was all too familiar. A slight dent held a dark stain, and my mind flashed back to the frozen blood on my front door. As I tried to puzzle out the reason for the damage to my car, a luminescent outline took form near the back fender.

The glow shaped and solidified until it became a man. "It's okay, Fia. It's me, Daniel Clark."

"Daniel? What the hell—I thought you'd moved on." Part of me was delighted, but the other part of me was annoyed that he was still here. Daniel Clark had been a sheriff's deputy and a local hero in the mountains of North Carolina. That is, until Alzheimer's Disease claimed his mind and then his life, and he became a confused and restless spirit that Cam, Zackie and I tried to help.

Daniel, in uniform and in the prime of his life, gave a rueful grin. "Not movin' on just yet, darlin'. There's always folks out there who can't keep their hands to themselves and leave other people alone."

"You have anything to do with this?" I pointed toward the dent coated with blood.

The grin grew wider. "Little bit. The bastard was setting up your tire to have a flat. Putting a big ol' nail right there in front, so you'd roll over it." Daniel stuck his thumbs in his belt and chuckled. "I gave him a little nudge to let him know what's what."

"You ever give him a little nudge before? Like maybe around my house?" I crossed my arms and tilted my head, starting to put two and two together.

"Sure did, ma'am. Couple of times. Hip checked him into the back of your house once and then gave him something to think about when he was fiddling with your front door." Daniel jutted his chin toward the bloody dent. "Only the little f-ff—sorry, the little bastard can't seem to learn."

"Three time's a charm, you think?"

Daniel sucked his teeth and gave a half shake of his head. "Doubt it. But you be rest assured, I'll have your six. Don't you worry about him none."

With that, Daniel faded into the growing night. I got into my car and breathed a sigh of relief. My body had stood down when Daniel drew on my excess energy to help him manifest. The adrenaline-fueled, frantic edge had receded. My heart was beating normally again. Best of all, I felt secure knowing Daniel had my back. Still, I locked my doors and checked the rearview mirror before pulling out. I'd call Cam when I got home and let him know the mystery of the blood on my door was solved.

#

The theme from *The Good, the Bad and the Ugly* shrilled from my phone and made my hand jerk as I tried to thread the needle for the third time. Sitting at my card table, I'd used an iron-on to patch the hole in the pants that tore during the search for Millie, and I was just about to stitch the small rip on my coat. Frustration with all things domestic was at an all-time high, so Cam's timing was impeccable.

I stuck the needle in the fabric, so I wouldn't lose it and picked up my phone. "Howzit Brah?"

"I beg your pardon?"

I sighed. How was I ever going to learn to speak a new language if no one let me practice? "Nothing. Just something I picked up from Goose. So, what's up?"

"We have a special guest appearance from Lucas at tonight's dinner. He's going to give us an update."

"So, now he's calling *you* for dinner dates? Something has gone very wrong…." I was only half joking about this. Maybe Lucas really was upset that nothing happened between us the other night, and I hadn't read him right.

Cam chuckled. "It's not you, it's him. He only had time for one call and needed to know if it was okay with Lenora if we all met for dinner at six. Figured I'd manage the invitations once she'd approved the event."

"Okay, I'll be there, but he better not start hitting on Lenora in front of me." I had a mental image of Lenora jabbing Lucas with her cane and demanding a bouquet of roses.

"So, erm, should we maybe plan on paying Phebe a visit afterwards?"

"I dunno, Cam. Is it worth it? I mean, I'm up for it, but I'm a little disappointed with her level of truthiness. Maybe we should just focus on Phillis. Phebe ought to move on after Phillis goes, don't you think?"

Cam exhaled noisily through his nose and didn't answer right away. "I think it will be a relief to her if Phillis finds her rest, but Phebe is likely suffering under a burden of guilt. She might linger to punish herself for betraying Mark and Phillis during the trial." He paused again. "I sense you're a bit reluctant to work with Phebe."

"Yeah, I suppose. She's kind of a con artist. I don't think she's ever going to give us a straight story."

"And how is this different from many of the others we've worked with?" Cam's voice took on the patient, pedagogical tone I've come to expect right before he hits me with a bit of wisdom related to the unseen world.

I took a moment to sort out my thoughts. "I think the others were either self-deluding or in a place where they couldn't think straight, even if they wanted to. Phebe's knowingly feeding us a line."

"I won't argue with you on those points. But you need to consider her life's history. Do you think someone who is a slave can be straightforward in what they say, just speak their mind without fear of retribution?"

Damn it, Cam was making me feel sorry for her again. I closed my eyes and scrunched up my face, trying to swallow his logic. It was a bitter pill, and I had a hard time disregarding my personal feelings of having been conned by this spirit. "No, you're right. She's not going to trust us, and she'll deflect and redirect to keep herself out of trouble. Habits of a lifetime."

"So, given this situation, what do you suggest?"

129

"Well, she's never going to trust us. To her, we're no different than the sub-humans who bought and sold people like her. We should probably bring in someone she won't see as 'management.'" I grinned sheepishly and stopped air-quoting the word when I realized I was the only one who could see the gesture.

Cam made approving noises. "Very good. I think Lenora is an excellent candidate for the job."

"Really? I was thinking Ron." I pushed the coat toward the center of the card table, so I could lean on my elbows. "Think about it. Ron's this attractive guy about her age. She might behave herself and cooperate just to please him, maybe impress him."

"Hmm. That's a possibility, but from my perspective, I think Phillis was something of a mother figure for Phebe. She gave the girl that doll, after all. Lenora has that no-nonsense, maternal presence needed to make Phebe remember her manners."

"You might be right." I rubbed my lower lip as I considered. "But the beauty of the situation is, we have a two-fer—Ron and Lenora are a package deal, so we don't really have to choose. Something ought to work for us, right?"

Lucas's hands ran along my ribs as we kissed, caressing slowly upward. Teasing my earlobe, he whispered, "I think I'm addicted to you—"

I never heard the rest. With uncanny precision, Cam interrupted us, issuing orders to stop our snogging and come in from the front porch. Dinner was ready, but so was I, and the timing couldn't have been worse. I took a few moments to compose myself, burrowing into Lucas's open coat and snuggling into his warmth.

"That's not helping, you know." Lucas made no move to dislodge me, but I sighed and then stepped away before taking him by the hand to lead him inside. Hanging back, he resisted my pull. "You go ahead. I'll just be minute. I forgot the report in the car."

This was perhaps a ruse to give him a little more time to cool down, but I nodded and entered Cam's house. The aroma of something tangy with the sweet scent of fresh bread captured my attention and drew me to the dining room.

Lenora sat at her customary place at the table, a look of challenge in her eye. Boxes of pizza covered the table from end to end. She caught my astonished look and shrugged. "I took a day off from cooking. So sue me."

"Everyone deserves a day off, *Uma*. Don't sweat it." Ron reached for a box and helped himself to three slices of pepperoni. Selecting another box, he added another three slices of sausage and pepper.

Not to be outdone, I copied Ron's method and loaded my plate with slices of pepperoni and the special with everything on it. The next time I looked up, Lucas was across from me, finishing the last few bites of a slice, a brown mailing envelope sitting at his elbow.

Cam stared pointedly at me. "Now that we're all present, maybe Lucas can provide his update."

Wiping his hands, Lucas nodded as he swallowed his last bite. While he was occupied with removing the document from the protective covering, I quickly wiped my face with a napkin and hoped he hadn't noticed the pizza sauce around my mouth.

"This is the lab report on the hair samples from that doll Fia found." Placing the document flat on the table, Lucas flipped back the cover page to reveal what looked like a summary of the analysis. "What they found was—"

"It was from a female of African descent?" Cam smiled, an amused glint in his eye.

Lucas sat back and crossed his arms. "Yes, West Africa. How did you know?"

"We've had dealings with someone who knew the hair donor." I went on to explain Phebe's story.

"The isotope analysis *was* consistent with the hair being a historical sample." Lucas shook his head, nonplussed. "'There are more things in heaven and earth, Horatio...'"

Lenora gave a disapproving grunt. "Poor Phebe. The Cherokee in Oklahoma kept slaves. They were generous and took in the Lenape when our people were forced out of Kansas, but they'd also kept slaves. Terrible thing."

"Wait, what?" This did not compute. I remembered from my college classes the Trail of Tears, a time of death and sorrow for the Cherokee as they were forced from their lands. The fact sat like a lump in my gut, that these mistreated people also abused others. *Hurt people…hurt people*. The sad refrain echoed in my mind.

"What he said. Hamlet had it right." Ron pointed his chin toward Lucas. "The Cherokee slaveholders either force-marched their African-American slaves on the Trail of Tears or had them shipped like cattle in cramped boats with the rest of their stuff." He shook his head, the corners of his mouth turning down in a deep scowl. "This kind of thing doesn't make it into the history books, probably 'cause it's so confusing. You don't know who to root for anymore."

Lenora sighed and slowly shook her head. "The descendants of the slaves got kicked out of the Nation a few years ago when that tribe voted you had to have Cherokee blood to be a citizen. The Black Cherokee had to sue to get their rights back."

Cam looked away, his expression weary. "Be that as it may, we can't save everybody from everything. Let's keep our focus on Phebe. Maybe we can at least bring some measure of peace to her and Phillis."

"I think Phebe's story would make an interesting episode for the show. We already have the hair analysis, so some film footage—" Lucas's attention was drawn by the vibrating phone that he pulled from his back pocket. Glancing at the screen, he frowned and stood up from the table. "Sorry, I have to take this."

As Lucas left the room, Cam continued, addressing his comments to Ron and Lenora. "Could we perhaps visit the Roseberry House together tonight? We think Phebe might relate better to you two and be more forthcoming."

"Thought you'd never ask." Ron rested his chin on a fist and batted his eyelashes like a seasoned flirt. "I was starting to think *Uma's* grandfather sent dreams telling her to stay, just so she could get some new recipes."

Lenora reached across the table and lightly cuffed Ron's ear. "You watch that attitude, boy. Big as you are, Grandfather'd have you over his knee and—"

"I'm just kidding, *Uma.* I take the dreams seriously, I promise." Ron rubbed his ear and shifted his chair to be out of Lenora's reach. "I'm just restless to do something."

Lucas had slipped back into the room and returned to his seat during Ron and Lenora's exchange. His next words made me forget all about post-pubescent disciplinary problems. "You might be interested to know that there's been a new development in the Scotland case."

Cam perked up. "Something else happened on that country lane? Has another jogger been savaged?"

"No, no new violent incidents. The investigative team found an interesting historical connection." Lucas sat forward, resting his forearms on the table. "It appears that in the sixteenth century, a local woman was executed for witchcraft. Her bones may be buried at that crossroad."

Great, I thought, *someone else who was persecuted and is now dishing it out.* Out loud, I shared different thoughts, because this sounded too maudlin even in my own head. "Were there other similar events at this crossroad? Other people being attacked? You'd think we would have heard about this crossroad before, if that were the case."

Lucas shook his head. "No previous reports of anything."

Ron stood up and began clearing dishes from the table. "So, if things were quiet, what riled her up? Why did it start up now?"

Lucas waggled his eyebrows. "Why indeed? Your questions would make an excellent teaser for the show." The phone, still in his hand, began to buzz again. After a few taps, Lucas pulled a face. "Damn. This is not what I signed on for."

"What's wrong?" I asked as he stood up again.

"It looks like I won't be able to help with Phebe. I have to go home and pack. They booked me on the next flight to Scotland." Lucas ran a hand through his hair, pushing it back with an irritated motion. "Let me give you a handheld camera before I go. I'd really appreciate it if one of you could take some footage for me."

"I'll do it." Ron carried the pile of dirty dishes to the kitchen. "Just let me get these into the dishwasher, and I'll take the camera from you." The industrious sounds of running water and clinking plates soon followed, along with some off-key whistling.

"How long will you be gone?" I fought to keep the whine out of my voice. This was work. It wasn't as if he had a choice, so I didn't want to make it more difficult for him.

Lucas shrugged miserably. "A few weeks, maybe

more."

I nodded and looked down, so he wouldn't see my disappointment. "Well, Scotland should be fun. Keep in touch and let us know how you like the haggis."

Maybe to cover his frustration with the situation, he began to energetically stack the empty pizza boxes. "I'll put these out with the trash." On his way out, he murmured in my ear. "I would have brought you pink roses this time."

I kept my head bowed, my eyes trained on my hands to prevent Cam and Lenora from seeing the blush inching up my hairline. Maybe things would have worked out for us this time if Lucas hadn't had to fly out. Then again, maybe Hannah would have shown up full of fury, or Lucas would have mysteriously backed out like before, or a badly timed callout would have interrupted us. Or maybe it would have been glorious.

I sighed quietly to myself and then got up to make coffee. It was going to be a long night for everyone, and I would have some long, empty days ahead of me until I saw Lucas again.

#

My lips still tingled from Lucas's farewell kiss. That man knew his stuff when it came to making an exit. I had definitely been left wanting more. Despite this burning distraction, I did my best to concentrate and focus my mind on Phebe, to entreat her to join us.

The Roseberry House was quiet. In the absence of an electrical storm to power the psychic recordings, there were no voices from the past replaying the history of the home. Just as well. Ron moved restlessly in a protective circle around Lenora, his eyes darting to follow the movement of every shadow that lurked along the ruined walls. Using the small, handheld video camera strapped to his wrist, he took sporadic, shaky video of nothing. Lucas was going to need a good film editor to get anything of value out of this footage. Hunched in a camp chair in the middle of the room, Lenora rubbed her arms obsessively against the unnatural cold, her face creased with worry. In contrast, Cam stood apart from everyone, leaning against the fireplace mantle and calmly waiting for the show to start.

I took a break from calling to Phebe. Ron's constant pacing was distracting me, making me nervous and uncertain about what we were about to do. I grabbed his sleeve as he strode by. "Would it kill you to stop doing that?"

Ron flashed a strained grin, his eyes wide with barely suppressed panic. "I'm just hoping being here won't kill me." He had been restless to do something, and now he was having second thoughts and was filled with unease.

"It's so cold!" Lenora huddled deeper into her coat.

Cam slipped off his down-padded jacket and draped it around her shoulders. "Here, take this. Another layer should help." The psychic cold could not penetrate the rhino-hide he had built up over many years of dealing with discarnate spirits.

I looked from Ron to Lenora. "I don't get it. It wasn't like this with He-Who-Counseled-the-Chief. What's different?"

Ron went still. The only thing about him that moved were his eyes, warily delving into the dark corners of the room. "I'm not gonna lie—this place freaks me out. It doesn't feel right here. We're somehow confined. Trapped. With He-Who-Counseled-the-Chief, at least we were outdoors. It was natural. Open...I don't know...."

I wondered if part of what he was picking up was the life of freedom the ancient Lenape man led compared to Phebe's enslavement.

Ron pushed his hair back with a shaky hand and tried again to explain. "Lenape people believe one of the souls, the blood soul, can do living people serious damage. Our elders teach us to avoid this thing. But we were connected to He-Who-Counseled-the-Chief like family, and he was careful with us. What we're doing here isn't healthy." Ron's eyebrows knit in consternation and he turned to Lenora. "What is your sense of this, *Uma*?"

Lenora looked up at Ron, her face troubled. "I don't like it. But Grandfather said we're needed here." Having said those words, her eyes hardened, and she nodded once. "We do this thing."

Ron took a deep breath and rubbed his face with his free hand. "Right. We do this thing." Pulling the camera up to eye level, he widened his stance and braced his feet as if standing his ground against some threat. "Go on, Fia."

I shot a look at Cam. He chewed his lip, watching Lenora and Ron with concern. "Are we doing right by them, Cam?"

Lenora, belligerent, answered for him. "You go on, little girl. Don't you worry 'bout us."

With a final uncertain glance to Cam, I oriented myself to face the site along the demolished wall where Phebe had first manifested. I focused my will on drawing her to us. Zackie sat at heel on my left side, her ears perked and alert.

This spirit did not want to come to us. It was like trying to extract a mass of tangled hair from a clogged drain. Parts of her were clinging to something and resisting the pull of the invitation, but I sensed this recalcitrance was mixed with a desire to be seen and heard. She came slowly, grudgingly.

The air near the wall wavered as if heat were rising, and a faint glow expanded to cast a sickly yellow light along the wall. Phebe gradually gained color and substance until she stood before us, head bowed and arms crossed in silent rebellion. She gazed at the ground, her expression sullen. My ambivalence toward her must have leaked through as I called her to us.

"What do you want of me?" Her voice was low and she set her lips in a tight line, as if these few words were forced out and good luck getting her to say more.

My gaze slid toward Ron and Lenora. While Lenora was so cold her teeth chattered, Ron stood rigidly, his eyes flitting like a hummingbird with its heart racing at ninety miles an hour. I did not have to tell them Phebe was with us.

Cam cleared his throat. "Phebe, allow us to introduce our friends, Ron and Lenora."

Phebe raised her head and regarded the pair, taking in their dusky skin and Ron's long, black hair. She cocked a skeptical eyebrow. "Friends, you say?"

"Yes, friends." I repeated this firmly, so there would be no mistake.

Phebe shook her head, not accepting this relationship. "Are they not beneath your station? Do they not do your bidding?"

Cam and I burst out laughing, startling Phebe and throwing her off her guard. Grinning, Cam approached Lenora and stood in front of her. "Phebe would like to know if you'll do my bidding."

Lenora peered out from under her layers and gave

him the stink-eye. "Kiss my ass, Kemosabe."

Ron, still wound tight, managed to crack a smile. "Isn't that a Lyle Lovett song?" His face sobered as he continued. "Ask Phebe what we can do for her, to help her."

Phebe dropped her defensive posture, and a look of cunning calculation appeared, but it was quickly hidden behind an expression of mild interest. She turned her head and gave Ron a look of frank appraisal, from the tips of his toes to the top of his head. A thin smile spread on her lips and then she modestly lowered her gaze. "I thank the young sir for his kind offer. It is true I have been here over long."

While Cam relayed Phebe's words to Lenora and Ron, I kept my eye on her. Something was not right. I didn't trust her mercurial change in attitude, from bitch-on-wheels to demure maiden. I slipped into interrogation mode but kept both my voice and the initial question easy, so she wouldn't feel threatened. Push too hard and this spirit was likely to go AWOL. "What brought you here, Phebe? The whole business with Mark and Phillis happened in Boston. How did you end up in New Jersey?"

Phebe breathed a dramatic sigh. Her eyes drifted to the gray, dingy walls stripped of whitewash, the plaster gouged and uneven. "This was once a beautiful house." She waved a graceful hand to an area of the wall separating the room from the hallway. "Do you see these stencils?"

Allowing her to evade my softball question for now, I looked where she pointed. Remnants of color stood out on the wall, barely recognizable as something that had once added beauty and character to the house. Squinting, I let the years drop away until I saw what she saw. Decorative rope borders edged the top and bottom of the wall in shades of blue, gray, and black. Gracefully weaving down between these borders, fancy chains of daisies alternated with strands of multicolored floral patterns, both repeating the blue-gray motif, but also adding a striking red to the palette. "I see them. These stencils must have been the centerpiece of the house."

Phebe's eyes dropped, her long lashes brushing her cheek. "I was long dead when the Roseberry's hired a man to decorate these walls. He traveled from town to town, painting signs for businesses and stenciling walls for people of means. I almost left with him. I wanted to follow him and see the world."

Cam picked up this lead and used the next question to provoke, trying to get something of substance from this spirit. "But you stayed—for what? To watch over dead children?"

Phebe's eyes snapped open and there was nothing placid in her gaze. Twin pinpoints of light burned in her pupils and her voice shook. "I watched them depart this life and move on to the next." Her lips twisted into a snarl. "It was so easy for them. I tried to suss out the riddle of how they made this happen. I tried to trail behind them, but I was denied."

Phebe fueled her rage by sucking away what little heat we had in the room. We could see our breath. Shivering, Ron's numb fingers struggled with the camera to capture the effect of the anomalous cold. "Dammit. Camera's frozen. Buttons won't depress." Taking a closer look at the device, his eyes widened in disbelief. "And now the battery's dead."

Lenora snugged further into the layers of coats and let out a small moan. From deep within the folds of fabric, Lenora's muffled voice sounded irritated and out of patience, the fear yielding to the discomfort. "Tell her to let the dog take her over. Works for Lenape, it'll work for her."

Approaching the spirit with a slowly wagging tail, Zackie radiated a warm compassion that dispelled the cold. All earthly woes would pass away if the spirit could accept what was offered.

With an effort, Phebe quelled her rage and dropped to her knees. Burying her face in her hands, she took a long, shuddering breath before meeting the gaze of the Psychopomp. "I would go with you, but I have learned my heart is chained to this earth until I make right what I have done."

The harsh edge had gone from her voice, and she spoke in the soft and submissive tones of a little girl. Zackie huffed a frustrated sigh and turned away from the mewling spirit. Before retreating into the shadows, she gave Cam and me a baleful glance to let us know the tedious job of convincing this spirit to cross over rested squarely on our shoulders.

"What's happened now?" Ron demanded, his eyes wild and fearing the worst.

Cam huffed out his own frustration. "She's refusing to move on until she's cleaned up the mess she created."

Ron took a deep breath and stared at the ceiling, maybe gathering his strength. His expression grew serious as he psyched himself up to let go of the fear. "We do this thing." Getting down on one knee, he guessed wrongly about the location of the spirit and like a blind man, he directed his words to empty space. "Phebe, we know about the trial. We know about Mark and Phillis. Don't be enslaved a second time by guilt. You can be free now."

Phebe stared at him, liquid sorrow filling her eyes. "You do not understand—I lived and they died. Because of me, they died." Her small fist hammered her chest, and I couldn't tell if these were crocodile tears and histrionics, or if she was sincere.

Ron listened to Cam's translation and tried again. "That was lifetimes ago, Phebe. *Lifetimes.* No one alive remembers this story anymore. The world has moved on and so can you." Ron paused, looking to see how his words played out with the spirit, and got only a sad shake of the head from Cam. "Look, we've all done things in our lives that we wish we could take back, somehow un-do. We can't. We can only try to do the right thing now."

Ron's face clouded over, and I couldn't help thinking that he was remembering the violence he had done in his youth. Ron grew up with serious anger issues. It had caused all sorts of trouble for the white couple that had adopted him. In desperation, they had sent him through an escalating series of psychiatric treatments, ultimately landing him in the same institution where I had been sent. When that didn't work, Ron was bundled off to Oklahoma to live with Lenora and a branch of the Lenape tribe. Between Lenora's influence and reclaiming his tribal roots, Ron had transformed into the type of man who would disregard crippling fear to try and help a wayward spirit.

Phebe set her jaw, her whole posture stiffening. "I was to be transported to the Indies for my crimes and lose the *easy* life of a house slave." Her lips curled into a bitter smile.

Cam stared at the spirit with hard eyes. "But this didn't happen, did it? Your name was not in the indictment or the record of judgment."

Shaking her head in wonderment at her dumb luck, Phebe continued as if Cam hadn't spoken. "I thought I would work the sugarcane until I died in the fields, but I escaped even that. Before the ship could sail, a man bribed the guard at the gaol and brought me to serve his wife on their New Jersey farm. Some years later when he owed money, I was given to Master Peter Kinney to cover the debt, and I came to this house." She waved a hand, dismissive, as if what followed was of little consequence. "I caught the ague the next winter."

I mentally grabbed at this piece of her history, because it seemed that a deep reason for remaining earthbound was right here. "So, let me get this straight. You turned on Mark and Phillis during the trial, and you feel guilty that they were executed because of your words against them." She nodded miserably, wiping tears from her cheeks with the back of her hand. She didn't bother to rise from the floor, trying to look meek and submissive. "Not only that, but you feel like you were never punished for your misdeeds."

Phebe hunched her shoulders, whining. "There was never justice for me. I almost envy Mark and Phillis. Their sins were wiped clean after killing a man."

I rolled my eyes at this. These were the words of a true coward, the words of someone who never had to face the flames or whatever horrible death Mark had suffered. And I'm supposed to believe she was feeling sorry for herself because she didn't have to endure torture? I struggled to sort through what she had conveyed to us so far. Some of it was real and sincere, but a lot of it felt like subterfuge and manipulation.

Beyond the tragedy of how the lives of two people ended, there was something more here, but I couldn't get enough of a grip on this slippery narrative to ask precise questions. I cast a helpless look to Cam, and his lips twisted in an expression that seemed to say he, too, was unsatisfied with what we'd learned so far.

Cam paced the length of the room, his hands behind his back. "Bear with me, Phebe, and help me understand your point." When his stride brought him even with the spirit, he paused and frowned. "Are you saying you'd prefer earthly justice to whatever may happen in the afterlife? Because your actions show you're rather comfortable escaping both forms of justice."

Phebe had the grace to squirm. "N-no, that is not true. I tried to follow the children when they left this earth."

Cam stroked his chin and feigned a thoughtful expression. "Did you? Did you really, now?"

Phebe dropped her gaze. She went back to the little girl voice, sounding pitiful and powerless. "I followed them to the threshold but did not attempt to go farther. But I—"

"Mmm…yes, I thought as much." Cam resumed his pacing and fired off another question, not giving her time to think. "And the doll, Phebe. You're not carrying it. What's become of your doll?"

Panic crept into Phebe's eyes and she climbed to her feet. "I-I lost it."

Cam looked askance at Phebe. "Again? But I thought this doll was precious to you."

The spirit shifted from foot to foot, her eyes furtive as she sought a way out of this interrogation. When Phebe took a sudden step backward into the shadows, I almost called out to warn Cam that we had a runner. Between one breath and the next, Zackie crouched before her, like a bay dog cutting off her prey from all means of escape. Zackie exposed the tips of her fangs as her lip curled in challenge. The message was unmistakable: *Try it. I dare you.*

Lenora flipped the coats back to better see Zackie. She had been following my translation of the conversation and now glanced at me for confirmation. "She tried to run?" When I nodded, Lenora shook her head in disgust. Turning back toward the standoff, she called to the unseen spirit. "Child, you stay put and don't give that dog a reason.

And you stop your lying. You hear me?"

"Yes, ma'am," Phebe mumbled automatically, never taking her eyes from Zackie.

After I told Lenora that Phebe was inclined to follow her orders, she gave me a knowing look. "Sure she will." Lenora shifted in the chair and returned her attention to the spirit. "Phebe, why's that doll got you running scared?"

Phebe was trapped, and she looked like she was about to cry real tears. Sniffing, she wiped a sleeve under her dripping nose. "It was from Phillis. I helped her cut her hair. She was terrified of going into the flames and her hair catching, so she asked me to cut it. We chipped a flake of stone off the wall in the gaol, and we sharpened it as best we could." Phebe worried her hands and held them tight against her belly. "I told her to use that sharp stone on herself so they couldn't send her into the fire, but she said one wrong death was enough. Stone wasn't near sharp enough anyway. Pulled out more hair than we cut."

Lenora grunted when I told her Phebe's response and then went quiet for a moment. "And she made you that doll from her hair?"

Phebe nodded. "She said it was a keepsake, to remember her. It would bring me comfort."

When I relayed Phebe's answer, Lenora narrowed her eyes and edged forward on her chair. "Because she thought you'd be executed after her, and she didn't want you to die alone? After she and Mark were gone?"

"Yes." Phebe sobbed quietly.

I nodded to Lenora to let her know the spirit's reply. Lenora spoke softly, but there was a fury burning in her eyes. "You lied to her the whole damn time. When did she learn that you'd be spared? When that man came to take you to New Jersey?"

Phebe nodded again and hiccupped. "She was so angry. She knew then I betrayed them, and she cursed me."

Rolling her eyes when she heard my translation, Lenora spat out the next question. "Child, then why'd you take the doll? If you parted so badly, why'd you take the doll?"

She didn't have a ready lie and I could almost see her mind racing. Phebe's gaze shifted, and she took a breath before answering. "Because I still loved Phillis and I wanted to remember her."

I told Lenora exactly what I heard and saw. Standing up, Lenora flung off her coverings and pointed a shaking finger toward the spirit. "Don't you lie to me again. Why'd you take that doll?"

Phebe stamped her foot, her hands clenched into fists and her face contorted into an ugly mask. "I didn't! It followed me. Everywhere I go, it follows me."

Cam's eyes shone with triumph. "I knew it." Coming up behind Lenora, he put a hand on her shoulder and bent to her ear to tell her what Phebe had said. "Well done, Lenora."

Lenora patted his hand and returned to her seat, breathing hard and muttering. "Thinks she can lie to me…"

Ron grabbed the coats from the floor and covered Lenora. "Let me get this straight. Phillis haunted Phebe after she was executed?"

Lenora looked at him like he was stupid. "You not listening, boy? Course she did. Wouldn't you, after being betrayed and lied to like that?"

Ron exhaled loudly and ignored the question.

"What I want to know is if that's still going on. The doll came back to Phebe, after all."

Cam beamed. "Excellent question, Ron. Exactly what I wanted to know." He faced Phebe and crossed his arms. "And, young lady? Does Phillis still harass you?"

Phebe's color was still high, and she brought her fists up like she wanted to hit something. "Yes, damn you. I cannot escape that harridan. She gives me no peace. When I am away from here in the other place..." The fight seemed to go out of her, and she lowered her arms, wrapping them protectively around her torso. She shrank into herself and whispered, as if she were afraid Phillis might hear. "I am surrounded by smoke, and I can smell her burnt flesh. She is somewhere in that dark cloud, and she grabs me, and it burns hotter than hell. I can feel the bones break through her charred hands as her hold tightens. When her skin cracks and breaks, the sound it makes..." Phebe shuddered and closed her eyes, grimacing.

Catching on at last, I put the question to her. "Is that why you want us to help Phillis cross over? So you'll be free of her?"

Phebe kept her eyes shut, and her face twisted in

pain as she nodded.

# # #

"How did you know Phebe was lying when she said she tried to follow the children through the portal?" We sat on the couch in Cam's living room, our feet up on his coffee table, sipping bottles of coconut water. Lenora and Ron had gone to bed, exhausted from the stress of their encounter with Phebe.

"She said she was denied, and I thought, 'Oh, come on. They let anyone in.'" He snorted and pointed at the dead hand. "They almost took you."

I hitched a shoulder and gave a noncommittal mumble that may or may not have questioned the legitimacy of his parentage. But his statement was true enough. Some of the worst people went straight through the portal after they died, while some of the nicest got stuck on this side. Go figure.

I listened to the fire hiss and pop, stretching my stockinged feet toward its warmth. "So, what are we going to do with this? We can't leave Phillis earthbound. She's suffered enough. But if we move her on, all we've done is make things comfy for Phebe. She's never going to cross over. You saw how frightened she was at the possibility of facing justice on the other side."

Cam grunted. "I wonder if we can appeal to Phillis's baser instincts and get her to increase the pressure. If we make things bad enough here, maybe Phebe will be less inclined to stay."

I almost choked on my coconut water. Coughing a few times, I wiped my mouth with my sleeve. "What, you think Phillis is holding back after everything that's been done to her? No way, dude. This is the worst she can do. Phebe might not like it, but it's not moving the needle on getting her to move on."

"Then maybe we just have to give up on Phebe, cut our losses. We concentrate on getting Phillis through the portal and call it a day." Cam turned his head and cast a weary eye on me. "I have to say, a spirit haunting another spirit is not something you encounter every day. I had no idea this was possible."

"Glad to hear you say it. I was thinking this was a little weird, but I don't have a lot to compare it to." I took another swig of the coconut water and wished it was something harder.

Cam sighed and stretched. "It's the curse of growing older. You eventually encounter all manner of things you wish you could un-see."

We sat in comfortable silence for a minute, and I watched the flames glide along the wood like a cat rubbing against a scratching post. "You know, she never mentions Mark. I guess he just passed on through and he's not our problem. How did he die anyway? Phebe said it was worse than what happened to Phillis."

"Mmm...I read about this and it's another thing I'd like to un-see. They hanged him—"

I gave Cam a quizzical look. "That doesn't sound worse than being burned alive. Look, all of this is a horror show, and I wouldn't volunteer for any of it. But if I had to choose..."

Cam sunk his head back into the pillowed headrest and stared at the ceiling. "After they hanged him, he was gibbeted. They tarred his body and hung it in chains, displaying it for all the world to see."

Maybe I had gotten habituated to all the gruesome ways a person could die, but I shrugged, still not impressed. "You have to remember I'm a graduate of the 'People Suck' lecture. Zackie's shown me the worst of the worst. So, gibbeting? Not great. But if he was already dead, how bad could it be? Phebe made it sound like they tortured him to death or something."

Cam gave me the side eye. "That's a bit cold, but I suppose with your modern perspective, you really don't get the horror." I shrugged again, confirming his assessment. "From Phebe's perspective, he was denied a Christian burial, so he would have no peace. He was also left to be shamed in the public's eye until his body rotted in full view of those who scorned him."

When he saw that my understanding was still left wanting, he continued. "Fia, he became a thing, no longer a human or something that once was human. There was no respect for his remains. You know about Paul Revere's ride?"

I nodded, the history major in me making an appearance. "It was 'the eighteenth of April in seventy-five,' according to the Longfellow poem—"

"Paul Revere wrote a letter about his ride. He said that when he was nearly opposite where Mark still hung in chains, he saw two men on horseback under a tree. Mark's body was just a landmark in the end."

My eyes widened as I finally got it. "Holy crap. That ride was like twenty years later."

Cam nodded. "Imagine if that were someone you knew, a friend or a family member. People go to great lengths to make sure a loved one is buried properly, and the body is treated with dignity."

Poor Mark. I was glad that he had crossed over and wasn't lingering. I hoped it hadn't taken him long. As I mulled this over, a feeling of doubt gnawed like a rat in my mind. "Cam? We should also go to where they hung Mark's body. Just to make sure."

Cam was about to take another sip from his bottle and his hand stopped midway to his mouth. His lips curved down and he stared at me with troubled eyes for a long moment before speaking. "Good idea. Just to make sure."

###

I found a note taped to my door when I returned home. It fluttered in the chilly breeze, and I plucked it clumsily with my mittens. The note was from Peyton, telling me to come over to Joel's place and not to worry about the time. Something had been delivered while I was away, and she had signed for me. I checked my watch and it was just past nine, not too late to be calling.

Zackie trotted behind me as I made my way to Joel's door. No longer the hell hound that gave Phebe what-for, she was still a welcome companion in the moonless night. I figured she could turn that beast thing on and off, and if we encountered any person of bad intent, he'd meet with the sharp end of the hound.

I tapped lightly on the door. Despite Peyton's open invitation, Joel's contractor job made for early mornings, and I didn't want to wake him. Even with my light touch, the frantic barking of multiple dogs exploded inside the house. So much for not waking Joel.

Peyton cracked the door and then shooed the three dogs away to allow Zackie and me entry. "Come on in." Heckle, Jeckle, and Simber, the furry furies responsible for the racket, backed away with low wagging tails and dipped their heads as Zackie passed. I received considerably less respect and accepted the licked greetings and paws on my chest as they competed for attention.

Sounds of snoring floated down the stairs and my guilt for rousing the dogs and waking the household evaporated. The house was warm and inviting. Burning wood hissed in a pot belly stove standing in the corner. Its squat, humble body complemented the earth tones in the décor and added to the feeling of coziness. Peyton wore Joel's tattered, navy blue robe, and she held a mug of aromatic tea in her hands. Her bright red hair was mussed, but her eyes were lively and alert. I hadn't interrupted her sleep either.

"Want some?" Peyton held her mug aloft.

"That's okay, I don't want to keep you up." Truth was, I didn't want to keep me up. I was eager to get home and crawl into bed after everything that had gone on with Phebe.

"Suit yourself. Let me get your delivery." Peyton put her mug down on the coffee table and padded into Joel's kitchen. I waved inquisitive dog muzzles away from her mug while I waited. Returning with a massive bouquet of pink roses wrapped in clear cellophane, she winked as she handed me the flowers. "Here you go."

I grinned like the village idiot, delighted by another sweet, romantic gesture. "Lucas…." I fumbled with the cellophane until a dab of adhesive released the little white card. The message was short, but my heart gave a flutter like a baby bird's wings. "Missing you already. Keep the bear spray handy and be careful."

Peyton smiled. "He's a keeper."

"Yeah, I'd like to keep him closer, but he just left for Scotland to do some filming." I sighed and tucked the card into my back pocket and then brushed my hand over the bear spray, a reassuring lump in my hip pocket. "How are things with Joel?"

"Oh, he's a keeper too." Her eyes shone, and a soft smile touched her lips. "It's really something, having this May-December romance."

My eyes strayed to the occasional gray hairs peeking through her locks along her temple, and she caught me looking. Self-consciously, she smoothed these hairs and then clenched her teeth as she reiterated her position in a menacing voice. "May-December. It's very romantic."

I took a step back, holding the bouquet like a shield against my chest as I struggled for words. "Yes, I, um—absolutely. You two make a cute couple. We should go out sometime, that is, when Lucas gets back…because, um, he's in Scotland?"

Peyton arched a brow. "So you've said."

While the other dogs had gone back to nosing Peyton's mug, Zackie sat in front of me, her mouth open in silent laughter. Ignoring the canine mirth, I cleared my throat and tried for a neutral topic. "How's the Roseberry House restoration going?"

Peyton prattled on about the progress with the house, animated now that she could talk about stone masonry. "…and after I watched the master stonemason repoint the exterior on the north side, he took me inside and showed me one of the interior walls. There was actual horse hair, you know, from the mane or tail—these long strands of hair in the plaster. They used it as a binding agent—oh, that reminds me." Peyton padded off to the kitchen again and returned with a brown paper bag.

"Is that my lunch for tomorrow?" As I took the bag from Peyton, Zackie nudged it with her muzzle and gave me a meaningful look.

Peyton picked up her mug and made a face as she plucked a dog hair from the lip. "Joel found that in one of the walls he was working on. The lath in that wall was just higgledy-piggledy, and he found that thing wedged between two slats. He said to give it to you. It kind of freaked him out, so I put it in a bag and hid it in a cabinet." She took a sip of the tea and made another face. "Blech. It's cold. Anyway, that thing's yours now."

Feeling unhappy that I was now the owner of whatever-it-was, I put the roses on the table and unrolled the top of the bag to look inside. As I tilted the sack to get better light, a musty odor rose up, and I wrinkled my nose. At the bottom of the bag, the crumpled form of the hair-doll lay with its limbs bent at random angles. It would have looked back at me if it had eyes. Probably would have winked, too. Dammit.

CHAPTER 3

Ron pounded his fist on the fender of Cam's truck. "No! I am not spending five hours with *that* next to me. Put it in the back with the luggage."

"Geez, all right already. I'll put it in the back. Just chill out." I grabbed my pack from the back seat and tossed it in the bed of the truck. All this drama from Ron because the hair-doll was stored in the pack. My plan was to give the doll to Phillis as an ice breaker to start the awkward conversation about Phebe.

Lenora sat in the front passenger seat, her enormous purse primly on her lap and her seatbelt buckled. Ron had stowed their half ton of luggage in the back of the truck at the crack of dawn. Maybe that was another reason he was being so pissy. It had looked effortless, but maybe he was one of those people who pretended to be stoic, at least during the unpleasant event, but then took it out on everyone else later. Or maybe he had a real aversion to the hair-doll because of its supernatural associations. I wasn't going to ask.

Ron sat behind Lenora with his arms folded and an unpleasant scowl on his face. I had grown accustomed to his almost constant, sunny disposition, but everyone can have an off day, so I just let it be. We had gone through the effort of calling our jobs and getting time off, planning the route, and finding a pet-friendly hotel. Cam even managed to research the historical areas relevant to the executions and gibbeting. I resolved to keep my mouth shut and not incite Ron further, so we could just get on with the trip.

Cam hesitated before climbing into the driver's seat. "Has everyone gone to the bathroom?" After a chorus of yes's rang out, Cam almost entered the truck, but paused again. "Are we all sure?" He leveled a gaze at Lenora that was loaded with expectation.

Lenora bit her lip. "I have to go again."

As she unfastened her seatbelt, Ron stepped out to hold her purse and help her down from the cab. When Cam followed Lenora back to the house to unlock the door, Ron threw the purse on her seat and then stood with his hands planted on his hips. His head was bowed, and he clenched his jaw, a small muscle twitching with the force of his thoughts.

"You all right?" Concerned, I walked over and gave his arm a tentative touch, afraid that he would blow up at me for intruding. Feeling a faint electrical buzzing on the surface of his skin, I withdrew my hand and stared at my fingertips as Ron blew out a breath and straightened.

"Yeah, I guess I'm not sleeping too well lately. It's making me cranky."

I looked up and examined his face, worried about what was behind this admission. "What's disturbing your sleep?"

Ron was silent, the only sounds were the early morning birdsong and the distant susurration of the constant New Jersey traffic. Shoving a hand through his hair, he looked lost for a moment. "Nothing's waking me up." Lines of worry wrinkled his forehead and the words came slowly, catching on the jagged edges of his uncertainty. "I'm just having some strange dreams. An old shaman. I think he's *Uma*'s grandfather."

169

A cold finger traced a path up the back of my neck. "What happens in these dreams? What does he tell you?"

Ron shook his head. "He doesn't speak, but he looks worried. He holds a bowl of burning tobacco, and he wafts the smoke at me with a feather."

"Why's this disturbing? Does it mean anything to you? Like maybe it's symbolic, something floating around in your subconscious?"

"I-I think it's literal. It's called smudging. You use smoke from a sacred plant to cleanse and purify, like before an important spiritual ceremony."

I tried to put a positive spin on things. "Maybe it's a benediction. You're getting a blessing before we 'do this thing.'" Hooking my fingers, I put air quotes on the words from our night in the Roseberry House to let him know I understood how unsavory this spirit work was for him. Getting the blessing of the old shaman might ease the burden of going against tribal teachings.

Ron forced a crooked smile. "Yeah, maybe." He didn't sound convinced.

Cam and Lenora emerged from the house, their

banter reaching our ears from across the lawn.

Lenora stepped carefully through the grass, using her cane to keep a steady gait. Looking over her shoulder, she called back to Cam. "You had to go too. Don't give me that look."

Cam responded with righteous indignation. "I merely took the opportunity to go, so we wouldn't have to stop too soon. I was being proactive."

"Yeah, yeah. Tell that to your prostate." Lenora reached the truck, and her lips curved down with disapproval as she approached Ron and me. "You two ready to go yet?" Like it was our fault we weren't on the road already.

"Yes, ma'am." Ron spoke mechanically without intonation and it made me stiffen. Before I could think too deeply about why this felt so wrong, we were back to normal. "We're ready to go now," he quipped and then sent me a surreptitious wink over Lenora's head as he helped her into the truck. I relaxed and gave an inward sigh of relief. Maybe talking about the dream helped and he'd be okay.

I slid into the back seat next to Zackie as Ron came

in from the opposite door. Turning in the driver's seat, Cam did a quick head count before starting the engine. As he pulled into the road, I grabbed my phone and sent Lucas a text to let him know we were en route to Boston to hopefully resolve the Roseberry House case. Ron would work the camera and get him something for the show, at the very least, some local color for the piece. I couldn't guarantee anything more than that. I finished the message by saying I missed him and then added some random emoticons, because it's always good to have a little mystery. Maybe this was why no one ever came to me for relationship advice.

A minute later, Lucas wrote back. A quick calculation told me that it was two o'clock in the afternoon in Scotland. He was probably busy with work, so it surprised me that he sent such a lengthy response. He missed me too and he assumed the emoticons indicated the depth of my despair without him. He told me to thank Ron for doing the filming and asked that we do our best to capture something his viewers would be able to accept as evidence of the supernatural. He also said things had kicked up a notch at his location, and we should try to get to Scotland with all deliberate speed. Plane tickets would be forthcoming, and updates on the case would come to us at our hotel in Boston, so I just needed to tell him where we'd be staying.

I quit reading and called out to Cam. "Stop! We have to go back."

"I told you to go before we left, why didn't you—"

Lenora interrupted him. Turning in her seat, she pursed her lips. "Shoulda gone before we left like I did."

"No, that's not it. We have to get our passports." I gave a hurried explanation of Lucas's text as Cam turned the truck around, taking right turns at the next two intersections.

"Bloody hell…we're going to have to go all the way back to your place too." Cam dragged a frustrated hand down his face as we sat at a red light. Giving me a sly look, Zackie put her head over his shoulder and then snuffled at his ear. "Oh, like hell. You do *not* have to pee."

Satisfied with her joke, Zackie sat back against the seat and huffed her amusement. I nudged her in the ribs with my elbow. "Good one."

We arrived back at Cam's house, and he admonished us to stay put. He would be back in only a minute, and he did not want to have to look for anyone when he returned. True to his word, he was back in the driver's seat before we had concluded our conversation on the relative merits of naan versus fried bread.

"And anyway, you're saying it wrong." Ron leaned past Zackie to emphasize his point and spelled it out for me. "It's f-r-y-bread. Not the adjective, like you use when you say 'fried chicken.'"

Cam made an exasperated sound and pulled out on to the road. "Do you people ever think of anything other than food?"

Ignoring Cam, I responded to Ron's revelation. "Huh. You mean, all this time I've been saying it wrong? Why didn't you correct me?"

Lenora shrugged. "We thought it was cute. Kinda like when a little kid says 'puh-sgetti.'"

I sat back and blinked a few times. "Did this perceived cuteness get me more 'frybread?'"

Ron tilted his head and thought. "Probably."

"Well, all right then." Considering this small humiliation a fair trade for more frybread, I nodded to myself and then picked up my phone to finish reading Lucas's text. "Get this. Lucas says they brought the cyclist who was attacked back to the crossroads for an interview, and all hell broke loose. They got some poltergeist-like activity on film before a flying rock trashed the camera." I paused and read to the end of the message. "A bunch of people on the crew got a little banged up, but nothing serious. The cyclist was okay because he set a land speed record getting out of there. Lucas says he's okay, he didn't get a scratch." I probably owed Hannah one for once again keeping Lucas out of harm's way.

The truck slowed, and Cam pulled into my parking space. "We're here. Hurry up and get your passport, so we can get back on the road."

"I'll make it quick." I forwarded to Lucas our hotel reservations and then took off the seatbelt before popping my door, leaving the phone on my seat.

Unbuckling his seatbelt and grinning, Ron made eye contact with Cam in the rearview mirror. "I have to use the bathroom." Zackie stretched out on the back seat as we closed the truck doors on Cam's vociferous swearing. He was going on about people with bladders the size of walnuts. Heading to the front door, Ron held on to his grin as he fell into step with me. "I don't really have to go. I'm just messing with him."

I chortled and looked down to pull the door key from my pocket. "Gotta keep him on his toes and let him practice his swearing 'cause—"

Something heavy slammed into me. I staggered backward, landing awkwardly on my butt. In slow motion, I watched Ron grab the back of Rory's jacket with both hands and throw him hard against the wall of my apartment. Rory reflexively brought up his forearms, shielding his head and face from the worst of it. Yanking his shoulder, Ron spun him around and grabbed him by the throat, lifting him. Only the tips of his toes touched the ground. Rory made a gurgling sound and struggled to fight back, but it was like a trapped moth beating against a window.

I scrambled to my feet and ran over to them. "Ron, I think you should let him down." Somewhere in the distance, Cam and Lenora were moving quickly toward us. Rory's struggles became weaker, his eyes bulging and his lips turning blue. "Ron, I'm serious. Let him down." Ron's eyes had gone dark, his pupils completely dilated, and a thin smile played on his lips. A look of eager delight gripped his features as he made a fist with his other hand and drew it back to land a killing blow. "Ron, please!"

Lenora grabbed his upper arm with both hands to stop the punch. "You put that boy down right now, you hear me?"

"Yes, ma'am." Ron's face was blank, and his words spilled out like an automaton. He lowered the limp body until the feet touched the ground and then let go. Rory collapsed in a heap.

Cam and I sprawled over the fallen man, checking to make sure he was still breathing. He was unconscious, but inhale followed exhale and his color was returning to normal. We explored his limbs and skull for deformities that would signal a broken bone. Aside from old bruises around his face and a healing laceration along his temple, we found no new wounds. Assured that immediate medical attention wasn't necessary, we placed him into the recovery position on his side and covered him with Cam's jacket.

"Damn. That boy got moves." Daniel Clark stood leaning casually against the wall, his thumbs hooked in his belt. He clucked his tongue and looked appreciatively at Ron. "He ever consider going into law enforcement?"

I stared at him glassy-eyed, then my jaw dropped and I shook my head in disbelief. "Ron was about to kill the guy. Just for running. How is that even close to law enforcement?"

Daniel snorted. "Not the killing part, baby girl. I'm talking about how he didn't let the perp get past him. Now, holdin' your own in a fight, that's also a good trait. The academy will teach you how to channel that to subdue a suspect." He jutted his chin toward Ron. "This boy here got all the right fundamentals. He just needs a little training to sand off the rough edges."

Still holding on to Ron's arm, Lenora wrinkled her brow and squinted at the empty space near the wall. "Who you talkin' to?" Ron's eyes seemed unfocused, but he stepped forward unsteadily to position himself slightly in front of her. One arm stretched out to support himself against the wall.

Getting to his feet, Cam dusted off his knees. "Lenora and Ron, allow me to introduce you to Daniel Clark, former sheriff's deputy out of North Carolina." He straightened and nodded to the spirit. "Daniel, always a pleasure. Fia told me you were around."

As Cam and Daniel exchanged pleasantries, I stayed on the ground and put a shaky hand to my chest, willing my heart to stop flailing and beat right. I kept running over the scene—Ron with his fist poised to take a life—and it made me shake. As a kid, Ron had been violent, but he lacked the strength to do any real harm. He'd grown from a string bean kid into a powerhouse from all the years of heavy lifting on Lenora's ranch. As a man, the possibility of lethal outcomes was almost a certainty if he lost control. And no one else had seen the expression on his face. That, more than anything else, left me quivering inside and frightened for Ron.

I shot a resentful glance at the unconscious Rory. Bastard. Daniel had done his level best to dissuade this creep from stalking me. How many warnings does a person need to back off? If anything bad happened to Ron, it would be Rory's fault for being such an unrelenting jerk.

But then my thoughts took a turn into ruthless introspection, with no self-deception and no place to hide. Did Rory really shoulder all the blame? Maybe Ron was backsliding into old habits because of the stress of dealing with the supernatural. Lots of people responded to stress that way, suddenly finding themselves unable to refrain from self-destructive behaviors when things got bad. And wouldn't that put me squarely in the crosshairs as the person to blame? I was the one who had started it all by asking Ron to come and help with the spirit of He-Who-Counseled-the-Chief. Ron would still be happily wrestling cattle, or doing whatever you do on a ranch, if it hadn't been for me.

Cam's words broke into my guilt trip. "So, what are we going to do with him? We can't just leave him here."

Lenora gave Cam a level look. "Why not?"

I picked myself up off the ground. "Well, for starters, it would be kind of rude to leave him for Joel or Peyton to deal with."

Lenora grunted agreement as Daniel squatted down to stare at Rory. The spirit cocked his head, and his eyes drifted along the prone form. After a moment, he tapped the side of his nose with an index finger and gazed up at us. "I tell you what—you take him to your local police and I guarantee a day's worth of questions on how he got this way. How 'bout you throw him in your truck bed and dump him somewhere else? He'll come to eventually and find his own way home. Won't be worse than a hangover."

After I translated Daniel's thoughts on the matter, Ron spoke up, his voice subdued and his expression guilty as hell. "No, let's take him to his house and make sure he can take care of himself before we leave."

Cam looked to the heavens for help. "You sure about this, Ron?" When Ron nodded, we exchanged helpless looks, since we all considered this above and beyond our duty. Cam finally shrugged. "Okay, Ron. Whatever makes you happy."

Daniel stood and considered Ron for a long moment, finally giving him an approving nod. "This one's nicer than he needs to be." Walking back toward the woods, he spat near where Rory lay and then gave us a wave. "Y'all can take it from here, I think. I'll be back if you need me."

We pulled Rory's wallet out of his back pocket. It was made of expensive, light tan calfskin, and it defied my experience with wallets. There were no Velcro closures. The driver's license was front and center, tucked in the first card slot. Even though Rory came from money, there was a marked absence of gold and platinum credit cards in the other slots—proof positive that he had been cut off. His family had finally reached their limit after Rory had literally played with fire and tried to burn down a family's home. This attempted arson had been his way of retaliating against a young woman who had refused to go out with him. At least Rory's kin drew the line somewhere. But it did not speak well of them that it had taken a near-homicidal act for them to finally withdraw their support.

Rory had a Washington, New Jersey address that would take us only a little out of our way on our drive to Boston. After carrying the man's limp form to the truck as if he weighed no more than a cat, Ron placed him with care in the back seat next to Zackie. Cam persuaded Zackie to relinquish her napping area altogether and ride in the truck bed, so Ron and I could sit on either side of Rory and keep him upright.

When we pulled up to a two-story house with flaking gray paint and a broken gutter, Ron nudged Rory and patted his cheek to wake him up. "Rory, you're home. Which floor do you live on?"

"Nnurph..."

Rory's reply wasn't informative, so Ron reached into the man's pocket and extracted his house keys. Tossing them to me, he asked, "Can you find the door these go to?"

As Ron and Cam wrestled Rory out of the truck, I went ahead to the house. Knocking on the lower level door, I received no response and failed to fit the key to the lock. Upstairs, I knocked again in case there was a roommate. All was quiet, so I unlocked the door and went inside. The apartment had one bedroom, one bath, and a small kitchen. The cracked linoleum floor made it look shabby, and despite the choice of white paint, the place had a dreary atmosphere. The living area was spartan. Only a small, scarred wooden table and one chair occupied the kitchen area. There were no personal items other than a tiny gold frame on the table. Maybe the trust fund was going to come due soon and Rory wasn't expecting to stay there long. I put Rory's keys on his table and picked up the tiny frame.

Lenora's halting steps sounded as she made her way through the door, leaning on her cane. "Had to be the upper level. Damned stairs…" Out of breath, she huffed and placed her voluminous purse on the kitchen counter before looking around. "Ewwww…" Muttering to herself about the crappy apartment, she rummaged through the cabinets until she found a mug and a pot. "We make him some honey tea. His throat's gonna hurt." After she filled the pot with water and set it to boil on the stove, she grabbed a kitchen towel and then went to investigate Rory's freezer.

Glancing over her shoulder at me, Lenora's eyes fell on the little frame I held. "What you got there?"

"It's a picture of an old man with a baby on his knee." The old man's mouth was pulled down in a sour expression, and his dark eyes seemed to glare back at me. His hands grasped the infant in a proprietary manner that left no room for affection. I put the frame back on the table when the sounds of heavy thumping met my ears. Stepping to the door, I held it open for Ron who was helping Rory make it up the stairs. One hand grasped Rory's belt, the other held on to his arm, which was slung over Ron's shoulders. Their steps were slow, and Ron kept up a steady stream of encouragement. Cam brought up the rear, issuing dire warnings that no one had better fall over backwards because he wouldn't catch them.

With her head in the freezer, Lenora made a sound of triumph. "Found it." Pulling out a bag of frozen peas, she wrapped it in the towel and walked over to the lone chair where she made Rory sit. He was still a little groggy but seemed stable enough. "Put this on your throat." Moving to the kitchen area, she hunted through her purse, eventually pulling out a tea bag. Next came a small bear-shaped plastic container full of an amber liquid, presumably honey. With her back toward us, she poured the hot water and set the tea to steep.

Ron crouched down next to Rory. "Are you feeling okay? Do you want us to take you to the hospital?"

Rory's voice sounded hoarse, but it was strong. "No. No hospitals." Rory probably didn't want to be interrogated about how he was injured any more than we did. He gave me a look like he hated me at the molecular level and that this whole thing was my fault. When I stared back impassive and bored, his gaze became furtive, ultimately focusing on the floor.

Cam rolled his eyes so hard I could hear it. "He'll be fine. You don't have to—" Reaching down to help Ron to his feet, Cam suddenly jerked his hand back as if he'd been burned. His expression registered alarm, but only for a moment before he smoothed his features and wrapped his fingers around Ron's arm to pull him up. "Up you go, then." Cam shot me a worried look but said nothing.

Rubbing the back of his neck, Ron fixed concerned eyes on Rory. Lenora pushed him out of her way with a nudge from her cane as she carried the mug of tea to the table. "Move. I talk to this one." Lenora placed the mug in front of Rory and cleared her throat to get his attention. When Rory stubbornly continued to stare at the floor, refusing to acknowledge her, Lenora slapped him lightly on the top of his head.

"Ow! You bi—"

Lenora waggled a finger at him. "Careful now. I stopped my grandson once. No guarantee I'll do it again." She crossed her arms as he glowered at her and met him glare for glare. "Drink the tea when it cools. Hot drink's no good for your throat. This is willow bark tea, natural aspirin, to keep your swelling down. Also has honey to soothe and a little brandy to make you sleep."

I stared with admiration at Lenora's purse sitting on the counter. "You have brandy in there?"

Other than giving me the side-eye, Lenora ignored me and continued lecturing Rory. "That girl can irritate. I give you that. But you gotta stop now. You know by now that this is no good for you."

Cam nodded and picked up her thread. "Listen to her, Rory. There are things you don't understand that can hurt you very badly. Even kill you if you keep provoking the situation." He put one palm flat on the table and leaning in, he traced the constellation of contusions on Rory's face with a wave of his finger. "All that mysterious bruising? That's only the beginning. Consider those love taps. Do yourself a favor and forget about Fia."

Rory's eyes widened, and a hand reached up to touch a purplish welt on his cheek. For a moment, I thought he'd come to his senses and would stop stalking me, if only to avoid Daniel's constant beatings. But then he glanced at the small framed picture, and his face hardened. "Get out. All of you. Get out of my house!"

Cam pushed off from the table and opened his hands, palms up. "Don't say you weren't warned." He gave Rory a final sad glance before slowly shaking his head and turning to open the door. Ron was the first one out, relief plain on his face to be away from Rory. As I passed through the doorway, Cam muttered, "Right then. Didn't think that would work."

When we reached Cam's truck, Zackie was again in the back seat and impatient to leave. We drove away in silence, uneasiness settling on us like a dank, gray cloud. Something was wrong with Ron, and I didn't know how to help him. He sat hunched with his eyes shut tight, quietly suffering. A geyser of hot acid shot through my gut, my body revealing the conflict between the urgency to act and the ambiguities that held me paralyzed.

Maybe the best thing to do would be to get him out of this supernatural stuff and back home to Oklahoma. Given a chance to de-stress and normalize, it was possible he'd go back to the way he was before I asked for his help to talk to the spirit of He-Who-Counseled-the-Chief. Maybe that experience had primed Ron, like the first bee sting for someone who would become severely allergic. When he had been confronted with Phebe's bad vibes, it was like the second sting that brings on anaphylaxis. He would have had no defenses. Getting Ron away from an environment where he could be stung yet again seemed like the stupid simple solution—until I thought more deeply.

I worried the cuticle on my thumb as I considered an alternative outcome to sending him home—Ron would be isolated and without a support network who understood the traumas of confronting the supernatural. If he tried to talk to someone who never experienced anything otherworldly, and they scoffed at him for his fanciful notions, that could be devastating to the healing process. If he instead kept it to himself and tried to bury the experiences, that might also damage him psychologically.

To speak and be dismissed, or to never speak and unburden yourself of the things that inhabit your nightmares? Either way led to isolation, the precursor to madness and suicide in this business.

And Ron's problems might not be wholly due to stress. Cam had felt something when he tried to help Ron to his feet at Rory's house. It would be foolish in the extreme to leave Ron on his own to deal with whatever had surprised Cam. But exposing Ron to more of this toxic environment wouldn't be good either. There was no clear path forward to help Ron that was guaranteed not to harm him further.

Unable to reach a resolution, I sidelined these thoughts on Ron because, on top of this problem, nothing was resolved with Rory—in fact, things had probably escalated. My friends were now on his radar, and it was my fault for allowing him into their lives. Maybe I should have kept quiet about his intrusions and dealt with Rory on my own. I slipped lower in my seat, weighed down by guilt.

It was only a matter of time before Rory would make another appearance. I touched the bear spray in my pocket, an almost ritualized gesture. Now that we had all done something to piss him off, Rory might feel compelled to find time for each of us in his busy schedule.

But as I dwelled on the unpleasant possibilities, it occurred to me that Daniel had nothing but time. He also had a growing contempt for Rory. I thought back to when we had first met, and the child molester that Daniel had been determined to hunt down. By now, all that was probably left of that guy were just a few bones scattered in the woods. As horrible as it sounds, this thought comforted me.

# # #

We stopped for lunch at a chain restaurant. The menu offered sustenance for the hungry traveler that lay somewhere between fast food and real food. The more you paid, the more real it got. I settled for a low-end burger that came with fries and coleslaw. No one else made much of an effort to find more interesting fare, and we all picked at our food, eating without enjoyment.

Looking at our reflection in the enormous mirrors lining an interior wall, I saw a group of people who appeared to be washed out and anemic. The garish red vinyl of our booth was a sharp contrast to our lack of verve and animation.

Throwing a fry back on to his mostly full plate, Cam rested his forearms on the table and surveyed the group. "I didn't want to say anything earlier because I didn't want to worry Lenora, but I've thought about it and she needs to know." His shoulders rose slightly and then dropped. "I think we have a problem with Ron."

Lenora stiffened and reached out to place her hand on Ron's arm. "He's a good boy." Her eyes were full of worry, but her voice was firm.

Ron looked up from his untouched plate with a hangdog expression. "No, *Uma*. He's right. Something's wrong with me."

Narrowing my eyes, I gazed at Cam. "You know." I leaned forward, adamant that he should tell us. "You know what's wrong with Ron. Spill it." My whole body was taut, anxious about what Cam would say.

Cam heaved a sigh and shrugged again. I didn't like what this gesture had to say. There was something helpless about it, and Cam always had the answers. Alarm bells rang in my head. The apprehension must have shown on my face because Cam waved a hand at me to calm down. "Don't look so stricken. He'll be all right. We just have to get Ron to my brother before he does anything foolish."

"But what's wrong with me? Am I relapsing?" Ron's voice was strained, and his eyes pleaded with Cam to say it wasn't anything serious.

Cam looked at him with sympathy. "You have a passenger, an unwanted houseguest."

Ron's eyes went wide. "I'm possessed?"

Cam shook his head. "No, not possessed. It's called spirit attachment." When Ron looked confused and no less frightened than when he thought he was possessed, Cam tried to explain. "Spirit attachment is the result of the dead being greedy for life. An entity will attach to people with habits or inclinations that can feed the spirit's obsessions."

Ron sucked in a breath and held it, his eyes closed and his lips forming a thin line. After a second, he exhaled slowly and opened his eyes, his gaze directed to the ceiling. "At least it's not me. I wanted to kill that guy, but it wasn't me."

Lenora touched his cheek and turned his face to her. "That's right. It wasn't you wanting to kill that guy. You're fine." Patting his cheek, she nodded. "You'll be more fine when we get rid of your passenger."

I ground my teeth, my hands closing into fists. "Who is it, Cam? Who's attached themselves to Ron?"

Cam rubbed his brow and then leaned back, crossing his arms over his chest. "Could be someone who was skulking in the background when we dealt with He-Who-Counseled-the-Chief. Or it might be an entity from the Roseberry House who was not inclined to make his or her presence known to us." He cast a speculative look at Ron. "It could be anyone, and we need to keep an open mind, but my money's on Phebe."

"That bitch!" I wanted to pound a fist on the table but controlled the impulse because we were in a public place.

Ron blinked owlishly, like this did not compute. "How do you figure it's Phebe?"

"Several things she said and did." Cam ticked off the list on his fingers. "Phebe mentioned an itinerant artist who stenciled designs on the walls of the Roseberry House after she passed. She said she wanted to follow him and see the world, so this was on her mind even then." Seeing this hit the mark with us, he went on. "When she's caught in a lie, Phebe will try to disarm you by playing the little girl if she thinks you are soft-hearted. She might also tell a convenient version of the truth that makes her look better than she is. But if you watch closely, you can see how angry she is that she's been caught, and that you've dared to confront her about it. Every now and then, the mask slips and you see the real Phebe. Remember how she raged when we forced her to admit the truth about Phillis and the doll?"

I was impressed with Cam's memory for details. He must have been thinking hard about this during the silence while we drove. As he recited the clues that led us to Phebe as the attaching spirit, a thought struck me. "Ron didn't want my backpack with the hair-doll next to him in the truck. I'm thinking that might have been Phebe too." I paused as a vivid recollection of one more thing came to the fore. "Phebe also gave Ron the once-over when they were introduced. I thought at the time maybe she just found him attractive, but there was also this sudden sea-change in behavior. It felt off—it just didn't sit right."

Cam gave me a shrewd look. "Exactly. I think she could tell right then that Ron had some buried anger issues. He was the perfect target for her—a big, strong man who could really do some damage. How frustrating it must be to exist as petite little Phebe, with all this rage bottled up inside and no way to lash out."

I blew a raspberry. "Oh, I think Phebe found a way to lash out just fine. It just wasn't physical. She's manipulative and probably did stuff like saying just the right words in the right ear to cause discord. And you barely have to lift a finger to poison someone."

Cam accepted this correction with good grace. "I'm sure you're right about that. But there is something intensely satisfying about being in the moment and reacting directly to a provocation. There is nothing quite as satisfying as 'punching someone's lights out,' as you Yanks say."

Lenora gasped as the significance of this spirit attachment hit her. "You mean this Rory was not a one-time thing? She uses my boy to live her dream, to hurt people? Ron can break someone's bones easy. He can kill someone." She had tears in her eyes and her hand shook where she grabbed Ron's sleeve. "They'll lock him up or someone'll come after him and kill him."

Lenora looked old and frail. It hurt my heart to see

her so distressed and overcome. I put my hand over hers and struggled to find some words of comfort. She was relying on Cam and me to do something that would save Ron, and I feared in the marrow of my bones that we were not enough. As my hand brushed against Ron's arm, I felt again the weird electrical buzzing that now made sense as the signature sign of an attached spirit. I concentrated and reached in to lock on to that spirit energy and yank it out of him. One second I was pouring my will into grabbing the invading spirit and the next second I was knocked back against my seat, my hand numb and useless. The hair on my head stood straight out as if someone were pulling on it. It was like I'd touched a live wire and almost been electrocuted.

I stared in shock at Cam and then frantically rubbed my tingling hand to get the sensation back. The last thing I needed was another hand that wasn't right. Cam rolled his eyes without a trace of sympathy. "Do you ever listen? I told you we need my brother. Neither you nor I can do anything about this." Cam turned away but then looked back at me. "And your hand will be fine."

Despite concerns about the long-term effects of getting zapped like a bug, I was unwilling to give up on finding some way to comfort Lenora. I racked my brain for something, anything that could help. Some days, my brain could amaze me; other days, I could be looking for my phone while I was holding it. Happily, it was a good day. As if on cue, the details surrounding the first time I'd felt that electrical buzzing sharpened into focus. "Tell them, Ron. Tell them about the dreams."

Ron shifted uneasily but related his disturbing dreams of Lenora's grandfather smudging him with tobacco smoke. Lenora listened to this story, not blinking and barely breathing until he finished. "Grandfather's trying to protect you and cleanse you of this spirit. That's good. We have help here." Her rigid posture relaxed, and she released her death-grip on Ron's sleeve, patting his arm. "He'll kick her ass. That man never did tolerate bullshit."

I slid a glance to Cam, looking for confirmation. "Sure, what the hell?" he said. I sunk my face into my palm and let it take the weight of my too-heavy head. So much for confirmation. Maybe I expected too much of him. This stuff was the definition of mystery, and a lot of it seemed to rely on intuition. If Cam didn't have a handle on it, the reason had to be because this was just too big and too complex to really know anything.

At least I was now clear on what we shouldn't do, and that was to send Ron home. But how should we proceed? Although I had my own ideas about what should come next, I lifted my face and broached the question to the group. "Assuming what Lenora's grandfather is doing controls Phebe to some degree, is Ron really stable enough for us to continue working on Phillis and Mark? Shouldn't we head straight to the UK and get in touch with Cam's brother?"

Lenora jumped all over this. "Yes! We go get Ron help with this spirit. No sense waiting. We should go now."

"No." Ron sat up straighter and seemed more focused. "Let's finish this business with Phillis and Mark. They've waited long enough, don't you think?"

Cam frowned. "Yes, but what about you? We could fly out from Logan and return via Boston to finish the job. It's been almost two hundred years for Phillis, and we don't even know for sure if Mark remains here. A few more days or weeks for them will not make a difference."

Ron shook his head, his jaw firm. "I'll be fine. Now that I know what I'm dealing with, I can second guess any impulses I feel. Maybe if I frustrate her, she'll leave on her own."

Cam looked doubtful. "Don't count on it."

I wasn't in the mood for Ron's act of self-sacrifice. I wanted him freed from this spirit and not having to check himself every time he felt something. Not being able to be your natural self, questioning your own genuine emotions, was damned unhealthy in my view. I decided to try subverting his altruism to get him to seek help sooner. "So, what about the entity in Scotland? That's a place with a pretty deep history. That spirit might have been trapped for many hundreds of years. Wouldn't it be even more unethical to make the Scottish spirit wait for the chance to move on?"

Ron didn't even take time to consider. "That one sounds like a real jerk. Maybe he or she had it coming, being earthbound and stuck here. As long as people aren't under constant attack by that spirit, we probably wouldn't be doing wrong by making it wait."

I knew I'd lost the battle when Lenora chimed in. Her face was a collection of worry lines, but she didn't argue. "You a good boy, Ron. We do as you say."

# # #

The hotel proclaimed itself to be in the Bunker Hill area of Boston, but the only thing I knew for sure was that we were in Somerville, on the south side of Washington Street in the business district. Just across the street was a pizza and sub shop, and with a few more steps in that direction, residential neighborhoods. If there was history here, it was so buried under modern influences that even someone like me, skilled in the art of seeing the past, had to struggle to locate it.

Pets were not permitted in the rooms, so we employed a little subterfuge to get Zackie past the front desk. Truthfully, this was all a bit of performance art for the sake of Ron and Lenora, who would otherwise think we left a poor, lonely dog unattended in the truck. The Psychopomp could pop in and out of our reality at will, to whatever location pleased her. It amused Zackie to play along with our ruse, so she put up with us dressing her in a service dog vest.

After everyone else had been assigned a room, Zackie and I took our turn at the check-in desk. A bored

Asian woman behind the counter glanced at Zackie and then pulled out a binder. She flipped to a tabbed page and recited what was written as she tucked a strand of her dark, salon-styled hair behind a delicate ear. "Is this animal needed because of a disability?"

Without blinking, I answered. "Yes." After spending years in psychiatric care, it wouldn't be hard to claim this as a disability. Legally, the hotel staff could not ask for specifics, but I had oodles of information for them if it became necessary to smooth our way.

"What work or tasks has this animal been trained to do?" The desk clerk closed the binder and waited.

I tried to look affable. Reading the woman's name tag on the red jacket of her uniform, I decided to personalize my response. "How do I put this, Rhonda? Zackie deals with things that I can see but you can't."

Rhonda raised her perfect eyebrows. Probably afraid of legal repercussions if she said the wrong thing, she declined to ask the questions that were plain in her eyes. "Credit card?"

When I unfastened the Velcro on my wallet and extracted my card, Zackie grabbed it from my hand and then placed her front paws on the counter to present it to the woman. I coughed to cover my laugh as Rhonda gingerly pulled the credit card from the dog's mouth with the tips of her manicured red nails. Rhonda made a face when she had to wipe the saliva off with a tissue before inserting the card into the reader. When the reader beeped, the desk clerk took the card and looked confused for a moment before handing the card back to Zackie. Rhonda's face scrunched in disgust as she withdrew her hand and then grabbed another tissue to wipe her fingers. Jumping down from the counter, Zackie returned the card to me and sat at heel, feigning a devoted look as she gazed up into my face.

With her lips still twisted in revulsion, Rhonda clicked through some screens on her monitor and then swiped a room card through a magnetic reader before slipping it into a small white envelope. She scribbled on the envelope and gave Zackie a warning look as she stretched her arm to hand me the key card directly. "Take the elevators over there to the third floor. Your room number is written inside the envelope."

As our group turned to go, Rhonda grabbed a pump bottle of hand sanitizer and gave herself a liberal dose. Not missing this slight, Zackie made sure Rhonda was watching when we reached the elevator bank. Jumping up, she pushed the "up" button with a paw and then balanced on her back legs long enough to give the elevator buttons a healthy lick.

#

The color palette for the walls and bedding in the room was competing shades of gray. For a second, my heart froze with the thought that the sudden muting of color meant someone had committed suicide in the room. When Zackie stretched out on the bed and the mushroomy taste didn't take up residence in my sinuses, I knew it was okay—probably only some hospitality industry psychologist trying to calm the guests by removing anything that might be visually stimulating.

Other than the color scheme, the room was pretty nice. I wheeled my luggage into a corner near the bed and decided against unpacking. I'd just grab what I needed on the fly. Wrinkles be damned. The backpack went in the same corner. Peeling off my coat, I put it on top of this pile and felt suitably moved in. I flopped down on the bed next to Zackie and reached for the phone in the leg pocket of my cargo pants. Lucas needed to know that we had arrived and maybe also that I missed him. I found the key card, but no phone, so I checked my other pockets, my coat, and then the backpack.

When I still came up empty, I thought back to the last time I used it—I had texted Lucas where we'd be staying just before I got out of the truck to get my passport. I tried to remember if I put it in my pocket after that, but I had no distinct memory of doing this. I must have left it in the truck.

Moseying over to Cam's room, I pounded on the door until he opened it. "I need to borrow your keys. I left my phone in the truck."

He reached into his pocket and pulled out the keys, slapping them into my open palm. "Fine. Just don't lose these as well." Cam closed the door in my face.

When I opened the rear passenger door of the truck, the seat was empty. I checked on the floor, under the front seats, and then on the floor by the front seats. Nada. Just for grins, I searched the truck bed and still couldn't find the phone.

I jogged back into the hotel lobby, gripped in the first signs of phone withdrawal. My chest was tight, my thumbs twitchy, and I felt a phantom vibration in my cargo pocket. This was not good. I hurried to the elevator and punched the up button, forgetting in my panic that it would still be sticky with Zackie spit. The ride up was spent wiping my fingers on my pants. Maybe I should have taken the time to ask Rhonda for some hand sanitizer.

Outside Cam's room, I pounded on the door. It must have sounded urgent, because when Cam appeared, his eyes were wide with concern. "I lost it, Cam. I can't find my phone."

Cam narrowed his eyes, and his bushy brows drew together. "Oh for—is that what all the pounding is about? I thought something terrible had happened." He exhaled roughly and ushered me in. "Do you have the locator app installed?"

I handed over the truck keys as I entered his room. "Yeah, I installed it after the phone slipped out of my pocket during SAR training. People got really pissed when I asked them to grid the woods to help me find it."

Cam's room held the same gray lack of appeal that

my room offered. Walking to the television console, he turned down the volume on the news program, and then snatched up his cell phone lying adjacent to the big screen. He punched in his password and then handed me the phone. "I hope you used a sufficiently complex password?"

I gave Cam a cheesy grin. "Not unless you count 'Fia123' as complex." Tapping in the website for the locator app, I entered 'FiaIsGreat' in the password field and let the app do its thing. "And what do you use as a password? Zackie-something-or-other?"

Cam colored. "With a mixture of caps and lowercase and other alphanumeric characters…"

"Uh-huh." I looked back at the screen and it showed a map with a red dot for where my phone was located. I tapped on the minus sign to pull back until I had some landmarks that made sense to me. "According to this, my phone's in a park in Washington—not Washington Street outside—our Washington, back in New Jersey. That doesn't make sense. We've never been to that park." I hit refresh and came up with the same location.

Cam sat on the edge of his bed. "When was the last time you're sure you had your phone?"

"Yeah, I thought about that. I texted Lucas right before I went to get my passport. I either put it in my pocket or I left it in your truck. I can't remember."

Cam crossed his arms. His mouth drew taut. "I think you left it in the truck and Rory took it. That's the simplest explanation, don't you think?"

I gave him a blank stare as my mind raced through all the information Rory could have gotten that could cause me trouble: Passwords to other accounts, email, texts, credit card number… I sat down at Cam's desk and logged into my bank and credit card accounts, checking for irregularities and the loss of my life's savings. Nothing looked out of whack, but I changed the passwords to something I'd never remember, writing the characters on a memo pad with the hotel logo. I next called the bank and the credit card company. A stop was placed on the current credit and ATM cards, and both institutions said new cards would be sent overnight.

Once my financials were secured, I sent Lucas a quick text to let him know we arrived and that he'd have to contact me through Cam until my phone issue was resolved. Next, I got the coordinates for my lost phone from the app and sent a text to Peyton, explaining that I needed her to practice her SAR skills and go get my phone. I ended this exercise in aggravation by changing the passwords on all my other accounts. Transcribing the alphanumeric nonsense with care on the memo pad, I prayed I wouldn't lose this cheat sheet.

Cam grew bored watching me click away on his phone and turned his attention back to watching the local news. When he bolted upright and demanded his phone back, I knew I'd missed something vital. "What's happened?"

Cam waved me off and tapped away, reading from the phone's screen and grunting affirmation after he'd found what he was looking for. "Just what I thought. Those fires?"

I stood up and came toward him, my arms flung wide. "What fires? What are you talking about?"

"On the news. There were a series of fires on Walnut Avenue near Porter Square. They think there's an arsonist on the loose."

I shook my head, putting my hands up in surrender and confusion. I hadn't been listening to the news. Cam rolled his eyes, tapped on the screen, and then handed me his phone. "Read."

The screen showed the feed for a Boston news channel. Images of fires burning in a residential area and firefighters in full turnout gear crowded the reports. No injuries, but a few houses had incurred damage. I looked up, only slightly less clueless. "That sucks, but at least it's only property. No one was hurt."

Stress lines formed across Cam's forehead. "Yet. The operative word is yet." When he saw I was still unable to follow his line of thought, he rubbed a frustrated hand down his face and then took back the phone. Tapping on the screen again, he gave the phone back to me. "Here's the map. I sent you all this before we left. You didn't read it?" When I shook my head, he raised his brows, incredulous, and muttered something about my utter lack of preparation. Cam pointed on the screen to a neighborhood in Cambridge labeled Avon Hill. Walnut Avenue was a short street that ran north-south in the area. "This place here? Used to be known as Jones Hill and before that," he paused for effect, "Gallows Hill. This is where they executed Phillis and Mark."

My mouth hung open as I finally realized the implication. "Fire... Phillis knows we're here."

"Right. And there's no hope of making it out there tonight, what with all the police and arson investigators on scene."

Arson investigations could take anywhere from hours to months, depending on the size of the blaze. Gallows Hill wasn't that big a space. If I assumed a worst-case scenario of a few weeks...I did a quick calculation of hotel room cost per night versus my bank account. I found myself seated on Cam's bed, a whoosh escaping from my lungs due to the sudden impact after my knees gave way. "Not good. Not good at all. I might need to find a cheaper hotel. Maybe live out of your truck."

Cam took his phone from my limp hands. "We do what we can do." He gave me a concerned look. "Right now, we can do an early dinner. You always feel better after eating. And maybe we can take care of some business after we dine."

I shook my head, no. "Dine? Like with a wine list? No can do."

"Relax. I was planning on the pizza and sub shop across the street. Let me show you something that will prove my genius." Cam fiddled with the phone and then held it up so I could see a map from a blog post about Paul Revere's ride. "A long time ago, this area was known as Charlestown Commons. Paul Revere was forced to change direction outside this hotel when two British officers on horseback spotted him."

"No kidding?" I took the phone back and browsed the post. It took me another moment before the pieces fell into place. "So, those were the same men on horseback you told me about, near where Mark still hung in chains?"

Cam nodded, his eyes grave. "That pizza place is where they hung Mark's body."

I had given the little restaurant a quick look when we pulled into the hotel parking lot and nothing had struck me as interesting. "You think he's there, not at Gallows Hill?"

Cam stood from the bed and took his phone back. "No way to know for sure without looking. I suggest we do this after we eat and it's a bit darker."

I got up and followed him out the door. After rounding up Zackie, Lenora and Ron, we left the hotel under Rhonda's steely gaze. Zackie did her best ultimate hound impression as we passed, raising her nose to issue a wet snuffle at Rhonda when we walked by and then allowing a string of drool to drop with a resounding splat on to the floor.

Catching Cam's eye as we exited the lobby, I giggled, half in amusement and half in embarrassment. "Why's she doing this?"

Cam winked. "Is there a better way to spend immortality than to screw with people?"

#

Washington Street was a lively two-way thoroughfare, flanked by bike lanes where the foolhardy could test their luck. The rush hour traffic was endless, and it made me yearn for Jersey. We opted for the crosswalk to prevent any unfortunate accidents due to, as Cam put it, "Mass-hole drivers with no respect for human life." After a desperate dash across Mt. Vernon Street, we turned left and approached the narrow, two-story building housing the pizza shop. We were directly across the street from the hotel and a historical sign on the edge of its parking lot. I had missed this sign when we arrived. It gave details about Paul Revere's midnight ride and pointed out that this place, this spot right here, had been his turnaround point.

I suspected Cam had not missed the sign and had not figured out the Paul Revere thing on the fly. I began to doubt his genius. He caught me staring at the historical marker and guessed my thoughts. "Okay, maybe not genius, but I did research the area and the executions before we departed. We did not reserve rooms in this particular hotel without reason."

"You did good. No complaints here." I patted his arm and then turned to survey the pizzeria and surrounding area.

On one side of the restaurant, a steep, rickety flight of wooden stairs led to a door accessing what must have been living space above the shop. While the exterior of the second floor was white clapboard, the first-floor business was enclosed in brick. A narrow sign extended over two sets of windows flanking the shop's door. White lettering on a Spanish red background declared that they would deliver, and Greek salads and calzones were among the offerings. On the other side, a squat building sat cheek by jowl to the pizza shop. It was a classic bunker building— a nondescript block of gray concrete with no discernible architectural features. The only thing of potential interest was a narrow alley between the two buildings that was separated from the sidewalk by a chain link gate.

I hoped the view had been more welcoming when the place was known as Charlestown Commons. The thought of Mark enduring lonely centuries in this gritty corner, pressed between relentless traffic and dismal, utilitarian businesses…this was too depressing to contemplate. The only thing that might have offered comfort to a lost soul was the aroma of food when this pizzeria claimed the building. As we entered the pizza and sub shop, I inhaled the scent of zesty tomato sauce and the homey tang of yeast from freshly baked bread.

We pulled metal stools up to a curved counter that surrounded both the serving area and kitchen. The Psychopomp still wore her service dog vest, and this passport allowed her to accompany us into the little shop. Zackie curled into a comfortable lump between my seat and Cam's. Our server was Nicos, a round man with a pleasant smile. He informed us that he liked dogs, and service dogs were particularly welcome. When Nicos offered Zackie a warm, crusty breadstick, my stomach growled with envy.

The choices for dinner were written on blackboards lining the walls behind the counter. After a disappointing

214

lunch fraught with tension and worry, we ordered pizzas, pastas, and salads to quell our hunger and ease our nerves. The food was everything I liked—tasty, plentiful, and affordable.

Nicos chatted amiably with us about visiting Boston and gave us his list of must-see sights: Faneuil Hall, Harvard Square, the Freedom Trail, and Fenway Park. He was fascinated by Lenora and Ron, exotic people from the Wild West, and they bonded over the foods they each cherished. Nicos listened with rapt attention as Lenora told him how to make venison stew and the simple, but soul-satisfying frybread, so like his beloved pizza dough. Lenora, in turn, was spellbound as Nicos shared recipes for Greek food, from the honeyed perfection of loukoumades to spanakopita, a crispy, layered phyllo stuffed with spinach, herbs, and feta. I was hoping she would remember every detail of these recipes that made my mouth water despite my full belly.

Cam tried to share his recipe for beans on toast. When his culinary expertise was met with a lukewarm response, he turned the conversation to the history of the building, asking if Nicos ever had any unusual experiences.

Nicos spread his hands and turned his head to look

at Cam from the corner of his eye. "Okay, but you tell no one, all right? The building, it's not so old. Maybe 1920 it went up." He leaned his forearms on the counter. "But this is a very old city. Very old. Who knows what came before? Some nights, I hear maybe wind chimes, but it's heavy, not delicate like wind chimes. And the air is heavy too, you know what I mean? It's…depressing." Nicos shook his head, like he was trying to dispel a bad feeling. "Me? I'm a happy guy, but this brings me down."

I kept my tone nonchalant, trying not to scare him off with a rabid interest. "Does the sound come from somewhere in the building?"

"Could be coming from anywhere." Nicos lifted a shoulder, noncommittal. "Maybe it's the ductwork, just carrying in noise from the street." His eyes shifted and his voice trailed off. He didn't sound persuaded by this possibility.

Zackie sat up, interested by the conversation. Convinced she wanted another breadstick, Nicos smiled and gave her two. "I used to have a little dog I named Zeus. He was the god of thunder, all right. Little dog could fart like nobody's business." Nicos reached under the counter and found a bowl that he filled with water. He handed it over the counter for Cam to give Zackie and then continued. "Anyway, Zeus, he never liked to go outside to do his business. I had to walk him up the street before he'd go. And when I heard the chimes or rattling or whatever it is, the hair on his shoulders would stand. Never made a noise, but the hair would stand right up."

Cam straightened after placing the bowl on the floor. "Interesting. Do you hear that sound at any particular time?"

"It's worse in the fall, but that's when it starts getting cold and I shut the door, so maybe I hear the ducts more. And it's usually at night, but not always." The phone rang, and Nicos excused himself to answer it, scribbling an order for takeout on a nearby pad. Tearing off the sheet, he called to someone named Sal in the back and handed off the order to be filled. When he returned to the counter, he held a carafe of coffee. "You guys want more coffee?"

We all declined, but thanked Nicos for a wonderful meal and asked to settle our bill. As we filed out the door, Ron paused. "Do you think it'd be okay if we poke around outside to see if we can hear the weird sound?"

Nicos, about to pick up the ringing phone again,

waved a dismissive hand. "Yeah, yeah, sure. Knock yourselves out. And tell Lenora I'll be trying that frybread real soon."

The streets were dark except for the headlights from passing cars and the weak illumination from a dying streetlamp. We kept to the shadows. Maneuvering around the wooden stairs, we looked above to the small porch near the door, our ears tuned to any sounds that matched Nicos's descriptions. All the while, we watched Zackie for any signs that she detected the presence of something otherworldly. We crept along the back of the building and approached a small parking area with caution. A hint of jangling metal sounded and then was gone.

I froze. "Was that chains on the hitch of a truck maybe?"

Ron paused and closed his eyes, then shook his head. "I can't pin down where the sound came from. But it's back here somewhere, not from the street."

Cam had heard it too. "That was definitely not a wind chime." He walked to the side of the parking lot and stopped when he hit the edge near the street. "Okay, I want everyone to form a line from where I stand to that building next door. And space yourselves evenly."

I knew right away what he planned. I took my place nearest the bunker building and positioned Ron and Lenora between us before I explained what would happen. "We do this in SAR all the time—it's called a tight grid search. We're going to do a staggered start. Cam will step off first and let us know by calling out. As soon as he's at about a forty-five-degree angle to Ron, Ron should step off and let us know. And then Lenora and then me. We keep moving forward unless someone says to stop."

Cam continued the explanation. "I want everyone to pretend there is a box around them as they move forward. Look and listen not just in front of you, but to each side, above and behind. Our line will form a diagonal and will give us a fair bit of overlap between our search areas to maximize our ability to find the source of this sound."

"How about if Zackie runs the perimeter?" I asked. "Make sure he doesn't make a break for it, if it is Mark."

Cam nodded and pointed to the edges of our area and then issued a vague command that probably sounded real to Ron and Lenora. Zackie began to lope around the parking area, nose alternately up into the wind and then dipping down toward the ground to look for scent. Cam faced forward. "Ready? One, stepping off."

As soon as Cam had taken a few paces, Ron called out and began to advance. "Two, stepping off."

Lenora and I followed suit, one after the other. We moved forward in our lanes, making little sound and slowly turning in place as we checked all around us. The jangling sound fluttered faintly in the night's breeze, and Cam told us to hold the line. We listened and turned, trying to locate the sound's origin.

I raised my arm and pointed to my right, where I thought I heard the muffled clanking. Lenora pointed upwards, Ron thought he heard it coming from his left, but Cam shrugged and shook his head, unable to make a determination. After waiting a minute and hearing no other sounds, we advanced again, calling out as we stepped off.

Another minute passed before we heard the distinct ringing of metal links hitting each other. This time, the noise was loud and clear but was abruptly cut off. We held our positions, and we each pointed behind us in the direction from where we heard chains clattering. This time, all of our pointing reinforced each other. Whatever it was, it existed near the center of our area and was elevated.

I walked to the approximate area and reached out my senses to find the source of the sounds. Normal. Everything was normal. "Why don't we have a visual on it, Cam? And why did the sound get cut off?"

"Please, the spirit is not an 'it'—I believe we've had this discussion in the past." Cam approached the center of the parking lot with Ron and Lenora following. "I'm almost certain this is Mark and *he* is deliberately closing the door on us."

Ron pulled out the video camera from his jacket and turned on the unit and its attached light. He walked around the periphery of the area, filming and peering through the camera at the center of the lot, but maybe unconsciously keeping his distance. "I don't follow. What door?"

I squeezed my eyes shut and dredged up the words to explain something that had no true physical representation in our world. The task was harder because this concept had become intuitive to me. "He means…there's this in-between space that spirits can occupy. It's not the true afterlife, and it's not our here and now. Honestly, I don't know what it is, but there's something like a door that they use to move between this in-between space and us."

Ron stopped filming and worked his shoulders, as if his muscles were tight or he had an itch between his shoulder blades. "And you and Cam can draw them out from there?"

"We can call them. Whether they come out or not is their own decision. But yeah, we can be persuasive." I watched as Cam stretched his hands out, seeking the door by feel like a dowser hunting for groundwater. Ron put the camera back to work to capture the moment.

"Ah-ha! Right here." Cam demonstrated an awful lot of confidence for a man waving his hands over a section of air. But Zackie must have believed him. She came trotting over to investigate, poking her muzzle under his hands and wagging her tail.

The wind shifted and a jagged sound, like a dark carillon, emerged from the area near Cam. Instead of harmony, there was discord. The bright, hopeful sound of bells was replaced by the high tone of metal links striking each other. The door had opened, and the atmosphere around us became oppressive with a feeling of futility and desolation. Lenora began to weep as the emotion leaking through the door overcame her. Grasping her shoulders, Ron pulled her away from the epicenter of grief just as a powerful smell, acrid and oily, suffused the air.

"Pine tar." Cam coughed, and he strained to speak. "I think we've found our man."

I rubbed at my nose to diffuse the offending odor from my sinuses, but I only succeeded in lodging the taste of pine tar deep in the back of my throat. Grimacing, I strode forward to stand beside Cam. "Do you think he'll come out now?"

"I think we should both call to him before he shuts the door in our faces." Cam grabbed my hand to encourage a psychic link between us, reinforcing and amplifying our efforts. As we focused our minds to pull this spirit forth, our hands first warmed where we touched and then grew unbearably hot as the energy thrummed through us. Zackie stood between us, baying in a voice that sent shivers up and down my spine. She sensed her quarry.

Sweat broke out on my brow. "Wow, that is some serious resistance." I planted my feet and mentally leaned into the wall that was Mark's will. "Mark, it's time to end this. Come out. We can help you cross over."

"Don't push back, Fia—pull!" Cam psychically 'leaned back,' and something solid and massive began to move like a glacier out of that unknowable space where spirits hide. I followed his lead and mentally rocked back on my heels as Cam urged Mark to come to our side of the void. After that first shift, Mark countered our efforts and dug in again. I feared that the door would slam shut, and we would lose our chance to save him, so I dug in with everything I had. I was tiring when Cam changed tack and attempted to lure the spirit out with a question—a question that would have weighed heavily on his conscience over the centuries, one he would feel compelled to answer. "Mark, you need to tell us why you did it. Why did you murder that man?"

These were the magic words. Mark let go. I felt another seismic shift that sent me staggering, and I lost my grip on Cam's hand. A physical shock struck me like a blow to my breastbone when that massive, shifting thing forced through to our side. The psychic sonic boom made my eyes quiver in their sockets. At first, I could not focus—I stared at the ground, taking shallow breaths, waiting for stability. But all the while, I sensed something moving above me that I did not want to see. I hunched my shoulders, praying that it wouldn't touch me.

Take it slow, I cautioned myself. *One step at a time.* My eyes crept along the ground inch by inch until I saw the base of something crude and wooden, like a square, rough-hewn telephone pole. I concentrated on it, allowing my eyes to follow the pole up a good twenty to thirty feet until I saw a horizontal beam braced to the top by a short diagonal beam. The L-shaped gibbet loomed over us, and I craned my neck to trace along the extended tail until I reached the chains looped through a hole at the end.

A blackened corpse hung, suspended from the chains of the gibbet, twisting silently in the Stygian gloom. Eight bands of metal wrapped around the body from feet to shoulders, holding the legs together and capturing the arms to the sides. An open mask of metal bands encased the head. The skin was like old leather, dried and cracking.

Cam nudged me and spoke in a low voice. "Try not to stare. He's spent enough time on display. Possibly why he stays hidden behind the door."

Embarrassed, I shifted my eyes and ended up looking directly into the light of Ron's camera. Being on display didn't work for me, either. I turned away and stared fixedly at the base of the main pole where Zackie sat, alert with her eyes aimed upward. "But *she* can stare at him."

"Of course *she* can stare at him, you numpty. He's probably been desperate to see her. We just need to sort out a few things for him, and he'll be good to go with her." Cam glanced up before looking away and raising his voice. "Mark, thank you for coming here. I know this can't be comfortable for you."

The hanging body continued to twist above us, unresponsive. While we hoped and waited for Mark to collect himself after that wrenching transition, Lenora wiped her eyes with the back of her hand and took a hesitant step forward. "What d'you see?" We explained to her that Mark had manifested, and he remained chained to the gibbet, so far not responding. "Oh, that poor man. He must really feel awful if even I can feel his suffering."

Ron worked his shoulders again and made the camera light jump. "*Uma*, maybe you shouldn't get so close. Come on back over here and stand by me."

Lenora looked at him over her shoulder. "Nah, I'm all right." Turning back to Cam and me, she made a rolling gesture with her hand. "You two get on with it."

My eyes drifted upward and locked on the still form of Mark. Still no action from that grim, hanging mass. I looked away, stymied by his silence, and tried to sort through my impressions. He wanted to tell us about the murder, or why else would he have come? Something was preventing him from communicating with us. Was it the hopelessness that clung to him like a shroud? Maybe he was so drained by it that he was unable to speak or reach out to us. Or maybe he spent so many years being treated like an object that he no longer remembered how to be animate? I sensed we needed something to shock him out of this torpor.

I shared my thoughts in a quiet voice with Cam. "Can Zackie do something to get him to react?" I remembered how the Psychopomp had applied her version of tough love to Maggie, the spirit of a suicide victim who would flee from us whenever things became too intense. It was effective but hard to watch.

Cam quirked his lips and whispered back. "By all means. Give Zackie a command to awaken Mark. Let's see how she responds."

"That's not what I meant," I hissed. "Why can't you—" In the middle of my complaint, my dead hand shot past Cam and grabbed the main pole. A shudder ran up the pole emanating from this point of contact, and the entire gibbet began to quake. Zackie jumped up barking furiously as the quaking became frenzied. Beams shrieked in protest as wood fought against wood—the gibbet's voice an unsettling accompaniment to the discordant chinking of swaying chains.

Overhead, the corpse swung wildly. I ducked, my shoulders reaching my ears, even though the body hung a good two stories above me. The creaking sound of dry, ancient leather flexing made me look up again. Big mistake. Just as my eyes locked on the desiccated face, the jaw on the corpse unhinged with a sudden crack.

A hollow groan escaped from the dark cavern of his mouth, making the fine hairs on the back of my neck rise in waves. The body began to writhe, and I had nowhere to hide when flakes of skin and tar rained down on me. Gagging, I slapped a hand over my mouth and nose, trying not to breathe as the smell—a sharp and bitter odor of tar mingled with the sulfur-sweet stench of rotting flesh— threatened to suffocate me.

When words poured out of that unmoving, open maw, I wanted to cover my ears as well. The raw pain in Mark's plea throbbed like an infected wound in my brain. "Nathaniel," he croaked, "leave me. I beg you."

Cam's eyes were wide as he watched the animated corpse. "I bloody well hate surprises. Who is Nathaniel?"

"How the hell should I know?" As the words left my mouth, an itching paranoia slithered up my spine. I looked at the dead hand, still gripping the main pole. "Damn it." Grunting with effort, I peeled the dead hand off the post with my good hand. The tremors running up the main pole stopped the second the hand let go. While the corpse continued to swing, the motion was winding down. But the distressed sounds of the corpse muttering and moaning went on unabated, as did the manic barking. "Whoever Nathaniel is, he's coming through the hand."

Lenora added to the chaos of the moment, calling over from a few paces behind us. "What's going on?"

Cam replied over his shoulder in a calmer voice. "It's all right, Lenora. Just give us a second to sort something out." To me, he raised his eyebrows, staring pointedly at the dead hand. "And?"

"And? And we knew anyone and everyone from the afterlife can act through this thing." I let go of the dead hand, since its energy seemed to be spent. "I have to say I'm kind of shocked, though. I had no idea it could do *this*." In addition to sporadically acting independently of me, both when I was awake and asleep, we knew it could also communicate through a sort of automatic writing— depending, of course, if the party controlling it at the time was literate. That had been the limit of our knowledge until this incident. Now we knew better. Mind officially blown.

Cam's agile thoughts brought him to an interesting possibility. "You were the one who said Mark needed to be shocked into reacting. Apparently, Nathaniel obliged you. Do you think he was responsible for bringing us the hair-doll?"

"No idea. Maybe. Probably." I shook my head, trying to think through the noise of the barking and wailing. "I'd have a better feel for it if we knew more about him."

Lenora, tired of waiting, came a few steps closer to ground zero. "Well?"

"*Uma*, you're too close. Don't get so close. Let's move back." Ron closed the gap between them, taking a few involuntary steps forward. Unease etched his face, and the light from the camera danced around us in his agitation to protect Lenora.

Cam barked orders to calm the situation. "Let's everyone stay where they are. Zackie, if you please, I can't hear myself think." He waited until the bedlam died down. "There, that's better. Mark is awake now, and we're going to try to talk to him."

I took Cam's cue. Looking up at the gibbeted man, I repeated the question we knew he should be eager to answer. "Mark, why did you murder John Russell?"

The chains clamored as Mark shifted and stretched against his confinement. "It is true. I was responsible for his death. I obtained the poison and gave it to Phillis and Phebe. Were it not for me, none of this would have happened." His voice rasped, and I was again disturbed by that dangling jaw that never moved as he spoke. "I read the Bible. It said that if blood was not spilt, if we did not lay violent hands on him, it was not murder. This was not true."

Cam relayed Mark's words to Lenora and Ron. It was clear Mark was evading the question, so I tried again, taking it slower this time. "Were you enslaved to this man all your life?"

"I was not." Mark was giving nothing away.

Cam made an exasperated noise, exhaling loudly. "But you were enslaved to another before this?" When Mark confirmed that he was bought from a plantation in the West Indies, Cam shared this information and continued. "So what changed in your life that things became unbearable? What led you to want to kill this man? Did he beat you?"

Mark's bitter laugh was chilling. "Of course he beat me. So did the other master. What is a slave's life except constant beatings?"

Ron let out a low groan. I spun around as the camera light bounced crazily and he dropped to one knee. "My back—it's burning!"

Phebe emerged from behind him. With one hand pressed against Ron's back, she urged him to his feet and marched him forward. Lenora's hands flew to her mouth, her eyes wide and fearful as she watched Ron's stiff-legged progress across the parking lot. I put a hand up to tell her to stay where she was and explained that it looked like Phebe wanted to speak.

When the two drew even with the gibbet, I could see Phebe's hand deeply embedded in Ron's back. She was not letting him go. Ron's hands reached to touch the tender spot where she invaded his back. He worked his shoulders to relieve the discomfort, and his face told the story of how wrong this felt. Ron bit his lip, stifling his pain and any thoughts he might have had on being hijacked.

"Tell them the truth," Phebe said. "Mark, you tell them all of it." She turned her fierce eyes on Cam and me. "The day before John Russell died, Phillis had to dress Mark's eye because master had struck Mark with his stick. That man deserved to die."

As Cam translated what was said for Ron and Lenora, I looked from Phebe to Mark. I wanted to keep up the momentum of questioning. "The beatings became too much? Too frequent? Is that why you poisoned him?"

Phebe bared her teeth, her eyes fiery with hate. "Arsenic was too good for that man. Too quick. I wish he'd suffered more."

Mark breathed a long, sorrowful sigh. His neck made a cracking noise as he shook his head. "That girl is all piss and salt and vinegar. I could stand the beatings. I would not have committed a mortal sin and killed a man for that." His voice grew harsh, and he spat the next words. "I would not have caused my sister to die in the flames for a beating."

This took me aback. I repeated what I'd heard for Lenora and Ron and then tried to pursue this information about Phillis. "Phillis was your sister?"

Before Mark could answer, Phebe pointed a demanding finger at him, not allowing us to be distracted by talk of Phillis. "Tell them about your family. Tell them why you burned down the workshop."

That broke him. His body sagged. He was done resisting. "He sold my family." Oily drops fell from the chained man as he began to weep. "That whoreson sold my wife and children. I begged him to sell me too so I could be with them, but he said I was too valuable. I was skilled and I could build what was needed with wood. John Russell sold what I made and put coin in his pockets from my labor. So I burned the damned workshop."

Cam spoke softly. "You thought if you were no longer able to work wood, he would sell you to the one who owned your family. But it didn't work out that way."

Mark shook his head and took a shuddering breath. "No. If anything, it turned him hard against letting me be with my family."

Cam looked up at Mark, compassion burning in his eyes. "So you gambled that you would be sold after his death. You felt you had no choice but to murder the man."

Phebe nodded, a look of grim satisfaction on her face. "None of us ever had a choice in this." With those words, she stepped behind Ron and disappeared as she reclaimed her host.

It wasn't necessary, but I warned Ron that Phebe was back in residence. He only nodded, resigned that she would not leave him. Ransacking her purse, Lenora dug out a lighter and a bundle of tobacco. She lit the bundle and began chanting as she approached the center of the parking lot. Ron relaxed and looked more at peace as she smudged him with the smoke.

Unable to help, I gave in to feeling sick about the injustices surrounding Mark's life and death. I doubt I would have reacted differently if I were placed in the same no-win situation. Families had been torn apart so others could make a profit. It was inhumane. This was people actively choosing to do something evil, even though they could see with their own eyes the evidence of their cruelty. And it had harmed generations of people who were denied the family ties that brought a sense of security and identity.

I thought of my upbringing in a close-minded, adoptive family. It was not their fault, but they had no frame of reference other than psychiatric illness to understand my abilities. When I compared this to Cam's close-knit family and their tradition of understanding and mentoring the unique gifts in every generation, I felt a keen sense of loss and isolation.

With these thoughts in mind, I wanted to finish this. I knew a part of the answer before I asked the next question. "What were the names of your children?"

Mark's voice caressed the names he spoke. "Emma was my sweet girl with a voice like a nightingale. Felix was the youngest and he was such a strong little man. And my oldest, Nathaniel..." His voice broke. "I told him to take care of his mamma when they took them from me."

I wiped a tear before it could trail down my face. "Nathaniel's trying to take care of you now. He wants you to come to him. Are you ready to finally be with your family, Mark?"

"How can I? I am not deserving after killing a man. My punishment is to be chained here." Mark hung his head. "Always a slave in chains."

Cam shook his head. "No, Mark. It's enough now. No more punishing yourself. You need to be with your family. Are you ready for Zackie to take you?"

"Oh God Almighty, yes! Please let me be with them." Mark strained at his bonds, sobbing. "I can't break them. How can I be freed?"

Zackie slammed against the main pole with her front paws, shattering the wood and breaking the structure into pieces. Marks body tumbled to the ground in front of us. As he writhed and strained, futilely trying to break the bonds that held him, Zackie ran to his side and bit through the chain that bound him to the gibbet. Mark cried aloud with triumph. Using her claws, she tore through the metal bands, finally freeing him from all restraints.

While Zackie comforted Mark, licking his face and leaning in to his embrace, Cam explained what had happened. Lenora approached with the lit tobacco. "Where is he?"

We pointed to where Mark sat with Zackie, rubbing his arms, face and chest, desperate to remove the tar now that the chains were gone. Lenora sang and wafted the tobacco smoke where we indicated. Shaking himself and squaring his shoulders, Ron tried to banish the influence of Phebe. When he joined Lenora in the chant, his voice was strong. As the burning bundle neared its end, Lenora placed it on the ground. The smoke grew thicker around Mark, clinging to him until we saw only his outline.

The chant ended as the tobacco finished burning. When the smoke cleared, Mark reappeared. His skin was clean of the tar, and he looked human again after all the long centuries of suffering. Pulling Zackie back into his embrace, he wept with joy into her fur. "Thank you. Thank you all."

Zackie nudged him to his feet, and he placed a hand on her back, allowing her to guide him. Cam and I turned away to shield our eyes as the portal opened, releasing a blinding light. From the other side, we heard a joyous cry. "Papa!"

# # #

We drank a few gallons of coconut water. Cam sprawled on his bed with Zackie at his side, the empty bottles scattered around them. I sat on the couch, semi-conscious with my feet propped up on the coffee table. My empties littered the floor. If it hadn't been for the fancy hotel room decor—the monochromatic gray being the exception— it might have been a scene from skid row.

"Why'd she do it, Cam? Why'd she even bother?" I slurred my words, my electrolytes still wildly out of whack.

Cam yawned, not bothering to cover his mouth. "Who do you mean? Phebe?"

"Yeah. What's it to her if Mark crossed over into the afterlife or stayed here another hundred years, swinging on the gibbet?"

Cam folded his hands over his belly and closed his eyes. "It's not that she doesn't care about what happened. I do think she feels guilty about how they died and that she testified against them. She just cares more about herself. But it cost her nothing to see Mark on his way. No downside for her. You see what I mean?"

"I guess." I nodded, even though he couldn't see me. I sat quietly for a minute and drank some more coconut water. "You know what cracked me up?"

"What?" Cam spoke with his eyes still shut.

"When Zackie went through the portal, and Lenora said she had run off into the night and you'd better go get your dog." I sniggered.

Cam cast his arm out and turned his head in a dramatic pose. "Poor Zackie—lost in a strange city and all alone." Zackie groaned and stretched her long legs, pushing Cam toward the edge of the bed. "Cut that out, you bloody hound."

As Cam pushed back in a vain attempt to center himself on the bed, his phone went off. He swore and sat up. Plastic bottles crunched as he maneuvered his legs off the bed and grabbed the phone on the nightstand. After a few rapid pokes at the screen, he looked at me with bloodshot eyes. "Peyton just sent a text for you. She says she recovered your phone, but the screen is smashed in and you need to get another one."

I made a face. "Can you look if there's a store near here? Oh, and can you thank Peyton for getting the phone?"

Cam poked at the screen, and after some additional swiping and poking, eventually found a store on Washington Street within walking distance of the hotel. I'd deal with it in the morning. Having been drained by spirit encounters before, I knew I'd be in no shape the next day to do much else that was useful. It was just as well that the arson investigation was blocking our access to Phillis.

Despite feeling completely drained, we were too tightly wound to sleep. Cam turned on the television, angled it toward the couch, and then joined me there in vegetating. We spent the next hour watching reruns of old sitcoms and adding to the collection of coconut water bottles on the floor. When the local news came on, a teaser told us there was a new development in the Walnut Avenue fire story and to stay tuned for an update. We sat through stories about internet cats, how coleslaw was the new brain food, and the salacious details of celebrity breakups. Finally, the newscaster announced a suspect had been arrested in connection with the fires. The suspect had a prior arrest for arson but no conviction.

I raised my eyebrows at Cam. "Not Phillis, then?"

Cam made a scritching sound as he rubbed his stubbled jaw. "I don't know. I find it all just a bit odd. To me, the timing of the fires was definitely a statement. And it smacks of Phillis." He sighed. "But I could be wrong, and this is just a run-of-the-mill, conventional crime."

With the news program over and nothing more to be learned about the fires, we gathered the mountain of empties into a bin and called it a night.

I looked at the overflowing bin. "We seriously need to buy stock in coconut water."

My first text on the new phone was to Lucas. Standing outside the store, I found some shade from the bright autumn sun, so I could see my screen well enough to tap out a quick message. Lucas needed to know I had a new phone and that he could go back to texting me directly.

My thumbs slowed as I considered how Cam had received nothing for me on his phone the previous day except for Peyton's message. Maybe Lucas felt inhibited with Cam as an intermediary. Or maybe he met a bonnie, red-haired lassie and he had been having a night out at the pub with her. Shaking my head, I rejected the thought.

242

Hannah would never stand for it. As another idea bubbled to the surface on the roiling waters of my insecurities, I raised my eyes from the screen and stared unseeing at the passing traffic. What if Hannah had found a way to make her presence known to Lucas and that was why he was incommunicado? All things considered, the bonnie lassie was less horrifying to me than the second coming of Lucas's wife, the love of his life.

I returned my attention to the phone. Tapping a little more forcefully than necessary, I finished the message by saying I missed him and then tagged on a few random emojis. After I hit send, I stood staring stupidly at the phone, willing Lucas to text me back. I had just about given up when the phone buzzed in my hand. My smile faded when I saw it was Cam calling. I really needed to fix my ringtones.

I poked the screen to accept the call. "What?"

"You'll never guess who they picked up for the arson." Cam sounded like he was about to burst.

I took a breath, not in the mood to play twenty questions with him. "You're right. I never will. Why don't you just tell me?"

"Rory. He was skulking around the scene and the police must have thought there was something suspicious about him. The idiot tried to run when the police said they wanted to question him."

"You think he followed us here?" I was torn between guilt and anger. There was no way Rory had set the fires. The timing was completely off—he would have had to make it up here before us if he were responsible. Rory was innocent, at least of this. But what the hell was he doing up here?

Cam huffed. "I think that's obvious. He's not given up on stalking you."

"But how would he know to go there? *I* didn't know we were going to Walnut Avenue."

Cam probably rolled his eyes so hard I should have felt a shift in the Earth's orbit. "Are you going to make me call you a numpty again? He read it in your phone messages. You know, the ones you *didn't* read in preparation for this trip."

Embarrassed by this reminder, I turned a few shades of pink. "Oh."

"Yes, 'oh.'" Cam's end was silent for a few moments, and then he sighed. "Bugger it all. I suppose there's no help for it. We'll need to talk to the police. We can't let him rot in jail."

"Um, I think we can." My internal battle between guilt and anger was over. The final score was anger one, guilt zero.

"No, Fia, we can't. Besides, it's not to our benefit for the authorities to believe they have their man."

I started walking back to the hotel. "Why? Wouldn't they clear out of the area and stand down once they had someone to pin the fires on?"

Cam's voice took on the patient and didactic tone he used when he needed to explain something to a simpleton. I hated that tone. "No, not at all. The arson investigators will redouble their efforts to find evidence specifically linking Rory to the fires. They'll assign more resources to Gallows Hill, not less, making it even harder for us to meet with Phillis."

I grunted, unwilling to admit he was probably right. "Did you at least see the perp walk?"

"Yes, yes I did. And I have to say, he looked guilty as hell." Despite Cam's insistence on taking the high road, his words sang with schadenfreude.

I stepped off the curb to cross the street and was almost sideswiped by a turning car. The driver casually flipped me off as he drove away. Without missing a beat, the dead hand shot up and returned the gesture. The hand's motion was so supple and fluid, it made me wonder if some past resident of New Jersey might be at the controls. "Cam, I need my full attention just to cross the street around here. I'm going to hang up. I'll be back at the hotel in a few minutes."

I crossed the street without further need to issue a rude gesture and walked the last two blocks to the hotel. With impeccable timing, Zackie met me outside the door, and we walked in together. It wouldn't have looked good for me to be seen without my service dog, and as it turned out, Rhonda was back on shift. She watched us make our way across the lobby to the elevators. Out of the corner of my eye, I saw her lips compress as she reached for the bottle of hand sanitizer.

At the elevators, a new sign was posted above the call buttons: ONLY USE YOUR FINGERS TO PRESS

ELEVATOR BUTTONS. I wondered what other people made of that. Grinning, I took out my phone and snapped a picture of the sign. While we rode up to the third floor, I posted it to my brand-new social media account with the caption, *Don't even want to know the story behind this sign.*

Cam answered his door on the first knock and emerged with Ron and Lenora in tow. He spouted plans as he shooed us back toward the elevators. "The Somerville police station is on Washington Street, a fifteen-minute drive from here. I believe Rory is being held in the jail for questioning."

"Geez, is there anything here *not* on Washington Street?" When no one offered a response, I allowed myself to be swept along by Cam's ardent shooing. "What about lunch? Can we stop somewhere to get lunch?"

Cam held the elevator door open with his palm and gestured for us to enter. "We'll get something afterwards."

I put on an impish face. "Will you invite Rory out to lunch with us if you get him out of jail?"

Ron snorted. "Rich bastard should take us to lunch."

"Pfff-ffft—the more they got, the tighter they hold

on to it." Lenora poked the button for the ground floor with the handle of her cane.

"Do be careful with that." Cam joined us in the elevator and pointed to Lenora's cane. "They've put up a new sign saying we're only to use our fingers to operate the elevator."

Lenora looked at Cam from under her brows and then slid her eyes to Zackie. "You know that's not what Rhonda's sign's about."

Cam stared at Zackie with tired eyes, as if greatly put upon after decades of dealing with her antics. "I've identified an alternate hotel for us, should it come to that. Nevertheless, let us try not to get thrown out of this one. Obey the letter of the law, if you please." Zackie did not share Cam's concerns, returning his look with a wagging tail and a playful grin that showed the tips of her canines.

The elevator door opened and deposited us in the lobby. Busy checking in new guests, Rhonda had her eyes glued to a computer screen and did not notice us. Rather than hurry and possibly engage her prey drive, Cam set a leisurely pace to the exit, allowing inattentional blindness to complete our camouflage. We sauntered out the door and made it to the truck without getting the stink-eye from Rhonda.

The Somerville police department was housed in a brick structure with a tall arch over the main entrance. Finding no parking near the building, we spent twenty minutes searching the surrounding neighborhood of multi-family homes for a space large enough to accommodate the truck. Cam squeezed into a space precariously close to a fire hydrant, on a street almost certain to be on the patrol route of Somerville's Finest. Curling up on the seat, Zackie made it clear that the whole thing bored her, and she declined to accompany us.

As we approached the police station on foot, there were no news vans or reporters with cameras. Interest from the local press seemed to have died down—a lucky break for us. Nothing was visible through the tinted windows on the front of the building, and I took that for another good omen. I didn't know what we would need to disclose or how this was going to pan out, so anything offering discretion and privacy was welcome.

"What's your plan?" I whispered to Cam as he opened the door. A rush of stagnant air tinged with stale coffee and decades of nervous sweat settled over us.

He waved his hand in a cavalier gesture and muttered, "Don't really have one. Playing it by ear."

Cam walked up to the front desk with a brisk stride and an air of confidence—undeserved, in my opinion, given his lack of planning. The desk sergeant held up a finger asking us for a moment as he concluded his phone conversation. My ears struggled to adjust to his strong Southie accent as I eavesdropped on his call. He spoke rapidly, the words melting together as *r*'s dropped out in favor of broad *ah*'s and at one point, I swear I heard him say the word "wicked," but I was disappointed when it wasn't followed up with "sinners." It appeared that all vestiges of the founding Puritans had vanished from the language.

Cam began to speak as soon as the sergeant put the phone down. "Officer, would you be holding one Rory Craymore? As much as I regret doing this, I believe we have information we are obligated to provide that would exonerate—"

The grizzled desk sergeant put up a hand. "Save it. The kid's frickin' grandfather already sprung him." He motioned over his shoulder to a desk along the white cinder block wall.

Rory sat on a straight back chair speaking to a
police officer with a skeptical look on her face. Her dark
hair was pulled back in a tight bun, and she leaned forward
in her seat as if she were compelling a confession from
Rory. Behind the chair stood the old man from the tiny
gold-framed picture in Rory's apartment. Although he
leaned heavily on his cane, there was nothing weak about
him. His expensive attire was a deliberate statement meant
to clash with the humble cinder blocks. The perfectly fitted
navy suit and polished leather shoes sent a clarion call for
the peasants to settle down and bow to his birthright. He
had a shock of white hair and dark, penetrating eyes that
glared at the officer who dared to detain one of her betters.
The old man's hand grasped Rory's shoulder as if he
owned him.

Lenora took in the scene and then glanced at Ron. A
worry line formed between her brows. "Guess we know
how he used his one phone call." She turned her attention
to the desk sergeant. Glancing at his nameplate, she tipped
her head toward Rory's grandfather. "Sergeant Murphy,
what'd he say to get that boy off?"

The officer pursed his lips like he had just sucked
on a lemon. "The kid's E-ZPass showed he was driving

through tolls when the fires were set. We also caught him behind the wheel on a traffic camera on Mass Ave." He shook his head. "Maybe we can't make him for torching that neighborhood, but that kid ain't clean. I'd bet my badge on it."

Cam met the officer's eyes. "Indeed. But none of it took place, as they say, on your patch." Shifting his weight, he angled his body toward the exit. "Being that there's nothing further, I think we'll be off."

I was delighted by the way things turned out. We were free and clear of any moral obligation to spring Rory, and no disclosures had to be made to the police. As we were about to ride off into the sunset, Rory called out from across the room. "That's him! That's the guy who did this to my face."

Crap. We had been so close to making it out the door. The crazy thought of making a run for it flitted through my mind, but Lenora would never be able to keep up. As a group, we returned to the front desk. I stood shoulder to shoulder with Lenora, forming a defensive line in front of Ron. Cam protected his back.

I could feel the tension vibrating off Ron. I knew

this wasn't the first time he'd been in a police station accused of something violent. It also wasn't the first time for Lenora to endure this ordeal. She held her cane in a white-knuckled grip. Her face was taut as Rory, his grandfather, and the interviewing officer came toward us.

The officer held her hand palm up in an apologetic gesture. "I'm Officer O'Malley. Very sorry to hold you folks up, but Mr. Craymore here seems to think one of you may have been involved in an assault on him."

Rory flushed red. "I don't *think* I was assaulted—"

Cam interrupted with a soft, superior tone that is a British specialty. "Well, if you don't think you were assaulted, why are you wasting the time of these good officers?"

Rory clenched his teeth and raised his voice. "I *know* I was assaulted."

Officer O'Malley tightened her lips and looked at Rory out of the corner of her eye. "Keep your voice down!" The force of her directive easily overpowered Rory's mewling complaint. In another life, she might have been an opera singer.

I could tell she wanted to say something different, probably involving expletives, and my gut unclenched a little. I didn't know how long she had been dealing with Rory, but she was hanging on to her professionalism by a thread where he was concerned.

With a visible effort, Officer O'Malley reduced her volume. "You haven't been able to give me a straight story up until now about how you got those injuries. And suddenly you're telling me—"

Rory's grandfather showed yellowed teeth as he parted his lips in a sneering smile and appealed to the desk sergeant. "Obviously not a good time of the month for this little lady. I don't know why they let women conduct police business when they can be so emotional."

Sergeant Murphy's mouth hung open for a split second as he stared wide-eyed at Rory's grandfather. With an abrupt shake of his head, he snapped his jaw shut and turned his back on the old man. Busying himself with a stack of paperwork, he called to the Officer. "O'Malley, if you shoot 'em, I'll forgive you."

I burst out laughing, and this only seemed to further incense the old guy.

"How dare you! You are a public servant, and you must serve me. Don't you ever turn your back on me!" The old man screamed at the desk sergeant in a hoarse voice, flecks of spittle spotting the counter.

Rory's grandfather had no subtlety and no finesse. I had been worried that he would be all sharp and slippery, and a major threat to us. But watching him in action, there was an absence of clever in how he approached the world. I felt sure nothing would come of this interview, and Ron would be safe.

Officer O'Malley rubbed her forehead and muttered to herself. "…not paying me enough to deal with this sh—" Looking up, she focused first on the old geezer. "You, quiet down. Milo Hardwick, you have the right to remain silent and I strongly suggest you take me up on that." She next fixed her scowl on Rory. "You. You're telling me you were assaulted. Who did it? When and where did it happen?"

Rory jabbed his index finger at Ron. "This one—he punched me in the face yesterday. We were in New Jersey. I want him arrested for assault."

Ron looked him in the eye, and then made eye contact with each of the officers. "It's not true. I never punched him in the face."

Eyes blazing, Milo Hardwick looked Ron up and down, and then curled his lip in disgust. "Just look at you. You're a lying savage!" The old man spat at Lenora's feet. "You people need to go back to the reservation."

I sensed something like a seething volcano rumbling beneath Ron's skin. His face was tight but held in a carefully neutral expression. I became frightened when I noticed Ron's hands bunched into tight fists, ready to hammer flesh into pulp. Then I saw the tiny, barely perceptible tremors in his arms, and I knew he was putting all his effort into holding back. Ron needed to keep control over both his own reaction and over Phebe's influence. I prayed he wouldn't lose it in front of the cops.

The room went silent. Even Rory looked uncomfortable for a moment, but then he rallied and tried to play the victim. "It's a free country. My grandpa can say whatever he thinks. You're just all a bunch of PC pussies looking out for each other. I'm never going to get any justice here."

Officer O'Malley leveled a dark look at Rory that stopped his babbling. In a swift move, she spun Hardwick around to move him back to her desk. With a hand still on his upper arm, Officer O'Malley spoke to Lenora. "This man assaulted you by spitting. Do you wish to press charges?"

Lenora took one look at Ron and, breathing hard, she clamped her mouth shut on whatever she was going to say to that sexist, racist bastard. Just like me, she was afraid that this could turn into a bloodbath. To Officer O'Malley, she gave a one-word answer. "No."

Officer O'Malley nodded, accepting Lenora's decision, but her eyes were sad. "Your choice." As she marched Rory and his grandfather back to her desk, she informed Hardwick that he also had a choice. She could either issue him some paper towels and a spray bottle of disinfectant or a citation for a misdemeanor.

Cam put a steadying hand on Ron's shoulder, and despite everything, he had a spark of triumph in his eye. Cam kept his voice quiet as he addressed the desk sergeant. "I think we all know what this is about."

Sergeant Murphy was white-lipped, and his brows formed an angry V. "If there really was an assault in New Jersey, it's New Jersey's problem. Sir, you and your friends are free to go. Have a nice day."

He didn't have to tell us twice.

# # #

I was stress eating, not that anyone noticed. After what happened at the police station, I felt the need to soothe my frayed nerves with lots of carbs. We sat silently, squished into a booth at a family chain restaurant. We had tacitly agreed not to talk until the food was served and everyone had a chance to steady their blood sugar.

With my mouth full of fries, I turned to my friends and said what we were all thinking. "And what the hell was that all about?"

"Letter of the law." Ron gave a firm nod.

I cocked my head. "Huh? Not following."

"I did what Cam said to do when I told them I never punched him in the face. Sure, I throttled him. But punch him? Never. Letter of the law." Ron brought his burger to his mouth to take another bite and then paused. "Rory was probably too punch drunk to remember what really happened."

Cam sipped his tea and then gave a low chuckle. "More likely, he didn't want to reveal to the officer what strange and violent things can occur when you trespass while in the act of stalking someone."

"Yeah, not really what I was getting at, but Ron did a good job doing the letter of the law thing." I swallowed the fries and washed it down with some coffee, watching the object of my praise out of the corner of my eye. He looked like he had just won a title fight—a little ragged around the edges, but overall, Ron had the vibe of someone who had triumphed. It finally clicked in my brain that he had won this bout against Phebe—she hadn't gotten her bloodbath despite the worst kind of provocation. Ron probably felt confident that he now had her number.

Cam must have been thinking along the same lines. He raised his mug to Ron in salute. "And good on you for keeping Phebe under control. That couldn't have been easy."

Ron clinked his mug of hot cocoa against our mugs. "A toast to bratty spirits everywhere who are gonna learn that they're not always gonna get their way."

I drank to his toast and then circled back to my original question. "What I meant to say before…what's up with Rory's grandfather? He had to have known he was pissing off the cops."

Cam handed me a napkin from the dispenser and motioned to an area on my cheek. "It was rather odd behavior. Self-defeating. Rory wouldn't have thought of his E-ZPass records himself, so he was lucky his grandfather provided this alibi. Mr. Milo Hardwick was at least thinking straight on that bit." Cam nibbled on a chicken nugget and then frowned. "But this proves Hardwick's behavior isn't just due to his age and senility."

Ron helped himself to some fries from my plate. "Personal experience says he's just an asshat."

When he went in for another helping, I jabbed at his hand with my fork. "Speaking of asshats."

Ron hunched his shoulders, expecting Lenora to swat him one for stealing food. His eyes went round when he noticed she sat quietly, picking at her lunch. "*Uma*, what's wrong?"

Lenora set her fork down on her plate with hardly a noise. "Nothin' changes. Been putting up with that 'savage' shit my whole damn life. Tired of it."

"I'm sorry, *Uma.*" Ron hung his head and seemed to deflate. "I should have done something. I failed both of us."

Lenora focused her ire on Ron. "And what you gonna do, boy? Hit an old man? I didn't raise you like that. You did right. It would've got out of hand for you if you did anything."

She was bristling with pent up frustration and anger, so I didn't touch her. But I felt for her and wanted to say something to make it better. "I know it seems like the world isn't making any progress, but he's just one crazy old man. Maybe the last of his kind."

"And think about it, Lenora." Cam leaned forward to peer into her face. "He got no traction with his ranting. He got nothing but the enmity of the officers. Surely this shows he's an aberration."

Ron shook his head. "No. Sorry to say there's plenty like him. I might have met them all growing up."

Lenora rolled her eyes. "And getting arrested after tangling with 'em."

The corner of Ron's mouth hitched up a notch. "If there's anything in life worth throwing down over...."

I gave him a sharp look. "You don't have that luxury with Phebe on board, so wipe that grin off your face."

"Yes, *Uma*—I mean, Fia." Ron's eyes twinkled with mischief, but I didn't fire off a retort. I wasn't sure anymore if his jab was really an insult.

While I pondered how weird this felt, Lenora piped up. "You calling her *Uma*? You watch your mouth, boy." The words were biting, but a small smile played on her lips. I was glad to see she was bouncing back.

Preoccupied with Ron and Lenora, I missed it when Cam also stole fries from my plate. Waving away my dismayed look, he wiped his fingers on a napkin and then tapped at his phone's screen. "While you folks were busy discussing the finer points of strategic violence, I found some very interesting information about Milo Hardwick online."

While we ate, Cam gave us the lowdown on Milo. Much of what he related was no surprise. "Says here, Milo is wealthy. He got his start through the time-honored tradition of inheriting money. He was CEO of the family business for a while and managed dozens of manufacturing plants."

"What did they manufacture? Wait, let me guess— was it overpriced pharmaceuticals? No? How about pornography?" I figured it had to be something unsavory.

Cam shook his head. "They processed and packaged health food." He scrolled down a bit and then continued. "Looks like Milo was able to evade the public spotlight until his daughter, Amelia, came of age."

Cam tapped his screen and began reading from another website. What Amelia lacked in work ethic, she made up for in her insatiable desire for jet-setting to celebrity-studded, all-night parties. Her increasingly outrageous behavior became a favorite topic for the celebrity rags, and they gleefully reported stories of her going from one boy-toy to the next. Amelia eventually married and settled down long enough to have Rory, but then went on to several high-profile marriages and divorces. In the interim, she neglected Rory badly enough that an ugly custody battle ensued. Milo ended up taking responsibility for the boy.

Lenora shook her head with disgust. "Those were the people who raised him? Boy never stood a chance."

As much as I detested Rory, I couldn't dispute her claim. Cam surprised me when he disagreed. "By all reports, Milo proved to be a stabilizing influence in Rory's life." He read from his screen for a moment before going on with the story. "All was well until Rory turned eleven. That's when an industrial accident occurred at one of Hardwick Industry's plants. Milo was on the floor inspecting operations and he suffered a major head injury. The doctors weren't confident he would recover, but Milo defied their expectations. He eventually walked out of the rehabilitation center under his own steam. Thing is, he was a changed man."

Ron gave a quizzical look. "What's that supposed to mean? You hear that and you think he found God or something."

"Quite the opposite," Cam replied. "He became erratic, vulgar, and completely intolerable. For a while, Hardwick Industries was able to suppress the gossip about Milo's behavior. But eventually, playing on people's sympathies and quietly settling hostile work environment lawsuits proved ineffective. Stories abounded about how

Milo had become this century's Phineas Gage."

Ron leaned forward and put his palms up. "And what's that supposed to mean? Who's Phineas Gage?"

The history major in me took over, and I launched into a mini-lecture. "It was in the 1800's. Gage survived a really horrible railroad construction accident. There was an explosion and an iron rod went flying and drove right through his skull. It destroyed a good chunk of his brain, but somehow, he lived. The guy was never the same after that. His behavior completely changed. People who knew him before the accident said he'd been a great guy, but afterward, he became a total asshat."

According to Cam's website, just like his predecessor, Milo suffered brain injuries that had a major impact on his personality and behavior. In Milo's case, he completely lost his verbal filter—anything and everything came pouring out of his mouth.

Many former employees insisted he was only saying out loud what he'd always been thinking. The company's stock plummeted as these accounts went public. Forced to step down as CEO after a particularly egregious incident during a shareholders' meeting, Milo maintained a position on the board of directors and continued to earn millions operating in the shadows.

Lenora's expression became thoughtful. "So, where was Rory during all this?"

Cam's voice grew quiet and there was sympathy for the young Rory in his eyes. "He never left Milo's side. All throughout Milo's treatment and recovery, the boy refused to leave his grandfather. And as Rory grew older, the two remained inseparable." He quirked his lips. "Problem is, the boy grew up under Milo's dubious tutelage."

Cam found his place on the website's post and read to us the final bits of the entry. While Rory's love and loyalty for the old man was commendable, he made the mistake of publicly defending anything Milo said, effectively eliminating any possibility of someday taking on the mantle of company CEO. This might have been just as well, since Rory had also inherited his mother's wild streak. Other than his commitment to his grandfather, Rory demonstrated no predisposition toward anything good, productive, or useful. Had he been born poor, Rory would have had a lengthy rap sheet and a deep, personal acquaintance with the penal system.

We sat around in silence, trying to absorb all this. Cam put the phone down and frowned, deep furrows running along the sides of his mouth. "Perhaps this is what happens when a person acquires so much wealth that decency becomes optional."

I closed my eyes and gave a sharp shake of my head. I could almost feel nuggets of Milo and Rory's story ricocheting inside of my skull. "I honestly don't know how to file this info. Are they jerks because they choose to be, or is it all circumstance?"

Ron gave a half smile. "Who knows? We're probably all a mixed bag of nature, nurture, and free will." He made a clicking sound with his tongue. "And in my case, with Phebe on board, multiply that by two."

"Not buying it." Lenora's jaw was set. "There's always a choice."

Hurt people…hurt people. The refrain swam up through the murky waters of my subconscious and forced me to consider Rory in light of his horrible upbringing. But did that give him a pass every time he did something to harm someone else? I thought not and tended to side with Lenora on this. He had a choice, but based on what I'd seen, it appeared he repeatedly made the wrong one. The latest example was when Rory had shown a moment of discomfort after Milo spouted his racist comments. He could have tried to talk his grandfather down from the confrontation, but instead he took the path of least resistance and reverted to his childhood programming. How do you break from that?

And what about Milo? What, besides the accident, brought him to his current state? According to people who had worked with him, the accident had only loosened his tongue and not changed his mindset. If that were true, who or what in Milo's life taught him to be such a pitiful excuse for a human? But just because it was written somewhere on the bathroom wall of the internet didn't make it true. The people who spoke against him may have had a grudge. Maybe Milo wasn't a racist, misogynist pig before the accident, and it was all a side effect of a damaged brain.

Maybe all evil was just a bunch of flawed connections between the wrong neurons created by things like a dysfunctional upbringing, actual physical trauma, or some other negative life experience. But somewhere in there, I felt strongly that personal responsibility still existed—Lenora's idea that we always had a choice rang true to me. Maybe it wasn't black and white. What if the *degree* of personal responsibility was dependent on circumstance, and it wasn't purely circumstance dictating whether a person had any responsibility for their actions?

I was too tired for this. Thinking about cause and effect, right and wrong, the origins of human suffering— this was too much heavy lifting for my poor brain, and it was making my head pound.

Ron tapped my arm. "You all right? You're rubbing your forehead like it hurts."

"Yeah, it's just a headache." I pushed my hair out of my eyes and sat back in the booth.

Cam eyed me with mock concern. "Maybe we should head back to the hotel and get some rest before the next meal. You'll need all your strength if you're to eat a proper dinner."

I snorted and grabbed one of his cookies. "You're right. I have to keep my strength up." With my mouth full of cookie, I pulled out my wallet and dropped some bills on the table to cover my share of lunch. I was ready for a nap.

#

The hotel was on fire.

I had fallen asleep on a small corner of the mattress because Zackie had expanded out to her maximum bed-hogging capacity. She must have stretched her legs and pushed me overboard while I was in the middle of a really good dream about Lucas. I woke up on the floor in a dazed heap. Zackie, her expression unreadable, stood for a moment looking down at me from the bed before leaping off the other side. When I took a deep breath to broadcast my discontent, I got a lungful of smoke that made my throat constrict and sent me into a coughing fit.

The smoke had a strange acrid, sulfurous odor and I clamped one hand over my mouth and nose. Without thinking, I scrambled to get my legs under me so I could stand, but then thought better of it. The air higher up would probably be a whole lot worse. While I crawled on my hands and knees to the door, I found everything I owned littering the floor instead of tucked away in my bags. This was a trivial concern at that moment. I ignored the weirdness of someone having riffled through my stuff while I slept and forged ahead to the door. But then I encountered the hair-doll, and the weirdness took center stage.

The doll was engulfed in flames so intense that it should have been turned into a pile of ash in seconds. It made no sense how it could withstand a fire that hot, but the burning hair explained the stench, even if the blaze did not consume it. I stared mesmerized by the twirling flames, losing precious time when I should have been making good my escape. I flinched when the doll suddenly lurched upright, its limbs making spasmodic jerking motions, like a grotesque dance. My flesh crawled, and I leaned away but ended up flinging myself backward when flames exploded from the tiny figure.

I landed on my back, and I tried to crab walk away from the inferno of heat roaring toward the ceiling. I had barely taken one scuttling step backward when flames reached out like tendrils from either side of the writhing doll and began feeding on the carpet. The advancing flames cast a circle around me and stretched toward the ceiling. I was trapped, and the wretched doll capered madly in a danse macabre, mocking me. Dark laughter echoed from somewhere beyond the wall of flames. The world blurred as tears streamed from my eyes. I didn't know if I was crying because I was about to die or if my eyes were scorched and melting from the heat and smoke.

"Zackie!" I cried out in desperation, the smoke searing my lungs. If I was going to die, I knew she wouldn't let me suffer. She would lead me through the portal and out of the flames and that would be all right.

A flare of light momentarily overwhelmed the flames, and I felt a thud when she landed next to me. My body slumped with relief, knowing I would be spared the pain of being eaten alive by the flames. Instead of opening the portal, I sensed her lunge through the wall of fire to snatch the squirming doll in her jaws. The blaze before me died when she shook it violently with a vicious snarl before hurling it into the flames behind us. Grabbing the back of my shirt as if it were the scruff of my neck, she dragged me to the door and then leaped back into the room, baying ferociously at a dark, predatory being gliding through the flames.

Dying a fiery death became secondary to escaping the thing lurking in the fire. Whimpering, I fought to control my panic and resist the urge to throw the door open and charge into the hallway. I first brought the back of my shaking hand toward the door, trying to sense heat without touching the surface, imagining an even more intense fire on the other side that would blast through the open door and char me to a cinder. When I felt no heat radiating from the door, I brushed my hand along the crack and the doorknob. Both seemed cool compared to what I experienced in the room, so I risked cracking open the door.

The brightly lit hallway appeared normal, though blurred and indistinct through my streaming eyes. I sprang from my crouch like an Olympic sprinter, making it a few uncontrolled, stumbling steps before collapsing.

"Cam! Fire!" My voice was hoarse from inhaling the smoke, and I immediately started coughing, but my cry had been loud and anyone who heard me would know this was an emergency. Something tall and Cam-shaped burst out of his room and paused in the middle of the hall before lunging to the wall and pulling the fire alarm. Running past me, he yanked my room door closed before returning to pull me to my feet.

"No, Cam! Zackie's still in the room," I croaked. "We have to get her out."

"Don't be ridiculous. She'll be fine." Cam half dragged, half carried me down the hall. Stopping in front of

Lenora's room, we could hear her swearing and Ron bellowing. Cam pounded his fist on the door until it opened.

"She wouldn't leave without her purse." Ron's voice sounded tense, and I got the sense he was forcing Lenora along in front of him. I wiped my eyes and made out the enormous purse looped around Ron's neck before my vision grew watery again.

I babbled to Cam about what happened in my room as we made our way out. Between my smoke-filled eyes and Lenora's bum leg, we weren't the fastest to escape. A handful of people ran past us in the smoky hall. Thankfully, most of the guests had been out of the hotel during that late afternoon. As we passed the elevator, a sudden bright, hot flare made me turn back to look.

"Shit!" Cam forced me around and pulled me toward the stairs. "That was Rhonda's 'hands only' sign." A painting on the wall burst into flames as he spoke. "She's starting fires everywhere. Phillis is going to destroy this place."

We struggled to the stairway door, and someone brave held it open for us before they disappeared down the stairs. With no one behind us, we allowed the door to slam shut as we began our descent. We were only three floors up, but it felt much longer as the air grew smoky around us. To her credit, Rhonda was at the bottom of the stairs, frantically urging people toward a fire exit that led to the outside world and safety.

We ended up sitting on a curb a long way from the building, huddling together against the autumn chill. Despite our distance, smoke laced with that foul, acrid odor swept into my sinuses with every breath. The scream of sirens and car horns sounded far away as emergency vehicles forced their way through traffic to get to the scene. In the press of other bodies near us, I heard snatches of both curses and prayers from those who had escaped the fire. Rubbing at my eyes, I was desperate to see what was going on.

Lenora mumbled to Ron and he struggled to pull the purse's strap over his head before handing it to her. Rooting around in its voluminous folds, she swore fluently until she finally found what she wanted. As my vision again succumbed to tears, she grabbed my wrist and forced a plastic bottle into my hand. "Wash out your eyes."

A few squirts of the mysterious liquid and I felt a

blessed relief. When I looked up to thank Lenora and return the bottle, my vision was clear, until Zackie stuck her wet nose into my face. "I'm okay…it's okay…you can stop doing that."

I put my hands up to fend off another muzzle attack and caught Cam's raised eyebrow and bemused expression. Looking her over, she was untouched by the fire, but her vest had been singed black and the edges showed where the flames had eaten the fabric. The lettering identifying her as a service dog had melted, and the plastic snap buckle on the belt had fused into a solid block. We were going to have to cut her out of that vest when this was all over.

When I turned to look at the hotel, I couldn't help gawking at the thick, black smoke enveloping the building. The fire had metastasized to every floor, flames licking behind windows that would soon shatter from the intense heat. It had all happened so quickly.

My stomach twisted as I thought of that malevolent little doll dancing in the flames, taunting me. I was certain Phillis had found us because of that hair-doll. She had given it to Phebe to mark the girl, and she had sensed Phebe was near because I had brought it with us. Phillis had homed in on the last piece of her earthly body left on this planet and used it to come looking for Phebe. I felt like retching when I realized how I had endangered all the people in the hotel because of my carelessness. I should have known better. I should have done better.

I hoped Cam's quick action in pulling the alarm had gotten everyone out of the building. I scanned the former guests, now hotel refugees, that gathered near us. Many just stared vacantly at the burning hotel, others spoke excitedly on their cell phones or took videos of the disaster. No one appeared anxious, only relieved to be away from the fire. A handful of hotel employees, identifiable by their smart red jackets, formed their own little cluster. Their faces told a different story—etched with worry, some wide-eyed with hands covering their mouths, others agitated and pointing to the building. Rhonda was not among them.

With my gaze still fixed on the hotel staff, I nudged Cam and stood up. "We need to get Rhonda out."

"She's still in there? But she was right next to the fire exit." Cam craned his neck to look at the staff. Seeing their distress, he got up and stood next to me. Together, we surveyed the hotel, trying to come up with a plan.

Ron rose to his feet and joined us. "I'll come with

you."

"No!" The word flew from my mouth. "You can't. You'll make it worse. Phebe's with you and this is Phillis's fire."

"She's right." Cam motioned for him to sit with Lenora. "Phillis is the cause of this, and she'll roast you alive to get to Phebe."

Ron looked uncertain but then nodded, accepting the truth. His eyes wide with concern as he scanned the building with us. "It looks bad, really bad in there. Maybe only go as far as the fire exit and look for her. If she's not there, just call it and get out."

I swallowed hard, trying to quiet the paralyzing fear that was inching up my spine. I knew what we were going to face. My palms began to sweat as I flashed back to being surrounded by the suffocating smoke and blistering heat from the wall of flames. Escaping that fire once seemed a stroke of pure luck, and I really, really didn't want to go back. I reached for humor to control my fear. "You know, hand sanitizer's highly flammable. I hope Rhonda wasn't carrying any."

Cam played along. "She might want it later to get

the soot off. We can stop at the hotel gift store and grab some on our way out." With that, he handed his truck keys to Ron. With nothing left except Lenora's purse, they could at least drive home if we didn't make it out.

Ron said nothing, only shaking his head with the knowledge that we wouldn't listen to his advice—it wasn't going to be a quick peek from the fire door followed by a quicker exit. He knew better than to argue. His face was grim.

Cam and I walked to the fire exit, projecting the attitude that we had the absolute right to do what we were doing. No one stopped us, probably because those with authority were still fighting traffic. Zackie walked at Cam's side. It was decent of her to come along, but for all we knew, she'd soon be needed to take one or more of us through the portal. I was disturbed by how easily this thought came to me after I had faced it once.

Standing at the door, we took deep breaths and savored the relative purity of the air we inhaled. I tested for radiating heat with the back of my hand to make sure we wouldn't feed the fire by opening the door and giving it oxygen. Grasping the door handle, I shot a look at Cam. "Ready?"

Cam nodded, pulled out a handkerchief and tied it around his face. I stretched the neck of my t-shirt over my mouth and nose. We both knew this was not adequate protection, but it was what we had, and something was better than nothing. Taking our last breaths of mostly smoke-free air, we wedged the door open with an ornamental stone and stepped inside. Getting down on our hands and knees to find the least contaminated air, we crawled along the floor.

The smoke was much thicker than before, but at least the fire had not yet spread to the stairwell. We moved forward cautiously, calling for Rhonda and trying to see through the dense, dark cloud of smoke.

Behind the handkerchief, Cam's voice sounded muffled. "She can't have gone far. Just look at this place…"

"I am looking, and I'm not seeing much. This smoke… She could be collapsed nearby, and we'd never see her." I didn't say it out loud, but I was worried that Rhonda was already dead. I cast out my senses for her wandering spirit but did a rapid recoil when I blundered into a dark, brooding presence seething with fury. Phillis. "Oh fuck."

"Now you've done it. We're sure as hell f—" A malicious laugh froze Cam in mid expletive. The resounding clang that followed let us know the exit door had slammed shut. "Get to the door and prop it open. Don't let her seal us in here." He gave my shoulder a shove to get me moving. "Zackie! Where is that bloody hound..."

I scrambled to find the fire exit, my sense of direction muddled by the smoke. When I hit the wall, I hugged the firm contours of its surface to work my way in the direction of where I thought we'd entered. My knees ached from crawling along the hard floor and over sharp debris. I could hear Cam yelling at Zackie from somewhere in the smoke-filled room.

"Well, just do the search dog thing. How hard is that?" Cam paused as if listening and then growled his response. "No, I don't have a scent article, and I have no idea what Rhonda's scent smells like—wait, yes I do. Can you detect anything that smells like hand sanitizer?"

As they worked out how to find Rhonda, I groped blindly along the wall for the exit. I could visualize the metal panic bar that would unlatch the door and let in fresh air. I imagined what it would feel like to draw a deep breath and get a lungful of cool, clean air.

The sound of Zackie's nails clacking on the floor receded in the distance, and I panicked, thinking I had been left alone. "Cam, are you still here? Did you go with her?"

"Still here. She'll let us know if she finds—" One sharp bark told us all we needed to know.

I couldn't tell where the bark had come from, but I burst out with an idiot grin under my makeshift t-shirt mask. At least Rhonda had been found. "Now what?"

Cam started to answer, but he was interrupted by the sound of glass shattering as a window exploded on a floor above us. "Shit! We have to get out of here. Have you found the door yet?"

"Not yet, but I have to be close." At least, I hoped I was close. My eyes were beginning to sting and tear again, and my lungs felt hot and tight.

"Well, hurry up!" His voice was strained, and he wheezed as he spoke.

"Oh, you wanted this today? That wasn't clear to me, Cam." I was ready to let loose with some industrial-grade sarcasm, but the sound of something heavy being dragged across the floor shut me up. It had to be Zackie, pulling Rhonda along by her scruff like she had done for me. From experience, I knew it was slow, awkward work. I hoped the fabric on Rhonda's red jacket was good and strong.

Cam made a triumphant sound and then started coughing. "Zackie's brought Rhonda to me." After a pause, he gave me a reason to hope. "Shallow breathing, weak pulse, but she's still alive."

I made my own triumphant sound. "I've found it! I'm at the door." I hammered my hand against the panic bar and pushed. Then I did it three more times, wailing in frustration when it didn't budge. I began panting in my mounting terror and that made me cough. "It's not opening, Cam. She's locked us in."

"Okay. Stay where you are. We're coming to you. Keep talking so we can find you."

We played a short, tense game of Marco Polo, punctuating each call out with wheezing and coughing. Cam probably insisted on the yelling just to keep me busy so I wouldn't descend into panic. Zackie could have found me in a heartbeat, but she kept pace with Cam as he pulled Rhonda to the exit and gently laid her down. I felt infinitely better once they reached me and I wasn't alone.

It was irrational, but I made another futile attempt to open the door. When it refused to budge, I turned to Cam, who now saw for himself that we were trapped. "Now what?"

With the handkerchief over his face, I could only see his bushy eyebrows as they drew together in annoyance. "You seriously need to stop asking me that question."

Cam ran a rough hand through his mop of hair, his eyes worried. On his knees, he scanned the area in front of us as if he could find our salvation in the smoke. Facing the exit, he next tried the door himself without success and then, in frustration, slapped his palm on its surface. His shoulders sagged and he looked down, shaking his head. "Right, then. There's no help for it. We can't stay here much longer." Straightening, he turned away from the door and looked me in the eye. "Guard yourself, Fia."

With Cam's warning, I poured my will into constructing a safe zone for my psyche by visualizing a steel shark cage surrounding me that would keep out those with bad intent. The cage felt like little protection against the wrath of Phillis, and it was no defense at all against asphyxiating in the dense smoke. I glanced down at Rhonda. She had broken the nail on the index finger of her right hand. If she lived, she wasn't going to be happy about that. She was still breathing, but barely, and what she inhaled wasn't going to do her good. We had to get her out soon.

Cam centered himself and concentrated. When he called to her, his voice was strong. "Phillis, I've had enough of your nonsense. Come out and let's settle this."

I looked out through my hastily assembled mental shark cage and shuddered as a shadow passed through the smoke in the periphery of my vision. I spun to catch a view of the thing but lost it in the gloom. Sweat dripped out of every pore. Prickles of fear cascaded along my neck, making the fine hairs rise and stand ready to sense…what? The whistle of air just before the blade struck? The brush of cold fingers reaching around to crush my throat? I looked to Cam for reassurance, but he was fighting his own battle against these feelings of dread. His eyes were pinched, and his rapid breaths alternately blew the handkerchief outwards and then drew the cloth to his face. We exchanged a look and then placed ourselves in front of

Rhonda's prone form.

WHERE...IS...SHE

The words echoed and amplified in my head. I brought my fists to my temples to make it stop. In my rising panic, I thought about lying to her about Phebe. I thought about finding the broken window and jumping out. I thought about giving up and letting the smoke choke the life from me. But never once did I think of betraying Ron. When Cam spoke, I froze, mute and paralyzed by shock.

"I will give you the girl if you open this door." Cam sat with his back against the wall, his hands on his knees, fingers splayed out wide and stiff. Sweat beaded on his forehead. He took one shuddering breath after another, waiting for her response.

All I could manage was a weak, pitiful cry. "Cam...no." I tugged on his sleeve, pleading with him.

The message coming from his eyes said leave it alone. And I crawled backward, frightened of this man who was my friend and mentor. Despite the ferocity of his response, I could not go through with this. Some things were not worth living with. Giving Ron over to this demon woman in exchange for my life counted among them, but I had no way of stopping what Cam had set in motion.

The door's latch clicked and then swung open like the trapdoor of a gallows when the hanged man dropped. Cam wasted no time in hoisting Rhonda over his shoulder and carrying her into the fresh air. After he placed her on a strip of grass near the exit, he yanked out his cell phone from a pocket and stumbled as he took off, his long stride eating up the ground. The soot-covered handkerchief fluttered down to the cement sidewalk, forgotten.

I ran after him, hacking my lungs out, Zackie at my heels. I had no idea what else I should do, and I threw desperate glances back to where Rhonda lay, alone and possibly dying from smoke inhalation. As I pursued Cam, emergency vehicles pulled into the parking lot, and claws of guilt with Rhonda's name on them released their grip on my gut. But when I thought of Ron, another burning ache kept right on chewing through my stomach lining. Things were happening fast. I needed to think, to sort this out, but there was no time.

Cam put the phone to his ear, and I picked up my pace to get close enough to hear. "Ron, tell Lenora that Rhonda needs help. She's lying outside the emergency exit door. You need to meet me where Mark hung in chains. I don't have time to explain." Cam shoved the phone back into his pocket and charged across the street toward Nicos's restaurant. Cars screeched to a halt, horns blaring. I wiped sooty tears from my eyes and watched as Cam weaved through the oncoming traffic, miraculously emerging unscathed on the other side. I followed in his wake, apologizing as drivers swore and raised their middle fingers at his back.

I caught up with Cam in the parking area behind the restaurant. His face was flushed with exertion, and he was bent over, hands on knees, and wheezing. When he finally got his breath, he forced himself upright and stood hands on hips, staring into the distance with flinty eyes. His face had gone from red to pale, and I knew he was drawing on the last bit of his reserves. There was no hint of the witty curmudgeon I knew. It was like he'd run out of jokes.

Looking back over my shoulder, I could see Ron jogging toward us from across the street. "We could lie to her, Cam. Tell her we found the doll, but we have no idea who this Phebe person is." My voice was hoarse, and my throat felt like someone had massaged it with sandpaper.

Cam gave a short shake of his head but didn't spare me a glance. "We never lie to them," he croaked. "That's a cardinal rule in this business. They may lie to us, right up until the moment they wave us on as *we* go through the portal, but we must never lie."

I winced at his rebuke, but I wasn't going to let this go. "We can't just hand Ron off to her. You said it yourself—she'll roast him alive to get to Phebe."

"Yes, well…we'll see about that." His eyes shifted uncertainly.

Cam's lack of confidence convinced me.

I tried to power up and sputtered at first, a stab of panic making my heart skip. I was drained and exhausted. The energy was not flowing smoothly and easily, but I had to get this right or Ron was going to pay the price for my incompetence. I reached deep and concentrated, forcing a lethal amount of energy into my hands to fight this spirit. I hadn't done this in a very, very long time. There hadn't been a need. As Cam taught me to communicate with the spirits and understand their plights, I learned that resolving the issues that kept them earthbound required more brains than brawn. But Phillis was different. She was white-hot anger hungering for revenge.

I nervously flexed my fingers and felt the crackle of

power. Would it be enough? My stomach knotted, and I wished I had had more time to recharge after releasing Mark from the gibbet. Phillis was fueled by centuries of fury, and I'd need every ounce of energy I could muster for this showdown. She was not going to harm Ron if I had anything to say about it.

Cam stiffened and then flicked his eyes toward me before silently resuming his watch. He must have felt the energy shift and knew exactly what I was planning. I took his silence as acceptance, if not agreement.

Slowing to a halt in front of us, Ron wore a happy grin. But when he felt the vibe between Cam and me, a worried frown eclipsed his smile. "Lenora brought the paramedics to Rhonda, and it looks like you got her out in time. They're taking her to the hospital." His eyes darted from Cam to me and back again. "So, what's up here? Why do you need me?"

I clamped my lips into a firm line and looked Cam in the eye. "If there's no lying to them, I'm not gonna lie to Ron either." Turning to my childhood friend, I put a hand on his arm, and he flinched away, feeling the thrumming power waiting for release. "Sorry. I didn't mean to do that." I pulled my hand back. "You need to get ready. Phillis is coming and she wants Phebe."

Ron went pale and seeing his fear, Cam's eyes lost their hardness. "Ron, I am so sorry to have brought Phillis to you. I will do everything in my power to protect you. But you have to understand...I had no choice." He took a ragged breath. "Rhonda was dying. Firefighters would die. Phillis would have tried to spread her flames to incinerate everyone in the parking lot."

I gasped, finally understanding Cam's desperate choice. Cam faced me and his eyes were sad. "Sometimes there are no good choices, only catastrophically bad ones." He turned back to Ron and cast his gaze to the ground, staring at the weeds shooting up through the cracked asphalt. "Do you forgive me?"

Ron gripped his shoulder and brought Cam's eyes up to meet his own. "Nothing to forgive. I would have done the same." As he was about to say something more, Ron suddenly jerked, his hand flying toward his back. "Ow! Son of a bitch! Dammit, Phebe." He rubbed his back, and his expression darkened to anger. "I think she's digging in."

Cam reflexively reached out a hand to help, but then withdrew it, clenching his fist. There was nothing he could do to control Phebe. Squaring his shoulders, he sized me up and nodded, his gaze settling on my hands. "Ron, are you ready?"

"Nowhere near ready, but let's do this thing." His expression stoic, Ron planted his feet as if this were a physical fight.

That kind of chutzpah can get you through a lot in life. I hoped it counted for something in this situation. Cam gave a half smile when Ron repeated that rallying cry he shared with Lenora at the Roseberry House. It seemed so long ago when all this started. If my hands hadn't been charged, I would have given Ron a playful punch in the arm. I really admired his moxie. The best I could do was chime in. "Let's do this thing."

Cam took a moment to center himself and then drew a deep breath. "Phillis, if you please. We request your presence. I've brought you the girl, as promised."

Smoke wafted from the burning building across the street, first forming gauzy gray wisps around our ankles and then building in dark intensity as it rose. The thought of inhaling more smoke made lungs constrict, and my breaths grew shallow. By the time it reached our knees, the hot smoke was mottled like a purplish bruise. When it was chest high, I saw gangrenous streaks of angry red pulsing through the plumes. The acrid, sulfurous odor I had encountered as my room burned surrounded me again, but my stomach did not rebel until the smell of burnt flesh reached me. It was a bitter charcoal stench, tinged with the metallic smell and taste of coagulated blood. There was nowhere to escape Phillis's *odor mortis*, and I swallowed hard to keep from vomiting.

WHERE...IS...SHE

This time I was ready for her assault as Phillis invaded my senses. I held my peace, not wanting to tip her off that this could be a fight. Cam could do the talking and I'd conserve my energy. Concealed in the smoke, I sidled closer to Ron. Zackie sat next to us and made a huffing sound to express her impatience.

Cam gave an exasperated sigh, still wheezing a little, and then set the tone for our interaction with this spirit. "Phillis, please lower your voice. We will have a civil discussion or none at all." When she gave no response, Cam piled on another demand. "I also believe things will run more smoothly if we are able to see each other." He paused and didn't have to wait long.

A howl of outrage, like a rabid wolf, pierced the air. The smoke swirled around us, violent and disorienting. I closed my eyes before the stench and vertigo forced out the contents of my stomach. When I felt better in control of my churning gut, I opened my eyes to find Cam entertaining himself with his phone. Despite my discomfort, I had to smirk at his insouciance.

WHERE...IS...SHE

Ignoring Phillis, Cam held his phone so Ron and I could see. "You have to see this cat meme."

Ron, the whites of his eyes prominent as he gazed with unease at the churning smoke, stiffly nodded his approval when he glanced at the image. Even Zackie jumped up to see the black and white cat with a small patch of black fur on his upper lip that made him look like Hitler. The caption read, "I can has Poland?"

Under normal circumstances, the meme would have gotten a genuine chuckle from me. With my nervous system humming with dread at confronting Phillis, I had to force a laugh to match Cam's bravado. The fake laugh was cut short when the phone sparked and emitted a tiny electronic screech before going black. I gave Cam a sympathetic look. "Looks like you're also getting a new phone."

Cam harrumphed and then spoke in a low voice. "Give it a moment. I think she wants our full attention when she makes her entrance."

I was determined to stay loose while I waited, to be ready for anything, but my nerves and senses were stretched taut like piano wire. My eyes darted to each side, over my shoulder, and finally upward. Where I should have seen the autumn sky deepening into a dusky violet, I saw nothing but oppressive smoke.

The smoke bore down on me from all sides, muffling the street noises and awakening a latent claustrophobia. My heart pounded and sweat trickled down my brow, bringing with it the soot clinging to my face. After wiping away the wet, I stared with dismay at the black streaks on my hand. Distracted, I failed to check below and stifled a shriek when the damned hair-doll scuttled over my foot. Zackie snapped at the doll as it shot by her, then gave chase as the wretched thing disappeared into the haze.

"Son of a freakin' bitch!" I hopped on one foot,

shaking the other as if this could dispel the foulness.

Determined not to become part of whatever had just happened, Ron soft-stepped in a circle looking carefully at the ground. "What was it? Rats?"

"Ga-aaagh," was all I could choke out. I hopped a few more times and then gingerly placed my foot back on the ground. Then Cam put a hand on my shoulder, and I stilled my herky-jerky movements and looked where he pointed.

Phillis did not disappoint. She slipped through the swirling miasma, hovering a foot above the cracked asphalt. The tonsil-burning stench of charred flesh intensified as she drew closer, but it was nothing compared to its source—a blackened, brittle corpse, her head barely more than a skull, tufts of hair smoking like lit fuses. Her lips had been burned almost completely away and they formed a feral snarl over the exposed teeth. Every halting move of her twig-like limbs was accompanied by a sharp snap as the skin broke to reveal a flash of white bone. The only part of her that seemed alive was her eyes, glowing Lucifer yellow, a predator's eyes.

Every instinct screamed that I should back away. I

swallowed bile and instead, moved to plant myself between Ron and that burnt horror. Phillis narrowed her eyes and looked over my shoulder, assessing Ron. Nodding her head, her neck crackled with the motion. Smoke poured from her mouth as she hissed the name of her prey. "Phebe."

Ron jerked, arching his back and throwing his head back. He screwed his eyes shut and sucked in a breath. When he was able to straighten again, he shook his head. "That'll wake you up in the morning."

I took a step toward Ron but stopped short of touching him with my charged hands. I put my fists on my hips and directed my words to the spirit within him. "This has to stop, Phebe. You're hurting Ron."

Realizing our inability to control Phebe, Cam rubbed his face in frustration, smearing soot on to the clean part of his face that had been protected by the handkerchief. It made him look fierce when he glared at me. "Save your breath, Fia. Phebe doesn't give a rat's ass."

He glowered at the ground, breathing hard. I understood his worry—Ron stood between two dangers and we were ill-equipped to defend him from either. Maybe sensing our growing desperation, Zackie chose that moment to return through the smoke, doll hanging limply in her jaws. With a dangerous glint in her eye, she spat out the doll at Phillis's feet.

Cam exchanged a look with Zackie and then pointed a finger at Phillis in warning. "If you harm Ron to try to get to Phebe, I promise you'll never leave this earth. The Psychopomp will make sure of that. When Phebe is long gone into the afterlife, you will remain here in this world." He gave that a second to sink in while Zackie positioned herself to lie near Ron's feet. "Is that what you want? To stay in a world that becomes increasingly alien with every passing day? To spend eternity separated from friends and family? Look around you. Do you even understand this world? You are alone. Mark has moved on. Your brother is gone."

The glow in Phillis's eyes dimmed and the corners pulled down in grief. But she held her ground and forced a show of defiance. "If I am left here, I will make this world burn."

Cam scoffed. "There are things in this world that burn hotter than you. Can you remember the year 1945? Did you feel the heat from Hiroshima? You probably didn't understand it—but trust me when I say you are like a small spark to the sun."

The mysteries of the modern world must have made her feel small and insignificant. Her posture changed from defiant to uncertain, a being out of her time and alone in a world too complex.

When Phillis shifted uneasily, Cam turned back to address Phebe and pointed again. "And you? What will you do when, in the natural course of life, this man dies? For you, this will happen in the blink of an eye."

Ron turned another shade of pale. "Hey!"

Cam ignored him and kept hammering at Phebe. "You will no longer have the protection of his body. What will you do when Phillis comes for you? Because revenge is all she has, and you know she will dog your every step until Ron's time is up. She will be there that very moment you lose your host. Now that she's found you, you'll have no safe place." His tone softened. "Can't you see the futility? Step out, settle this with Phillis. Make peace and send her on her way. You'll have no peace otherwise."

A long minute passed before Ron answered for her. He tilted his head, squinting his eyes, as if he were listening to a far-off voice. "She won't come out. She's afraid of Phillis."

I dipped my gaze to my hands and made my decision. "I'll protect her." Raising my hands, I focused my will on directing the energy to forge a cage next to Ron, all the while wishing I had enough oomph in me to protect both Ron and Phebe. But I had my limits. I built a fabulous cage, my best one ever. And producing it left me completely vulnerable. With all my will poured into creating this cage for Phebe, I had nothing left if things went south. Sometimes there are no good choices.

Cam's face paled beneath the mask of soot and the wrinkles deepened around his eyes. We both knew if I had not taken this risk, we would have remained at a stalemate. Other than his unease, I sensed neither approval nor censure of my actions. Cam had no idea how this was going to play out. We were winging it.

Phebe trembled as she stepped from behind Ron and slid into the cage at his side. She stared wide-eyed at Phillis, terror chiseling deep hollows in her cheeks and under her eyes. One hand reaching through the cage remained embedded in Ron's back, making it obvious she wasn't going to give up her hold on him. I could forget any fantasies of getting her to cross over with Phillis—assuming we could even get Phillis to go through the portal when we denied her the fun of destroying Phebe.

The snarl on Phillis's face twisted into a sneer, and the scent of death intensified as she approached the cage. "Child, have you missed me? Do you hold me precious in your memory?"

Phebe shrank back and worried her free hand in the folds of her pale-yellow skirts. "Phillis, I am sorry for what I have done and I—"

Phillis cackled and stepped closer to the cage. "More likely sorry I've caught up to you. You were ever the slippery one, planting gossip in just the right ear, manipulating people to realize your ends. You manipulated these folks to rid yourself of me."

Shaking my head, I forced myself to look directly into the harsh glare of her eyes. "No, Phillis. We saw through her. We know she betrayed you and Mark, and we know you terrorize her when she retreats to the spirit's in-between place. Of course she'd want us to move you along."

Cam picked up the thread and began weaving his

tapestry of persuasion. "As much as it would benefit Phebe to have you move on, it would benefit you more. Let all this go, and walk through the portal with the Psychopomp. You deserve peace after all you've been through."

Phillis spun away from the cage, her gaze a scalpel, dissecting Cam and his soft words. The wisps of smoke rising from her skull congealed into thrashing, black plumes. "You? You dare to tell me what I deserve? I deserve vengeance. You know nothing of my suffering."

The Psychopomp stood as if she begged to differ, that she understood suffering. Approaching Phillis with her head and ears erect, her tail loose and stretched out behind her, she offered solace. Phillis took a step back and turned her face away, avoiding the offered communion. She would take no comfort from the Psychopomp.

Zackie huffed a sigh, and her ears descended. She returned to Ron, circled twice and lay again in front of him. Lowering her chin to rest on her paws, she twitched her eyebrows at Cam and me to compel us to continue to work on this stubborn spirit.

Having witnessed Zackie's advance and retreat, Ron raised his eyes from where she lay and stared unseeing into the smoke. "Phillis, my people believe a dog can guide our spirits to the afterlife. Why don't you let her take you?"

My blood chilled when the blackened wraith turned her attention to Ron. "Another child who thinks he knows what's best for someone else." She shook her head and the snapping sound of her skin breaking accompanied this hopeless gesture.

At this provocation, Phebe found her spine and looked up at Phillis from under her brow. Resentment and a childish hurt were stamped on her features. Still hunched protectively, she challenged Phillis. "You didn't have to help, Phillis. Mark helped because he wanted to be sold so he could be with his wife and children, and the master wouldn't sell him. I wanted the master's journeyman. He made eyes at me when no one watched, and with the master gone—"

Phillis shrieked with laughter. "The journeyman wanted the master's daughter, you little fool. Only reason he bought the poison was to get the master's daughter."

Phebe set her jaw and continued as if she hadn't heard Phillis. "With the master gone, the journeyman would have left and taken me with him when the master's daughter rejected him. But what was in it for you, Phillis? I never understood it. Why did you help to poison the master?"

Phillis's body went rigid, and a sudden realization spread across her face. She stormed to the cage, growling in her fury, the remains of her burnt hands clutching the bars and bending them. *Oh crap,* I thought. I had no energy left to reinforce the cage. If Phillis decided to go on a rampage, I couldn't stop her. My promise to protect Phebe meant nothing.

The burnt woman raged at Phebe. "It's high time *you* told the truth. It wasn't ever about no journeyman. The master wanted his daughter to marry up and find herself some rich merchant. And she wasn't ever going to lower herself and settle for some journeyman. *You* convinced him that he would have her if only he were rid of the master, so he would buy the poison." Phillis bored her eyes into Phebe. "I thought so. You planned the whole thing. We were all just your puppets."

Phebe was caught out. The girl hurried a hand from her skirts to cover her mouth as she whimpered, guilty tears cascading over her cheeks. Phillis did not relent. Flexing the bars, she leaned in and glowered at the girl. "Now, why did *you* want the master dead? Don't you turn away from me. You look me in the eye and tell me why you wanted him dead."

"Because he raped me!" Phebe rushed the bars and screamed at the other woman, all caution forgotten. Tears and mucus streamed down her face, her mouth open in a soundless wail. "That bastard raped me."

A slow and deadly smile formed in that charred face. "Child, you think you were the only one?"

Phebe closed her eyes in anguish and tilted her head back. Her hand fisted at her sides as she shook her head slowly. "I didn't know. God in heaven, Phillis, I did not know."

Phillis sighed with resignation. "Wouldn't have made no damn bit of difference if you had. We would have all done the same thing." She bent until her forehead touched the bars, appearing tired and defeated. "I, for one, don't regret killing him. Bastard used me to slake his lust, beat me, and sold my family. I might have enjoyed it more if I stuck a knife in him instead of feeding him poison, but that wouldn't a had a chance. People needed to believe his death was natural."

Ron cast a helpless look at me, unable to follow what was going on. In the fewest words I could manage, I summed up the bitter tale of Phebe and Phillis for him. Ron was an honorable man, and an impotent fury gripped his features. "That man deserved to die. I would have killed him myself."

Phillis straightened and turned to look at Ron for a long moment, a spark of approval and maybe hope in her eye. Then she hooted with laughter, hunching forward and beating her bony hands against her knees. I thought for a moment she had gone mad, but her words showed a fine mind with a dark appreciation for the absurdity of human monsters. "Boy, you would have challenged their imaginations to come up with a new way to kill you—a red man who dared raise a hand against a white man. They'd have to write the magistrates in England for advice."

Even Phebe grinned through her tears. "Master Ron, I chose you for a reason. You would have been my champion. You're a good man."

When I relayed the spirits' words to Ron, he blushed fiercely and ducked his head. Cam wore a thin smile, but his eyes were sad. I could almost read his mind—no one should need such a champion. Mark, Phebe, and Phillis never deserved the life they had been born to, and justice had not been served by the harsh punishments Phillis and Mark endured.

In my mind, the slave owner and villain in this story had too easy a death. How was that just? I looked at Zackie and wondered about that loud enough for her to hear my thoughts. Was there better justice beyond the portal? Zackie refused to comment and gave me her patented sphinx look—perfectly inscrutable and so very ancient. I averted my eyes, feeling silly and childish to be asking the same old question she'd heard from all my predecessors over the millennia.

Cam approached Phillis and raised his sad eyes to meet hers. "I deeply regret that nothing can be done to make right what was done to you. The most we can offer is to bear witness to your suffering." Watching her eyes brighten, he sighed and pushed a hand through his hair, releasing flakes of plaster and the reek of burning hotel.

Ron squinted through the smoke, his face impassioned. "But you're never gonna be made whole if you stay, Phillis. You can rage against this world. You can try to destroy Phebe because she betrayed you, but nothing's gonna change for you. Your life was spent in forced servitude, and it was cut short, and you died horribly. It will always be a life that wasn't valued and was denied a basic human dignity by the people of your time. Nothing changes for you. Nothing will be made better. Do you get it?"

Phillis watched Ron's reaction, maybe trusting him after he had declared himself her paladin. After he said his piece, Phillis bowed her head and closed her eyes, exhausted again. "So, I don't matter. Not then and not now. All that suffering for nothin'." She slowly shook her head, the skin crunching and breaking with every small move. "I'll go now. I know you want me to go." She sighed a fragile, white stream of smoke. "I hope with all my heart it just ends, and there is nothing on the other side."

Phebe reached out to her through the bars. "Oh, Phillis…" The burnt spirit did not respond and her back bent with the weight of her sorrow. Phebe looked to me, her eyes begging me to do something.

Zackie stood, ready to take Phillis over, but Phebe was right. I could not let her go like this, all broken and hopeless. I sensed she had been a proud, strong woman once and to see her like this seared my soul. Phillis deserved something from this world after all that it had taken from her.

Scrambling to find something to give her, my thoughts hit on how she brightened when Cam said we'd bear witness. "No, Phillis, it matters. Your story matters. Telling the truth about what happened to you is important." I edged closer and looked in her dimming eyes. "My friend Lucas has a television show. I don't know if you know what that means, but he reaches millions of people when he speaks. He will tell your story, and everyone will know what happened to you."

Phillis looked up, interested. "But why would it matter? Even if they listened, why would it matter?"

I moved forward and took her charred fingers in my hand. The familiar static that spirits release when I touch them danced along my nerves until my hands were buzzing. "Because we still haven't learned the lesson of what happens when people are dehumanized. Maybe if every story of injustice and brutality is told, one will eventually hit the right notes for someone. And maybe something changes. Because of you, maybe something changes."

Phillis searched my eyes, silent and thinking. "That woman in the building—does she still live?"

I nodded. "Yes, Ron said we got her out in time."

"I'm glad." Phillis let go of my hand and beckoned to the Psychopomp. "It's time I go."

I let the cage fade and raised my eyebrows at Phebe. As expected, she shook her head and stepped behind Ron. Ron grimaced as she made her way in, and he worked his shoulders to ease the discomfort. "She's baaaaack." Cam and I rolled our eyes at his *Poltergeist* reference, but then gave full attention to our departing spirit.

Phillis stood straight, holding her head up. Her nervous fingers trailed along the soft fur on Zackie's back. "I am unrepentant, so if there's nothing after this, so be it. If there's suffering," she shrugged her shoulders making small snicking sounds as the skin cracked, "I surely know how to shoulder that."

She was prepared for the worst, but I was hoping for the best. Zackie positioned herself at Phillis's side, ready to lead her from this earth. As the Psychopomp opened the portal, Cam and I turned away from the blinding light.

A cool, spring breeze blew out of the portal, dissipating the smoke and making the air fresh and clean. I took greedy gulps of this air, filling my lungs until I felt purged of the smoke and the odor of decay. The air was delicious, redolent of the green scent of growing things, and it held a dewy moisture, hinting of a gentle, cleansing rain. When the dew settled on me, it healed the small, angry burns from the fire.

I sensed Phillis taking a tentative step into the freshness and heard her delighted surprise. "Oh...oh my!" I listened for it, but there was no telltale cracking of her skin as she moved. I was sure she had also been renewed.

My heart almost burst when Mark called from the other side. "Phillis, hurry now. The children want to see their aunt."

#

I stood next to Cam and Zackie in Rhonda's hospital room. Her sleek, dark hair was mussed. Under normal circumstances, this would have seriously disturbed her. Dressed in my newly purchased cargo pants and hoodie, I was no fashion plate, but I had managed to run a comb through my hair before we came. I had considered it the ultimate sacrifice. My head hurt so much that even my hair felt sensitive. I had fallen prey to a very human impulse—believing that if a little was good, a lot must be better. No one had ever warned me that it was even possible to get a coconut water hangover.

After releasing Phillis, Ron had returned across the street to find Lenora and figure out where the hotel would relocate the guests. Cam and I had hobbled to a nearby bodega, freaking out the clerk with our fire-damaged clothes, faces smeared with soot, and a service dog in a melted vest. We bought every bottle of coconut water they stocked. We even sent the clerk into the back room to grab anything in the inventory, scoring a few more bottles.

Without wiping the soot from our faces, we staggered like drunken raccoons back to the burning hotel. With our clever little hands, we knocked together open bottles of coconut water and made clumsy, slurring toasts. Congratulating ourselves on our fortitude and quick thinking, we also sent our best wishes to Phillis and Mark in the afterlife. We were too exhausted and depleted from the spirit work to be of any use, so Ron became our designated driver and brought us to our new hotel. While he and Lenora went shopping to get us all some new clothes and a take-out dinner, Cam and I got so wasted on coconut water, we even got Zackie to drink some. By morning, she still hadn't forgiven us.

At the hospital, Zackie wore her backup service dog vest and stood at a polite distance from Rhonda's bed. She leaned against Cam's leg and gazed up at him, lifting her lip in disgust as he sipped from a bottle of coconut water. Displaying the depths of my poor judgment, I was about to ask for some hair of the dog when Rhonda spoke.

"Thank you for coming to visit." She fiddled with her nasal cannula and it made my monkey brain leap to wonder about Ralph and Millie, how they were getting on. I hoped Millie had recovered from being lost in the woods.

Rhonda elevated herself into a sitting position with the bed's handheld control and then smoothed the crisp, white sheets around her. She probably loved this semi-sterile environment. "That's better. Anyway, what I really wanted to thank you for is getting me out of that building. You saved my life."

I felt a blush creeping up my neck at her gratitude. Before I started squirming, I redirected the conversation. "We're just glad you're okay. We saw you sending everyone out the emergency exit, so you were right there by the door. When you didn't show up at the safe zone, we got worried. What happened?"

Rhonda's eyes slid to the side and her face pinched as she recalled the trauma. I felt guilty for asking her to relive the event, but she rallied and tried to piece together what happened. "I honestly don't know. I guess I got disoriented in the smoke. Not a lot of this makes sense. The sprinkler system should have gone off—it had just passed inspection. Smoke detectors failed too, but everything was in spec. I can't believe the hotel is gone." Her voice trailed off, and she pulled the sheets higher in a protective gesture. After a moment, Rhonda started again with a stronger voice, and her face relaxed. "My colleagues contacted Corporate and told them how you dragged me out of there, and how Ron and Lenora took care of me until the ambulance came. Corporate's comping all your hotel stays while you're in Boston."

Cam grinned and his eyes lit up at this unexpected windfall. "Well, that's very generous of them. Thank you, Rhonda."

She waved a hand. "Oh, please. It's the least that can be done after you risked your lives. I wish I could do something personally."

I shook my head, happy and smiling because now I wouldn't have to struggle to pay my rent this month. "All you need to do is get better. That's all we want."

Rhonda returned our smiles until she noticed the dead hand. Her expression alternated between guilt and disgust. "Oh, my God! Your poor hand! Did that happen in the fire?"

All my mortuary makeup had gone up in flames. When Lenora purchased my current ensemble, she did not think to buy me gloves. I had taken to pulling the sleeves of the hoodie down to my fingertips to hide the hand, but I hadn't noticed as the sleeve rode up and exposed the dead thing in all its grotesque glory.

I blushed hard, achieving what felt like an unbecoming shade of vermilion. "It's really not that bad. To tell you the truth, I'm a little embarrassed by how ugly it looks, but it doesn't hurt at all." I pulled the sleeve down to hide the hand.

Rhonda tried not to stare, forcing her eyes to look anywhere but the dead hand. Her gaze settled on Zackie, and she became speculative. "So, I heard it was your dog that found me."

Relieved to no longer be the center of attention, I went for broke to permanently remove myself. "Sure did. Would you like to pet her?"

Zackie took a step forward. Her tail wagged gently, but the tips of her canines showed as she pulled her mouth into an impish grin. Rhonda shrank back and raised her sheets like a shield. "Uh, no thanks. But reward her with a special steak or something, okay?"

Zackie's grin widened at the mention of steak, and Rhonda disappeared farther into the bedding. To encourage her recovery, we made our excuses and took our leave with the toothy Psychopomp.

We ended up replacing two dead cell phones. Cam's had been fried by an irate Phillis, while mine had gotten too close to the flames and something internal had melted. I was glad I'd never invested the time to personalize my ringtones. I was also filled with glee that I'd purchased the premium phone insurance plan.

When the service rep handed me my newest new

phone, I was thrilled to discover that Lucas had sent me a text. My heart plummeted when I saw the text was short, all business, and addressed to all of us. First radio silence and then a totally impersonal message devoid of warmth or feeling. I chewed my lip and worried as I re-read the text. Plane tickets to Scotland had been purchased and we would receive the itinerary by email. I checked my email and sure enough, the itinerary was in my inbox. Lucas, or more likely his administrative assistant, had booked the flight with equal parts optimism and practicality. The flight was scheduled to depart from Logan Airport the next night, but the purchased tickets were refundable.

I showed my screen to Cam. "I guess we're flying out. It's not like there's anything keeping us here anymore."

"I suppose I can sleep on the flight." Cam scrubbed his face with his palm and looked at me bleary-eyed. "It's probably for the best not to delay. My brother needs to perform a Phebe-ectomy on Ron at his earliest convenience."

"That's what I was thinking." But that wasn't all I was thinking. I tucked the phone in my cargo pocket and moved to the store's exit. Aside from freeing Ron, I needed to find out what was up with Lucas. Something wasn't right and despite feelings of exhaustion, I was suddenly eager to get on that plane.

CHAPTER 4

The airline's PA system sounded scratchy and occasionally cut out as it told me that passengers with disabilities could now board the aircraft. I could only hope the plane was in better repair.

Because I had been designated as a special needs passenger due to my service dog, our party moved to the gate in advance of the herd. The perky gate agent accepted my ticket and gushed over Zackie. "Oh, I just love dogs." Then she shifted into professional mode. "Please remember, your service dog must fit under the seat in front of you."

I nodded and shuffled on. I was still pretty wiped out and my carry-on felt heavy. It was a newly purchased backpack crammed with a change of clothes and some toiletries, including new mortuary makeup that had been shipped to me overnight.

As we entered the plane, a flight attendant with salt and pepper hair greeted us. Numerous pins on his uniform marked his years of service, and his nameplate identified him as Jeremy. As he checked our boarding passes, he sized us up with a practiced eye. I handed him mine, and he looked at the stub, pursing his lips. When he winked at me, the creases deepened around his mischievous blue eyes. "And you're in 18-D. Hope you have a pleasant flight." That seemed odd, but I was too tired to work up a decent paranoia, so I just thanked him.

I took a moment to appreciate the stale air on board as we made our way to our seats. Cam, Lenora, and I had been assigned adjoining seats, while Ron would sit right across the aisle from us.

When I reached 18-D, a bearded man already occupied my seat. The collar of his white Oxford shirt was stained with dried blood and soot. His face was marred with burn marks and signs of blunt trauma—abrasions as well as deeper cuts. He raised his clear plastic airline cup in a toast, sloshed some amber liquid, and smiled drunkenly at me. "Cheerz."

And that explained the wink.

"Cam, we have a problem." I nodded toward the stowaway spirit.

"Oh, for the love of…" Cam put his bag in the overhead bin before addressing the spirit. "And who might you be?"

The spirit shrugged like that should be obvious. "I am Zar. Pleazed to make your aquaintenz." Even with his slurring, a Russian or Eastern European accent came through.

Tired of carrying my pack, I shoved it into the bin and put my hands on my hips. "Well, Zar, you don't have to go home, but you can't stay here." I gave Cam a bemused look. "What the hell are we supposed to do with him?"

"Go to the bathroom in the back with Zackie." Cam stepped into the seating area behind ours to make space. "Zar, if you please, follow these two to the back of the plane."

Grinning and full of inebriated bonhomie, Zar stood and followed Zackie and me down the aisle. When I opened the door to the bathroom, Zackie opened the portal. Ducking my head and shielding my eyes against the light, I motioned blindly, urging Zar on.

"Dank you for your kindnez."

Not knowing what else to do after the little room went dark, I entered the bathroom and waited an appropriate amount of time before flushing and washing my hands. As I stepped out, bright light flashed behind me, and Zackie reappeared at my heels. To anyone who might have been watching, the need for a service dog was plain to see. I apparently couldn't even go to the bathroom without accompaniment.

Zackie and I made it back to our seat before the influx of general boarding passengers clogged the aisle. Occupying the window seat, Lenora watched as the baggage handlers filled the cargo area of the plane.

In the center seat, Cam fiddled with his seatbelt buckle. "They get your bags onboard yet, Lenora?"

"Not yet. But I keep watching 'til they do."

I waved Zackie in ahead of me. With a grunt, she crammed herself under the seat in front of 18-D and was gone after another flash of light.

"Works for me." I plunked myself into the seat and stretched my legs out. Cam settled in next to me, placing a small pillow behind his neck. We used his blanket to block the view to the "Zackie-occupied area." As we busied ourselves by exploring the fine selection of literature in the seat pocket, a commotion from first class reached our ears. Our fellow economy passengers pushed past the disturbance and advanced down the aisle, shaking their heads and muttering at someone's bad behavior.

That someone was extremely disgruntled, and his voice grew louder with every exchange. We finally caught the culmination of the guy's hissy fit. "Do you have any idea who I am?"

After a few seconds, I heard Jeremy's voice over the PA system. "Attention passengers. We have someone in first class who does not know who he is. If you think you can identify him, please come forward."

Lenora let loose with a belly laugh. The rest of us chuckled and joined the other passengers in a round of applause. Jeremy was my new hero.

When he came through with the beverage cart,

Jeremy made a point of asking me if everything was all right. I accepted my drink and winked at him. "No problems here."

He raised his eyebrows. "I felt sure I'd be finding you a new seat by now. Most passengers don't last ten minutes in that seat."

I raised my eyebrows back at him. "Any idea why?"

He leaned in and lowered his voice. "I think the seat has bad vibes. Someone told me that some of the seats on this plane were salvaged from a plane crash."

I feigned surprise. "Well, so far, so good. I'll let you know if I need a new seat, but I think I'm good."

"That's my girl. Low maintenance." With that, Jeremy continued to the next thirsty passenger.

#

I woke stiff but rested from a deep sleep. As I fidgeted in my seat, I envied Zackie, who I was sure was in a more comfortable environment than me. Cam was out cold, and I leaned past him to look out the window. Lenora slept curled against the wall, her head on the tiny airline pillow. She had pulled the shade down, so all I could tell was that there was no glow of sunlight coming through the covering. Sunrise was still some hours away. Glancing across the aisle, Ron slumbered with his head thrown back. The scrap of standard-issue blanket barely covered his chest.

Ron was in desperate need of sleep. I had never met anyone who could match Ron's strength and stamina. His most impressive quality was a stubborn ability to just suck it up when things went beyond even his reserves. And never once did he complain.

Counting off all the recent events, I realized how bad he'd had it. With Phebe a constant drain on his energy, Ron had still managed to face down Phillis and live to tell about it. Afterwards, he pulled himself together and acted as our chauffeur, hauling our sorry asses to the new hotel. Ron then took Lenora shopping to provide for everyone's after-fire needs and worked like a stevedore to move all our new luggage into and then out of the latest hotel. The stress alone would have killed an average person.

The last few days had whipped the stuffing out of Ron, and I hadn't noticed. Guilt washed over me. Even though I'd been running on empty, I had selfishly focused on my own needs as I tried to recover, and Ron had fallen between the cracks. He deserved better than this. Careful not to wake him up, I took my blanket and covered him.

Back in my seat, my head next filled with worries about Lucas. It had been almost a week since the last time I'd seen him, but it seemed longer. The old adage was that absence makes the heart grow fonder, but he hadn't said anything about being fond of me since the text exchange days ago as we drove to Boston. Maybe he was overwhelmed with trying to shoot the ghost show on location in a foreign country. That had to be more difficult than putting together a regular show.

I decided to stick with that explanation, shutting my mind to the possibility of a bonnie, red-haired lassie having her way with him. When Jeremy trundled down the aisle with the breakfast cart, food became a welcome distraction from my unpleasant thoughts. I nudged Cam awake, and he poked Lenora. We put our trays down in preparation for whatever reconstituted culinary delights were coming our way. I suspected Phebe roused Ron, since he sat up suddenly. Like any spirit, Phebe was starved for everything sensory. She would be eager to taste anything, even breakfast on a plane.

#

As we came in for a landing at Heathrow, Zackie reappeared under the seat in time to deplane, and we went through transit security together. We also faked a bathroom break for her and barely made our short connecting flight to Glasgow. Cam provided the customs agent at Glasgow a mountain of paperwork for Zackie, so she could avoid being quarantined for several months. I think plan B would have been to let them quarantine her, and then to act outraged when they called to tell us she had disappeared.

After we cleared customs, we were met by our driver, a wiry older man with a balding pate named Jimmy. His Scottish accent was so thick I had to listen closely to understand him. Jimmy would take us on the final leg to Inverness—another three to four hours, depending on traffic on the A9. I began to suspect Lucas's ghost show had found a way to save money on our travel expenses.

We helped Jimmy load the luggage into the back of the van, and then we piled in. I sat with Cam, Lenora rode shotgun next to Jimmy, and Ron and Zackie each occupied a row of their own. It was 8 A.M. and still mostly dark. The sun was only just starting to rise. Yawning, I slumped down in my seat, and my eyes slid toward Cam. "So, it's Camelot, then? Not just Cam?"

Cam was quiet for a moment. "How'd you find out?"

"I looked over your shoulder when you gave your passport to the customs agent."

He shrugged helplessly. "What can I say? My parents had some unusual ideas."

Ron leaned over the seatback. "Is it a Scottish thing, naming your kids something that stands out?"

Cam snorted. "No, Mr. Falling-Leaf, it is not."

Our driver chuckled. "Aye, it is not a Scottish thing. Look at me. Good solid name—Jimmy. Nothing exciting there."

Lenora cocked her head at him. "So, I'm interested— what's something Scottish?"

Ron called from the back. "Yeah, we're visiting from Oklahoma. Tell us, what's the most Scottish thing ever?"

Jimmy pulled the van into the flow of traffic and then stroked his chin. "Wee-ell...D'ye recall in 2007, there was a terrorist attack at the Glasgow Airport?"

Cam grinned and his eyes twinkled. "Yes, I do—a great story—but I'm not sure my friends know much about it."

Glancing over his shoulder at Cam, Jimmy grinned back and nodded. "Right then, I'll take it from the top." He paused for dramatic effect, and then launched into the story. "It actually started the day before in London. Two terrorists planted bombs there, but they failed to explode. Next, those two wankers thought they'd take their shite up 'ere. They rammed bomb-filled jeeps into the airport.

"A baggage handler named Smeaton saw the explosion and ran to the burning wreckage to batter the bastards." Jimmy shook his head, and his smile grew wider. "One of the bastards was on fire and tried to get past him, running into the terminal building. Coulda been wired with explosives—who knew? Smeaton shouted 'Fuckin' mon, then' and kicked the minger in the balls so hard he tore a tendon in his foot. Got the Queen's Gallantry Medal."

Cam leaned forward and clapped Jimmy on the shoulder. "And that, my friends, is the most Scottish thing ever."

When we arrived at Inverness, Lucas was out filming on location. I heaved a sigh, deeply disappointed that he was not there to welcome me, that I was not a priority. The analytical part of my brain tried to rationalize his absence—Lucas had a show to put together. He was on the clock, and I needed to cut the man some slack. I gave a vicious kick to a small stone in the parking area. My analytical brain needed to bite the big one.

Our hotel was a large, eighteenth century house with a jumble of rooflines. Sturdy chimneys sprouted from the major wings, relics from an age when fire was the only source of heat and comfort on a cold night in the Scottish Highlands. The sparkling white exterior was decorated with tall, narrow windows that looked out on eleven acres of grounds belonging to the house. Situated on a hill about ten miles from the center of Inverness, we had a spectacular panoramic view of the gold and russet autumn countryside.

I took deep breaths as a brisk breeze tousled my hair. After enduring many hours in cramped spaces with recirculated air, the fresh air revived me. I grabbed my bags and turned to enter the house, leaving the others to admire the grounds.

Although the exterior of the house promised old world charm, to my disappointment, the interior had been extensively renovated. Few historical features remained beyond the sweeping central staircase, high ceilings, and large, arched entryways separating some of the common rooms. With limbs heavy from disuse, I climbed the wide, winding staircase and dumped my luggage in my assigned room. The room was painted a cheerful yellow, a small fireplace tucked in a corner the only reminder of the home's age. The room would otherwise have seemed perfectly normal in an average home back in New Jersey.

As I descended the stairs, my stomach grumbled noisily, protesting the haphazard eating schedule of the last day. The lack of nearby restaurants in this isolated place worried me until I found the platter of sandwiches. The cook had set out an early lunch for us on the planks of a long wooden table in the dining room. We gorged ourselves on the sandwiches, famished after our travels. Zackie demanded a taste of the local cuisine, so I tossed her a sausage sandwich.

Jimmy proved to be an efficient eater, and I admired his style. He crammed a prawn and mayonnaise sandwich in his mouth and after chewing a few times, washed it down with some coffee. Before speaking, he dabbed delicately at his mouth with a napkin. "Lucas said to take you all to Inverness and go sightseeing this afternoon. Are ye up for it?"

Everyone seemed agreeable, but I was a little surprised. "He doesn't want us to start working on the case? He made it sound pretty urgent that we get here."

Jimmy folded his napkin on the table and arched a brow. "Lucas said to tell you to remember Hot Dog Johnny's if you brought up work. Sounds a bit cryptic to me, like you're a Russian spy or something, but there it is."

I paled as I thought back to how Hannah had almost killed me for kissing Lucas at Hot Dog Johnny's. It was either my first date or third date with Lucas, depending on how you counted. After that first earth-shattering kiss, I had the stunningly stupid idea that I had to square things with Hannah. Dead or not, she had been his wife. I felt badly that she had died so young and could only watch as another woman took up with her husband. Getting my ass kicked by Hannah happened right after some particularly demanding spirit work. I hadn't given myself enough time to recharge, and the encounter with Hannah drained me close to the point of death. I was lucky to survive. Lucas never knew exactly what made me so deathly ill, only that it was somehow related to overdoing it with spirit work.

Jimmy raised the other eyebrow as he watched the color drain from my face. "So, d'ye want to go to Inverness?"

"Yes, please."

The only thing I bought was a Loch Ness monster t-shirt. I had immediate buyer's remorse when Jimmy said they had better t-shirts at the Drumnadrochit Loch Ness Centre. I should have waited.

As we wandered along tourist-friendly High Street, Lenora went into every shop that sold Highland dress. She fingered the tartans, commenting on the fine weave and color combinations. At display cases in each of these stores, Ron's attention was drawn by the decorative, single-edged knives called *sgian-dubh*. Scotsmen in full regalia would tuck one of these small knives into the top of the kilt hose. When a salesclerk handed Ron one to examine, it turned out some of the knives weren't just decorative—the one he held was four inches of keenly sharp steel.

Ron sighed. "I love it, but I don't know about getting it through airport security."

The clerk shrugged and then returned the knife to the display case. "It's usually not a problem if you pack it in your checked luggage. But if you prefer, you can always order one through our online store once you've returned home." The salesclerk handed Ron the store's business card with their website.

After what seemed like hours of browsing, Lenora handed the clerk a merino wool scarf with a blue and green pattern. "This one. Clan Oliphant tartan. Close enough to Ottertooth. Don't need a bag. I'll wear it." As the clerk rang up the sale, Lenora motioned to the collection of plaid textiles and asked Cam, "Which one's your clan?"

Cam pointed out a black and blue pattern. "This is the ancient tartan for Clan Ramsay. The modern pattern is red and black. Don't ask me how that came to happen."

"Is the clan motto 'Start out bruised and end up bleeding'?" I offered with a winning smile.

Jimmy barked out a laugh. "Good one, lass."

Up until my quip, Zackie had played the part of a well-behaved service dog and quietly stayed in the background. She pressed her flank against Cam's leg and huffed, as if to say, *Ha, got you good.* She grinned at him, showing her long canines.

Surrounded by people enjoying themselves at his expense, Cam exchanged a long look with the salesclerk. "So...how much did you want for the *sgian-dubh*?"

The clerk put his nose in the air and faked a posh accent. "Sir, we have a strict policy against customers bleeding on the merchandise. You understand, ancient grudges among clans being what they are..."

Ignoring the banter, Lenora carefully counted out the pounds and pence to pay the clerk and then draped her new scarf around her neck. Before making her way to the exit, she gestured to the knives. "Maybe we buy two of those when we get home. Need one for my purse."

We meandered along the streets until we came to Castle Wynd and the Inverness Museum and Art Gallery. As a former history major, I was helpless against its draw and urged the others to join me. In contrast to the eighteenth and nineteenth century architecture on High Street that made me think of Dickens, the museum was a modern-looking structure with a glass-fronted entrance lobby. A curved section of the frontage was covered in striking amber panels depicting what I thought was Loch Ness at dusk. The exhibits inside proved to be a rich source of information on the natural history of the region, as well as Highland life and culture from the Neolithic to modern times. I was in heaven.

Ron and Lenora were drawn to the displays on the Jacobites, Bonnie Prince Charlie, and the disastrous Rising of 1745. Ron gazed at the weapons with a critical eye— leather-covered, wooden shields called targes, basket-hilted swords, dirks, axes, muskets, and pistols. Lenora and Ron probably felt a deep kinship with the Highlanders when the exhibit turned to the aftermath of the rebellion. Following the defeat of the Jacobites at Culloden, the British butchered the wounded on the field of battle and ruthlessly persecuted survivors and their families. A systematic purging of Highland culture resulted in prohibitions against traditions such as the bagpipes and plaid, all in an effort to weaken Gaelic culture and undermine the Scottish clan system. During the Highland Clearances, Highlanders were forcefully evicted from their ancestral lands.

Cam and Jimmy enjoyed the Viking exhibit. They were intrigued by the translations of rune stones, placed at crossroads to commemorate the honorable acts of long-dead warriors and adventurers. My new obsession was the Bronze Age. I was keen to see everything the museum had on cairns with their grave goods and the mysterious standing stones. Noticing my avid interest, a docent told me about Clava Cairns, a cluster of circular chamber tombs a few miles east of Inverness. I made a mental note not to leave the area before seeing this prehistoric site.

The highlight for Zackie was a Highland wolf, preserved through taxidermy in the natural history section of the museum. This creature was both chilling and magnificent, with its silver-gray fur and menacing eyes. Easily six feet long and three feet at the shoulder, it was the stuff of nightmares. Zackie's wistful expression grew as we examined the beautiful and enigmatic Ardross Wolf, a sixth century Pictish carved stone. The whorled strokes made by the ancient artist perfectly captured the power and drama of the wild wolf. Her eyes intent on the image, I sensed that Zackie identified strongly with the Highland wolf, and I could feel her longing. I wondered if this might have been a previous incarnation, another life for her.

Cam noticed Zackie's nostalgia as well. He gave her side a comforting pat, something I'd never seen him do. He caught me watching and murmured, "Sometimes the modern world is a bit too tame for her, and she yearns for the past." Straightening, he called out to the others. "How about we have our tea at the café here?"

Jimmy led the way to the museum's small restaurant that overlooked High Street. As we watched the shoppers roam up and down the street, I noticed some who belonged to different times—ladies hiking their skirts as they hurried along the street, men wrapped in plaids, soldiers from the Great War jostling each other in high spirited comradery. As the pageant of time paraded by the window, the waitress served an aromatic black tea from a huge pot into bone china teacups. Insisting we do a proper traditional tea, Cam ordered some buttery scones and suggested we drink our tea with milk and sugar. He fed a scone to Zackie, and she perked up, licking her chops and demanding another one.

I broke off a big piece of my scone and slathered it with butter and jam before popping it in my mouth. Soothed by the sugar, I daydreamed about the many thousands of years of human history in the Highlands. My head filled with romantic notions of all those lives spent so very differently than my own. What were their joys and sorrows? Did they rejoice just because they had meat in their pot? Was I spoiled because I took this for granted? If they got cold and wet, did they feel the same misery I felt, or were they more stoic and accepting? How did they meet their ends? Was death borne differently then than now?

Out of nowhere, the enormity of the task Lucas set before us invaded my musings. Sinking lower in my seat, I contemplated the layers of history we'd maybe have to sift through to get a feel for the haunting.

In general, the older the spirit, the stronger the spirit. But it was more than that. There was a whole cultural divide we needed to bridge in order to make headway with a spirit. Some things about humanity were universal and never changed, but there were other things that created a huge gulf in our ability to understand their reasoning and motivations. Would we be able to relate to someone from very long ago?

I thought back to our experiences with He-Who-Counseled-the-Chief. He was the oldest spirit I had dealt with so far, and he had died in the mid-1600's. While stateside hauntings had the potential to reach back as far as anything in Scotland, we'd lucked out so far. Lucas's case could easily reach back ten thousand years, and I wasn't sure our luck would hold. I had a hard time swallowing as this sank in. I stared glassy-eyed, my cheeks puffed out with scone.

I was jolted out of my thoughts by Cam's phone, shrilling out *Scotland the Brave* in synthesized bagpipes. As Cam fiddled with his phone, I noticed Jimmy staring at me. "Oh, good. You've snapped out of it." He fake-wiped drops of sweat from his brow. "I thought for a minute I'd have to give you the Heimlich."

Ron leaned across the table to look at my face. "Nah, she's all right."

I swallowed my half-chewed scone and nodded. "Yeah, I'm fine."

"If you're fine then, I'll be visiting the loo. Don't go choking or passing out 'til I'm back." Jimmy excused himself and got up from the table.

I was fine, but Ron looked a little worn around the edges. Phebe must have been weighing on him. He had dark circles beneath his eyes, but he otherwise seemed cheerful. I suspected the cheerfulness was a bit forced, so no one would worry. I offered him the other scone on my plate.

"Thanks!" He reached for the scone, but then stopped himself. "Wait, are you sure you're feeling all right? You're willingly giving up food."

I pushed the plate in front of him. "I'm saving room for dinner. I'm going for a double helping of haggis tonight." I must have been convincing. Ron shrugged and took the scone just as Cam muttered something I didn't catch. I assumed he doubted me. "Seriously? You're calling into question my ability to stuff my face?"

"No, nothing like that." Cam waved away this absurd suggestion, and a cloud formed over his brow. "My brother just texted that he is in the middle of something and can't make it here for a few days yet." He looked apologetically at Ron. "He said he was eager to meet you and regrets the delay."

Ron's face fell. Lenora put a comforting hand on his

arm, her face a mirror of his. After a moment, he patted her hand. "It's okay, *Uma*. I can wait a few days." He looked at Cam and forced a smile. "A few more days won't matter."

When Jimmy returned and asked if we were ready to head back to the hotel, no one objected. Our high spirits were flying low after Cam's news, and the jet lag was catching up with us.

#

I couldn't fault their timing. Lucas and the crew arrived at the hotel just as the sun began to set. It was about six in the evening, and the cook promised us dinner at seven. They came in two nondescript white vans that my bosses at the crime scene cleanup company would have approved.

I ran out to greet Lucas under the crimson and lavender sky, all resentment for the long day without him forgotten. As he stepped from the van, Hannah appeared at his side, possessively holding his arm, a smile on her lips. My headlong rush skidded to a halt. I couldn't very well throw myself into his arms with Hannah right there, staking her claim. Folding my arms around me to ward off the evening's chill, I approached slowly and got a real eyeful.

Lucas looked like hell. He had bags under bloodshot eyes, and even in the dim light, his skin looked sallow. It had only been a week, but I'd swear he'd lost weight.

He had to have been aware how awful he looked. I didn't want to waste time talking about it when I needed to do something about it. I schooled my face to hide the depth of my concern and smiled a greeting. "Lucas! At last!"

He opened his arms, and I folded into his stiff embrace. "How was your flight? Is everything resolved in Boston?"

"The flight was okay. Boston is mostly resolved." I kept my answers short and ushered him into the warmth of the hotel. Lucas wasn't up to listening to a long story, and I thought a little rest before dinner might do him good. He collapsed into a comfortable chair near the fireplace, the cheery blaze giving some false color to his cheeks. I brought us two hot mugs of tea from the sideboard, made Cam-style with plenty of milk and sugar, and sat in the overstuffed chair next to Lucas. Silently sipping the creamy, sweet drink, I gave him time to just sit and drink his tea in peace.

"Thanks. I needed that." Lucas placed his empty mug on the mahogany end table and sat back, stretching his feet toward the fire. "Maybe I'm coming down with something. I feel kind of out of it." He closed his eyes and sank into the cushions. Within seconds, Lucas was breathing deeply and drowsing in the chair. I pulled a throw from a neighboring settee and covered him.

Behind his chair, Hannah lingered with her hands resting lightly on the headrest. I watched her, speculating on her near-constant presence next to Lucas. It wasn't this way back home. She had wasted no time moving in on him in my absence.

After Cam and Ron made their way down the stairs, I shushed them and pointed to Lucas as they entered the room. "Where's Lenora?" I whispered.

Cam glanced at the exhausted Lucas and then frowned at Hannah before answering in a low voice. "She's in the kitchen with the cook."

"Said something about learning to cook Scottish." Ron stretched and yawned, waving a hand over his mouth. "Lucas has the right idea. This jet lag is kicking my ass."

We lounged near the fire, basking in its warmth while we waited for dinner to be announced. It had been a long day, but we all agreed the trip to Inverness had been interesting, and spending time out and about probably helped us adjust to the time difference.

Dinner was a subdued affair with many of us too tired to make conversation. Jimmy and the film crew talked softly among themselves, sensitive to our weariness. As we chowed down the haggis and neeps the cook had prepared, we promised to be better company after a good night's sleep.

To me, the turnips tasted like turnips, but the haggis tasted like some alien form of sausage, what with the crumbles of oats and unidentifiable bits of meat. I made Lenora promise not to tell me what was in it. Zackie ate the haggis without the neeps, and she seemed very pleased with the arrangement. Chocolate gateau for dessert rounded out the meal, and I thought I was done until the cook handed out the drams of scotch. And what a lovely burning sensation as it journeyed down my throat. Just the thing for a cold night.

The scotch was the final blow. My eyes grew heavy and I felt sure I'd be facedown on the flagstones if I didn't go to bed right away. Wishing everyone a good night, I lumbered up the stairs to my room, threw on some sweats to ward off the chill, and crawled into bed. I slept hard for several blissful hours until a woman's voice woke me in the wee hours of the night. Muffled by the thick walls, the voice was insistent and forceful, but I could not make out the words.

I got out of bed and opened my room door. The voice grew louder as I stole down the dark hallway, my feet silent in their thick socks. I followed the sound to one of the other rooms and stood with my ear pressed against the door. It was definitely Hannah's voice. Ready for my "Ah-ha!" moment, I gave no thought to the embarrassing scene if I were wrong about this and it wasn't Lucas's room I was barging into in the middle of the night. Testing the knob, I lucked out. It was unlocked and I slipped into the room.

Hannah sprawled on top of Lucas, who was out cold and insensate. She grasped his face in her hands, repeating loudly her fondest wish, forcing him to hear her. "Lucas, I'm here. If you open your eyes, you'll see me. I know you can hear me. Lucas, please. Do this for me."

Lucas groaned as if in pain and mumbled other sounds of distress in his sleep. Despite the cold drafts and frigid night, his hair was plastered against his forehead with sweat. His face contorted with anguish.

Lucas might have been asleep, but he was getting no rest. This was torture for him. Hannah must have been working on him non-stop the entire week, drawing from his energy like a parasite. I stormed over to the bed, grabbed Hannah by her shoulder and threw her to the floor, pinning her down with a knee to her chest.

"Stop this!" I hissed in her face. "You're going to kill him. Can't you see you're draining the life out of him?"

Her bald head lolled. She rolled her sunken eyes toward me, exhausted by her efforts to reach Lucas. "You'd do it, too, if you were in my place."

The fire went out of me, and I felt a stab of pity. She was so weak, so like when I first met her as she lay dying in the hospital. And then I thought back to our strange moment at the late-night diner. Pity was cheap. What Hannah needed was active compassion, not passive pity. "Hannah, let me help you talk to Lucas. He's never going to see you in this life. You know that. It's just not possible for him—he's not wired for it."

"No. I'm close. I know I'm close." Her voice faded

with her form.

I picked myself up from the floor and stood indecisively, despairing for everyone mired in this mess. I understood why Hannah wanted him so badly, why even in death she couldn't let him go. If the tables were turned, I couldn't be sure I wouldn't have followed the same selfish path. But I did know one thing for sure—this wasn't good for Lucas.

Slipping into his bed, I tucked against his side and scanned for any signs of Hannah. She was gone, at least for the moment. I lay for a long while on guard, protecting Lucas from this spirit who was hell-bent on having him, no matter the cost.

"Good morning." Lucas's gray eyes stared softly into my own. He looked better, less frail. The room was dim with pre-dawn light, and the distant sound of pots clanging in the kitchen carried up the stairs.

I cleared my throat. "Good morning. Bet you didn't expect to find me here."

"No, but I'm glad I did. That's the best night sleep I've had since I came here." He grinned, a prick of mischief in his eye. "We should sleep together more often."

I couldn't help it. I snorted when he said this. What happened the previous night was the furthest thing from my definition of sleeping together. But dressed in baggy sweats, I did not feel at all like the sultry seductress I wanted to be. Best to disappear before this look left a lasting impression.

Flipping the covers back, I sat up and planted my feet on the floor. "I should probably get back to my room before the rest of the world gets up."

I tiptoed down the hall, almost making it to my room undetected. A few feet from my door, Cam emerged from the room across from mine. He crossed his arms and raised his eyebrows.

"It's not what it looks like." I blushed to the roots of my hair, despite having no reason for embarrassment.

Cam smirked and then rolled his eyes. "Relax. I heard her too, and I'm glad you dealt with it. Lucas would have been much less happy to find me in his room this morning." He nudged me toward my door and out of his way. "Get dressed. I'll see you at breakfast."

I grabbed some clothes and a towel, and then headed to the shared bathroom. Once again, I lucked out—there was no line. After a quick shower, I threw the bath towel over the dead hand and headed back to my room to apply the mortuary makeup.

Ready for the day, I trotted downstairs, following my nose to the full Scottish breakfast set up in the fireplace room. Chafing dishes on the sideboard contained bacon, sausages, eggs, black pudding, baked beans, grilled tomatoes and mushrooms, and tattie scones. I piled my plate high, grabbed a mug of coffee, and joined Cam and Lenora at the long wooden table in the dining room. Zackie was occupied with her own plate under the table, but her nose came up like a periscope when she smelled my bacon. I gave her a crispy strip and then obeyed the social convention and said good morning before digging into my breakfast.

At the half-way point of my meal, Lucas and Ron joined us, followed by Jimmy and several crew members. Lucas crowded in close to me and my chewing slowed when I noticed Hannah dogging his every move. I glared at her, and she stepped back into a corner of the room but did not disappear. Not good, but not much I could do about it at that moment.

I went back to eating but tuned in again when Lucas spoke about the day's schedule. "We'll be filming at Culloden, and I think it would be good if you could join us," he said, referring to the four of us.

I put my fork down. "Isn't that where the final battle of the 1745 Rising took place?" When Lucas nodded, I thought we finally had a bead on the haunting. "So, the poltergeist activity that brought us here is associated with the battlefield?"

"No. We're just filming sites of interest for possible future shows. Need to show the producers they're getting their money's worth." Lucas brought a fork full of baked beans to his mouth and paused. "I may never get used to beans for breakfast."

Cam chuckled. "Beans on toast is another delicacy you should sample while you're here."

Lenora disagreed and surveyed Lucas's plate. "Too many other things worth eating. You don't like beans, eat the other stuff." She gave Lucas a sharp appraisal and shook her head. "Missing my cooking, boy? You got too skinny."

Lucas agreed that he spent nights craving her frybread, and then ate more of his eggs to please her. After taking a sip of coffee, he returned to the day's schedule. "Is there anything else you'd like to see while we're here? We'll take it easy today. Leave the real site for tomorrow to give you all a chance to rest some more before the work starts."

"How about Clava Cairns?" I asked, remembering the docent's advice. "They're a collection of Neolithic tombs. Probably make a good site to film."

Lucas considered it. "Sure. Why not? It's just a little south of Culloden."

Ron exchanged a worried look with Lenora. "We won't be disturbing someone's ancestors at these tombs?"

"Och, no, laddie." Jimmy pushed away his empty plate and dabbed his lips with a napkin. "The archaeologists have completely picked over that site. There's nothing there. The tombs were disassembled and reassembled to make them safe for tourists. You'll not be disturbing anyone, I guarantee it." He gave Ron a nod of approval. "But it's decent of you to be concerned. The site where you'll be wanting to be respectful is Culloden. Each clan has a mass grave containing the bones of the men who died that day. It's a solemn and sorrowful place."

Cam gave me a look at this bit of information, and I wondered how restful the day would be.

# # #

Culloden Moor seemed to stretch for miles under the low pewter sky. While the film crew assembled at a vantage point near the visitor's center to get panoramic shots of the moor, Lucas walked the battlefield with us. Hannah followed close behind, ignoring the dark looks I gave her.

Flags stood where the armies had once faced each other, but little else interrupted the bleak view. The most prominent feature was a tall cairn of large, rough stones erected to honor the fallen. It stood like a grim sentinel over the expanse of brown and amber fields. We approached the monument and read the plaque affixed to its base.

The Battle of Culloden was fought on
this moor 16th April 1746. The graves of

*the gallant Highlanders who fought for
Scotland & Prince Charlie are marked
by the names of their clans.*

It was just as Jimmy described. Scattered throughout the field, smaller stones had been placed to mark the mass graves of the 1,500 Highlanders who had perished in the battle. Each stone was etched with the name of a clan.

We wandered the narrow paths among the clan stones, passing markers for Fraser, Mackintosh, and Cameron. I stepped around the spirits of kilted men standing vigil at each stone, their plaids drawn over their bowed heads like cowls. Zackie trailed behind our group, and I watched her over my shoulder. When the Psychopomp stopped to acknowledge each spirit, the hooded men would nod their recognition and touch a forelock in respect before she moved on.

The energy from these spirits was overwhelming. As much as Cam had taught me to protect myself from a spirit's emotions and perimortem experiences, the images they projected were so powerful, I became awash in their memories. I could smell the gun powder and spilled blood. When the wind swept across the desolate land, I shivered, echoes of the brutal fight ringing in my ears—the boom of cannon, a sharp volley of musket fire, rhythmic thumping of broad swords against the leather faces of targes, shrill cries as hundreds charged, the clash of steel.

When we reached the stone marked "Well of the Dead" where the Chief of the MacGillivray clan fell, I was shaky from the visions swimming in my head. I took Cam aside and whispered, "What can we do for them?"

"Nothing. They wish to be the honor guard for their fallen kin. Honor their sacrifice by—"

Raucous laughter from across the moor interrupted him. An admonishing voice was overruled when a man shouted over it, "Do you have any idea who I am?" I had a sense of déjà vu when I realized it was the same voice as the irate first-class passenger on the plane.

We froze and then turned to stare down the line of clan stones. The cowled men went rigid, raising their heads, hands reaching for their swords. Zackie gave us a look of warning and then ran full tilt among the stones, circling and pressing to keep the spirits at their posts. Other clan stones were scattered throughout the battlefield, and I despaired at her being able to quell the angry spirits for long.

Cam and I ran headlong toward the shouting, both of us fearing the poltergeist storm that was about to be unleashed. As we took off, I heard Lenora urge Ron to leave her with Jimmy, that they'd catch up. Lucas sprinted after us and quickly drew even.

As we got closer to the fracas, red flags marking the Hanoverian battle lines dotted the field. The admonishing voice tried again. "Sir, this site is a war grave. I ask that you both behave with respect or leave the premises."

Standing near a camp chair, an elderly man in a kilt wearing a docent badge looked sternly at two drunks waving open bottles of whiskey. I was shocked to recognize Milo and Rory.

As our group edged in closer, Lucas realized who we were dealing with and groaned. "What's Rory doing here?"

"What, indeed?" Cam muttered, exchanging a suspicious look with Ron.

Hannah glanced from Lucas to the two inebriated men. Anticipating trouble, she stepped in front of Lucas and crossed her arms, promising a world of pain to anyone who tried to harm her man.

Milo sloshed the bottle at the docent and grinned as he tried to devil the man. "We only want to share this fine scotch with the Duke of Cumberland. Where is Cumberland's stone? We will pour out libations in his honor."

Done with harassing the docent for the moment, Milo squinted at us. "Ah, we meet again." A malicious smile spread across his face. "Thought we'd find you later, but no time like the present."

"Who the fuck is Cumberland?" Rory giggled and took a swig from his bottle. When he noticed me, his face took on a comical look of surprise. "What the fuck you doing here?"

I wanted to ask him the same question, but the elderly man wobbled toward Milo and Rory. Using a cane in each hand for support, he plowed forward. "If you wish to honor the Hanoverian soldiers and the clans who fought on that side, come back when you're sober." His eyes shot sparks at them. "If you are wanting to honor the Butcher Cumberland, his stone is outside the battlefield, off the B9006 toward Nairn. Take your drunken arses there, and good riddance to you."

Rory thrust his bottle in the docent's face. "Have a drink, you old fart, and calm the fuck down." The old man swatted the bottle out of Rory's hand and nearly lost his balance before Ron reached out to steady him. When the bottle shattered on a rock, Rory drew back a clenched fist to strike the old man. Before he could throw the punch, I reacted without thinking and kicked him in the balls so hard, I thought for a moment I tore a tendon. My aim was a little off, but it did the job.

Under a darkening sky, Rory doubled over, fell to his knees, and then on to his side. He writhed on the ground and retched, pathetic and miserable. The sudden shock of violence turned the old docent white and left him gasping. As Milo looked down at his grandson, his lips drew back in disgust, like the boy should have made a better show of it. Turning his attention to the docent, Milo pointed at me and screamed, spittle flying from his mouth. "Call the police! I want this woman arrested for assault."

To his credit, Ron was polite as he tried to shush Milo, but the old bastard was now fully committed to throwing a temper tantrum. Milo hurled invectives and racial slurs at Ron like it was an Olympic event. Ron's face hardened under the stream of insults. The telltale twitching of his shoulder blades told me the potential for violence was exciting Phebe.

With the ether trembling under the psychic strain of both Phebe and the spirit guards, we had to do something before the dam broke. I took a gamble. Standing in front of Milo to draw his attention away from Ron, I assumed a fighting stance as the bastard threw some florid language involving the female anatomy my way. Staring pointedly at his crotch, I yelled, "Fuckin' mon, then!"

Just as I'd hoped, Ron, Cam, and the docent recognized the reference and burst out laughing. The tension broke, and the atmosphere cleared—at least of Phebe's influence. The guardians of the graves were less than pleased by my ribaldry.

Gusts of freezing wind hurled withered leaves in our faces, and my scalp prickled. Cam stopped laughing and looked about uneasily. "Please. Decorum. We need to be respectful of this place." I put on a contrite face, but thought, *Oh, sure. Throw me under the bus.*

Abashed, the docent met Cam's eyes and colored with embarrassment. "I apologize, sir. This behavior is unbecoming." Pulling out his radio and speaking loudly over Milo's screeching, the docent requested help for an injured visitor. When the old Scot attempted to squat down on unsteady legs and clean up Rory's broken bottle, Lucas stopped him and took over the task. The bursts of wind died down, but the sky still roiled with storm clouds.

I played the penitent and got down on my knees to help pick up the broken glass. Ron understood better than anyone else why I went for the inappropriate laugh. Bending down, he gave me an affectionate pat on the head. "We'll go to Clava Cairns next and make it up to you."

I was grateful when the golf cart arrived to move Rory to the visitor's center. We loaded the victim of my violence into the back, but Milo only took his seat after demanding a full police investigation. His voice trailed off as the cart drove away. "This shit hole of a country doesn't know how to treat visitors. We saved your ass during WW2 and don't you forget it. Little pansies in skirts think they know how to fight…"

The golf cart rocked as the wind hit it, but we felt nothing. We watched as a dark mist gathered and followed the cart. A flutter of unease rippled through my gut.

#

At a tiny restaurant along the B9006 toward Nairn, we ordered fish and chips. We had left for lunch ahead of the filming crew and told them we'd meet them at Clava Cairns in a few hours. I ate my lunch with gusto, while I jiggled my ankle under the table to keep the joint loose.

Cam explained to Lenora and Jimmy what happened with the Culloden docent, explaining for Lucas and Jimmy the full Milo and Rory story. Lucas laughed out loud once he learned of the connection to the fiery terrorist incident at the Glasgow Airport. "That was brilliant, Fia." I wanted to bask in his compliment, but Hannah was near, sucking the joy out of things for me.

With a gap-toothed grin, Jimmy slapped his hand on the table. "Oy, I taught her that. I get some credit for this."

"How 'bout cheesecake? That a hero's dessert?" Lenora teased him.

Jimmy thought that would be fine. We ordered slices for everyone, including Zackie, and slid a plate under the table as soon the waitress turned her back.

After swallowing several forkfuls of the creamy

dessert, Jimmy gave voice to the nagging question in everyone's thoughts. "So, I've been told I'm fairly canny, and it seems an awful coincidence that these two show up now, visiting the same bit o' Scotland as you."

"You're not wrong there, Jimmy." Cam jabbed at the air with his fork. "It is odd, and I don't believe in coincidence."

I stopped eating cheesecake long enough to offer part of an explanation. "Probably my stolen phone. Rory read enough of my emails and texts to piece together our travel plans."

Ron pushed away his empty plate and sat back, a worried expression drawing his brows down. "That explains how, but we still don't know why."

We finished our desserts in silence, and I mulled over what Rory and Milo might be up to. Lucas offered his corporate credit card to pay for the meal and mumbled about needing to increase security for filming the ghost show.

Before we left, Jimmy warned us all to use the loo because there were no toilets at Clava Cairns. Bellies full and bladders empty, we piled into the van. After a five-minute drive along the B9006 and Culloden Road, we pulled into the parking lot. I dove out of the van, everyone else forgotten, eager to get my first glimpse of the Bronze Age burial ground.

Following a path that left the car park hidden from view, I found the first of the three chambered tombs, seemingly isolated from the modern age. I loved how Scotland preserved the views around these ancient monuments. The surrounding fields were beautiful in their autumn austerity, and I could imagine a solemn procession bringing a loved one to rest at this site.

I stared with wonder when I saw stone circles surrounding the cairns. The 4,000-year-old site was a study in gray, from the steely sky to the ash-colored stones. The center structure was a ring cairn, consisting of stones piled in a circular shape with a clearing in the center. There were no passages leading in, but it had somehow served as the site for cremation. In contrast, the burial chambers for the two cairns on the ends could be entered by crawling through short, stone covered passages.

Getting into an actual burial chamber was irresistible to me. As I got down on my hands and knees, small concave depressions decorating the entry stones drew my attention—no more than an inch or two across, these cup marks had been pecked into the rock surface. I crawled into the passageway, and it was surprisingly dark. A few worn rocks embedded in the dirt floor hurt my poor knees as I crawled forward, but I wasn't going to be dissuaded by a little pain. When I reached the low-ceilinged chamber, I stretched out my senses, eager to commune with whatever remained here. I allowed myself a moment of pride, recognizing how far I had come from the frightened, angry girl who was constantly at war with spirits.

Sitting with my back to the wall, I waited. And it was a long wait. I finally had to admit Jimmy was right about the tombs. After the archaeologists had finished with them, there was nothing left. Perhaps the place was sterile even before the researchers started. Disappointed, I crawled back out on my bruised knees and felt a twinge in my ankle as I stood up.

Blinded by the relative brightness of the overcast sky, I was surprised when Ron appeared and nudged me out of the way. "My turn." As he crawled in, I didn't warn him about protecting his knees from the rocks.

Cam and Lucas stood near the cairn's entrance, chuckling as I rubbed my sore knees. I saw Lenora and

Jimmy strolling in the distance on more level ground, deep in conversation and enjoying the bucolic scenery. Sniffing energetically, Zackie amused herself with the standing stones near the ring cairn. The film crew had not yet arrived, so things felt cozy and fun with our small group. If Hannah hadn't been standing with her hand tucked in Lucas's elbow, all would have been right with my world. Lucas was going to be exhausted by nightfall if she kept this up.

I was deep in thought, trying to figure out a way to get Lucas away from Hannah, when a voice roared from close behind me. "YOU BITCH!"

I was flung into Cam, who caught me and kept me on my feet. When I spun awkwardly on my bad ankle to see who had screamed and launched me into Cam, everything seemed to shift into slow motion. Lucas stood a little to the side and in front of me, and he was forcing Rory away as the bastard struggled to get to me. When Rory drew back his hand, a glint of light flashed on metal. He plunged a knife into Lucas and I screamed. Hannah just stood there. Her face was a mix of horror and hope, and her eyes bright and eager. My last coherent thought tore like lightning through my brain— *why isn't she protecting*

Lucas? She should be protecting Lucas.

Lucas was bleeding and holding his gut, but he refused to give way. He stood between me and Rory and the knife. Before Rory could stab him again, the dead hand reached around Lucas. It caught the blade through the palm as Rory slashed down. It closed around the knife, pulling it away from Rory. My body spun with the momentum, and Lucas, Rory, and I crashed to the ground. I untangled myself and shot to my feet, terrified of what Rory would do next.

Rory scrambled to his feet. His face was blotchy red and streaked with tears. He screamed, "IT'S YOUR FAULT!" When he lunged at me, a reddish blur met him in midair, barreling into his chest. Snarling teeth and a blinding flash caught me by surprise. I didn't look away.

I clutched my eyes with one hand. Anticipating the next attack, I reached with my free hand to block it. I couldn't see. I cried out in frustration and fear. Lucas was bleeding. I was defenseless. I heard nothing but my own harsh breathing. Then Cam's trembling voice. "Lucas, you will be all right. Just hang on, okay?" In a stronger voice, "Ron, get help. Tell Jimmy." The sound of running.

Tears streamed down my face. Was it from the bright light or was I crying? "Cam, what's happening?"

"It's all right, Fia. Zackie pushed him through the portal. He's gone. You're safe now."

Everything was blurry, and my eyes burned. Vision returned. Shadows became distinct. I didn't want to see.

Hannah knelt over Lucas. She sobbed. The same words over and over again. "Lucas, I'm sorry…I'm so sorry."

Lucas was curled on his side. Cam hovered over him, pressing on the wound. But blood seeped through. It pooled around his body. Lucas stirred. He opened his eyes and looked up. "Hannah?"

His eyes fluttered shut. I feared it was for the last time. "Lucas!" I was on the ground next to him. I slid a hand to his neck. He had a pulse. It was thready and weak, but he still had a pulse. "Stay here, Lucas. Don't go. Please don't go."

The police pulled me away. Paramedics rushed in. I never heard the sirens. I tried to wipe my face. The knife was still in the dead hand. I pulled it out. No blood. No pain. It was like when I slashed it on the thorns. I sobbed. Lucas gave me those roses. I threw the knife to the ground. It was a *sgian-dubh*. Such a little knife. How could it do so much damage?

#

We were in a hospital. Antiseptics and ammonia. It smelled like Hannah. Lucas was in surgery. He'd lost so much blood. Lenora put an arm around me. We waited.

#

Lucas survived the surgery and made it through the night. It was a close thing. The surgeon told us his belly had been filled with blood. Once they drained that, they found the stab wound. It had gone through the left lobe of his liver and created a huge hematoma that the doctors had to evacuate. The story got worse. Once the hematoma was cleaned up, the surgeon finally saw the three-centimeter lesion in Lucas's abdominal aorta, pumping out massive amounts of blood. Lucas wasn't leaving the hospital any time soon.

Cam and I did what we do best. We lied. We told the doctors I was Lucas's fiancée, so they'd let me see him. When I entered the room, Hannah stood weeping near the bed. I had no compassion for her left in me. I told her to get out.

Lucas lay so very still. Something beeped with a regular rhythm near the bed, and I decided the beeping was a good thing. He was unconscious and deathly pale, but his chest rose with each breath, and one breath followed another. I felt a little reassured. I held his hand and breathed with him until they made me leave.

# # #

The police eventually came back to interview me again. I told them I had nothing new to tell them, but they insisted on hearing it one more time, in case I forgot something. I stuck with the truth as much as I could and repeated everything I had told them the first time—Rory was a stalker, and they could get a police report from New Jersey; he followed me to Boston and then to Scotland; we had a run-in earlier in the day at Culloden; after stabbing Lucas, Rory ran into the woods behind the cairns.

I stared hard at my dead hand, artfully covered in mortuary makeup. The trauma and the pain on the day I put my hand through the portal came flooding back. I hoped it was like that for Rory.

When the silence stretched on, and it was clear I would say no more, the officer cleared his throat. "Miss Saunders, we want to reassure you that we are doing everything possible to find the attacker. We've put out an all-points bulletin for Rory Craymore, and he'll be stopped at any airport or train station, or any other way he may try to flee."

I stared through the officer, not really interested. I let him think I was still in shock. They were never going to find Rory. I felt badly that they were putting so much effort into the manhunt around Clava Cairns, but I couldn't tell them the truth. I sighed and thought I better say something. "Thank you, officer. I feel safer knowing you're looking."

Zackie put her head on my knee and looked up at me with concern. It wasn't all an act. I think having a service dog made the police go a little easier on me than they might have. The authorities were desperate to close the case before the tourist season picked up again.

The officer looked at me with pity, not acknowledging my flat tone. "There's one more thing. The grandfather he was traveling with? Turns out the old man had some sort of cardiac event or stroke after you saw them at Culloden Moor. The doctors are still trying to sort it out, but he's in this hospital. He's comatose, so we canna question him. He may not make it."

That got my attention, but I kept my face blank. At least this explained why Rory wanted to kill me.

#

Ten days after Lucas almost died, they discharged him from the hospital. Maybe we should have gone home, but I felt like he would get better attention with all of us constantly around him. Also, I didn't think traveling back and forth from the US was the best thing for Lucas. Because we'd have to come back eventually. Ron still needed to be freed from Phebe, and the violent poltergeist that brought us here remained a threat.

The production company was happy to oblige a longer stay. The show had gotten a huge amount of free publicity from the stabbing, and they could film Lucas's recovery at the charming country house. I was betting that in the near future, Lucas was going to be forced to do a show about how Rory disappeared through the standing stones near those ancient tombs. Because it could have happened. Lucas had been unconscious, after all, and could not be sure what had occurred. And it was just a hypothesis. Let the viewer decide.

When the film crew put the cameras down for the day, I sat with Lucas on the settee in front of a crackling fire as we waited for dinner to be served. Lucas was getting stronger every day, but there was a shadow in his eyes that seemed to be consuming him. I put my arms around him, but I held him gently. "I'm so glad you're out of the hospital."

"Me too." Lucas squeezed back, also gently. After a pause, he spoke softly, hesitantly, like he was confessing a sin. "I saw her, you know. I was pretty sure I was dying, and I opened my eyes, and I saw Hannah. She was kneeling next to me, and she was crying." Lucas shook his head, and the shadow deepened. "She looked like she had during those last days in the hospital."

I kept silent and let him get it out. Lucas had finally had a glimpse into my world, and I knew he needed to purge the vision. Like I'd told Hannah, he's not wired for it.

He swallowed hard and stared straight ahead. "You tried to tell me a few times, but I wouldn't listen. I needed to believe she had moved on. I didn't want to hear it because I didn't want her to suffer any more." Lucas looked at me, unshed tears in his eyes. "It's my fault, isn't it? I can't let her go, so she's stuck here."

He took a shuddering breath and gathered himself. "Did you know we had our honeymoon in Scotland? When I arrived here, all those memories came rushing at me. It was terrible. I missed her so much. But sometimes, it felt like she was still with me." Lucas stopped speaking and stared into the flames. "How do I let her go?"

I sighed. I hated that he still had such strong feelings for Hannah, but she had been his wife, and he truly loved her. Really, what did I expect? And in some ways, I encouraged this weird little triangle. I thought she could keep him safe when he entered blindly into areas with active spirits. He had no defenses in those situations, and if I couldn't be there, I relied on Hannah to protect him from harm. But unlike Ralph with his Millie, keeping her safe in the woods as she wandered in the fog of Alzheimer's,

Hannah wasn't willing to wait for Lucas. I had seen the look in her eyes as she stood by, watching as the knife went in.

Maybe she felt badly about it. I hadn't seen Hannah since I banished her from Lucas's hospital room. With a mental shrug, I decided to stop trying to second guess her motives. I definitely had to stop enabling her.

Regardless of how I felt about Hannah, I owed Lucas an honest answer. "Even if you let her go, that doesn't mean that she *will* go. Moving on to the afterlife is her decision. No one can force her to move on." I paused and chose my words carefully. "Thinking about her and grieving her loss isn't what's keeping her here. Hannah is not going into the afterlife because she feels cheated of the life she felt she'd been promised. And she really loves you and doesn't want to lose you. She's suffering because she wants something she can no longer have."

Lucas hung his head. My words had absolved him of his guilt, but Hannah's suffering remained an open wound. Only Hannah could fix Hannah.

#

Jimmy insisted we show our faces to the sun and enjoy the spectacular fall day. We had been cooped up inside long enough, and it was time we got out. Lucas had regained much of his stamina, but we still aimed for just a half day at the Drumnadrochit Loch Ness Centre and Exhibition. I felt destined to buy another Loch Ness monster t-shirt.

The exhibition was spectacular. We learned that monster sightings in Loch Ness had been going on for a very long time. The first recorded sighting was in the sixth century by St. Columba. While there were probably other sightings in the intervening years, the next one recorded was in 1863. A gameskeeper saw a large fish-like animal in the waters, but his report roused little attention. There had always been a local tradition of something big living in the loch, so no one was surprised.

But things changed dramatically after Mrs. Mackay saw a whale-like creature in 1933, and an amateur journalist/water bailiff from Fort Augustus wrote up the incident for the *Inverness Courier*. The story attracted interest from the London press on Fleet Street, and the reclusive Nessie achieved celebrity status—whether she wanted it or not.

"So, what do you think she is?" Ron asked after we saw the display with all the possible explanations. "A giant sturgeon makes sense. It said they can grow to three meters—that's almost ten feet long."

"Bah," said Jimmy. "That would be what Nessie eats while she's in the loch."

Lucas, ever the practical realist, made a tippling motion. "It's most likely a combination of good scotch and a seal pod sighting, if you ask me."

"I like the dinosaur." Lenora pointed to the picture with her cane.

"The plesiosaur?" Lucas stood next to Lenora and gazed up at the picture. "Even though it went extinct seventy million years ago?"

"Has the right look. That's what people say they saw." Lenora gave a single nod, as if the matter was settled.

We ambled on to the gift store where I found a t-shirt that tickled my fancy. I also fell in love with a pen holder that looked like a family of spotted Nessies. I asked the clerk to first wrap the pen holder in some tissue paper and then in the t-shirt. My heart would be broken if it didn't survive the trip back home. There were some things a woman cannot live without.

Jimmy next took us along the loch to the picturesque ruins of Urquhart Castle. He and Lenora sat chatting in the sun, while the rest of us scrambled like little kids around the fallen stones of the castle.

Holding tightly to a rope fixed to the wall, we climbed the tight, spiraling stairs to what remained of the keep. Cam and I looked out at the loch from a window with heavy bars, probably installed to prevent selfie-taking tourists from plummeting to their deaths. The water was a blue-gray expanse with sparkling crests on the small waves that reflected the sunlight. We had recently learned that at its deepest point, the loch reached an unfathomable 755 feet. With that kind of real estate, a monster was not out of the question in my mind.

Gazing out over the peaceful vista, I blinked twice when I saw it. Nudging Cam, I pointed to the proud neck and regal head bobbing through the waves at the center of the loch. "Do you see it?"

"I do. It's definitely her." Cam looked stunned and in awe of our finding. The serpentine body formed humps behind the head, appearing and disappearing as she swam effortlessly through the water.

Drawn by the commotion, Ron came to the window. "What are you pointing at?"

"I don't see anything," Lucas said, as he leaned in behind me, pressing his body close to mine and sighting down my pointing finger.

Ron scanned the loch with a hand shielding his eyes. "Me neither."

Cam winked at me. The spirit of the plesiosaur glided through the calm waters, happy in the warm sun.

****

If you enjoyed reading SOUL SIGN, please, please write a short review on Amazon and/or Goodreads. Your review is incredibly important—it is the currency that establishes a book's worth to other readers. Reviews also enable indie authors like me to qualify for desperately needed promotional opportunities. Please make the next book possible by leaving a review now.

Many thanks for reading and reviewing.

www.reynafavis.com

************************.

ACKNOWLEDGMENTS

I would like to express my sincere gratitude to the Schooleys Mountain Writers' Group at the Washington Township Public Library, the Phillipsburg Free Public Library Writer's Group, and the Belvidere Writers' Group for their patient support in reviewing early versions of this work and offering helpful feedback. Thanks also to beta readers Mark Christmas, Dana Geissler, Rich Kliman, and Sean O'Connor for generously donating their time and providing critique on the overall story structure, as well as catching typos that I swear will put an end to me. Special thanks to Lieutenant Mark Christmas (retired) of the New Jersey State Police, for help with questions regarding police procedure. All errors are my own.

AUTHOR'S NOTES

Roseberry Homestead
The Roseberry Homestead is real and is listed in the National Register of Historic Places. All the physical details of the house in the story are accurate. The association with Peter Kinney is also accurate. Kinney was a First Lieutenant in the First Regiment of the Sussex Militia of the Continental Army and owned the Roseberry Homestead in 1787. Historical research has shown that he owned two slaves, but any association with Phebe, also a real historical figure, was fabricated for the story.

The Roseberry Homestead is located in Phillipsburg, New Jersey. If you would like to contribute to the maintenance and restoration of this historic home, please contact the Phillipsburg Area Historical Society to make a donation. http://www.phillipsburghistory.com/donations.html

Inattentional Blindness
A fascinating phenomenon. How much of the world do we miss because of this?

Simons, D. (2012, September). But Did You See the Gorilla? The Problem With Inattentional Blindness. *Smithsonian Magazine*. Retrieved from

Mark, Phillis, and Phebe

Sigh. Mark, Phillis, and Phebe were real people who suffered greatly. Mark and Phillis's stories are accurately told. They died as described in the story and Mark's body did serve as a landmark for Paul Revere. Phebe really did testify against Mark and Phillis, and she was bound for the West Indies for her role in the murder. Her rescue at the last minute from the gaol and the hair-doll were created for the sake of the story.

If, like Cam, you Google "Mark Phillis Phebe," numerous entries describing the trial and punishment of these three people will appear. The slaveowner is frequently cited as Captain John Codman; however, the article at the end of this entry is written by John Codman and cites John Russell as the slaveowner. I think there was some confusion in the records, and like all things internet, it just propagated. I went with John Russell for the slaveowner's name.

For a map of the actual sites of Gallows Hill and where Mark hung in chains, go to www.reynafavis.com

Codman, J. (1891). A Story of Old Charlestown. *The New England Magazine, 3*(September 1890-February 1891). Retrieved from https://books.google.com/books?id=G2bCEsxjtDYC&lpg=PA801&ots=qf5-sq8R8q&dq=phoebe phyllis mark&pg=PA796#v=onepage&q=phoebe phyllis mark&f=false

Lenape and Cherokee

On July 4,1866, the final treaty to remove the Delawares to Oklahoma was signed. The Trail of Tears, when the Black Cherokees were transported like chattel to Oklahoma, occurred in the 1838 and 1839. The Cherokee Nation generously accepted Lenape into their Oklahoma territory; they also owned slaves. I still don't know who to root for.

Smith, R. P. (2018, March). How Native American Slaveholders Complicate the Trail of Tears Narrative. *Smithsonian Magazine.* Retrieved from https://www.smithsonianmag.com/smithsonian-institution/how-native-american-slaveholders-complicate-trail-tears-narrative-180968339/

Haake, C. (2002). Delaware Identity in the Cherokee Nation. *Indigenous Nations Studies Journal, 3*(1), 19–45. Retrieved from https://kuscholarworks.ku.edu/bitstream/handle/1808/5780/ins.v03.n1.19-45.pdf;sequence=1

Cooper, K. J. (2017, September 15). I'm a descendant of the Cherokee Nation's black slaves. Tribal citizenship is our birthright. *The Washington Post.* Retrieved from https://www.washingtonpost.com/news/post-nation/wp/2017/09/15/im-a-descendant-of-the-cherokee-nations-black-slaves-tribal-citizenship-is-our-birthright/?utm_term=.d42d9c69e1a1

Elevator Sign

This exact sign showed up in my Facebook feed some days after I wrote the scene where Zackie licked the elevator buttons. I couldn't resist adding the sign to the story. If you want to see the picture, go to Reyna Favis Author on Facebook and search for "Trigger warning."

Glasgow Airport Terror Attack

The event unfolded as described in the story. This is perhaps the most Scottish thing ever.
https://www.dailyrecord.co.uk/news/scottish-news/ten-years-glasgow-airport-terror-10716113

Clava Cairns

The real cairns are not roofed. For the sake of the story, I described Clava Cairns as being enclosed. Other Neolithic passage graves in Scotland are roofed, and I have crawled around inside a few of them.

Search and Rescue

While many of the locations described are real, no actual case histories of searches are used in *Soul Sign*. As part of the search community, I am committed to protecting the privacy of the missing and their families.

Zackie (true name Zackie-O) is a real search dog. She serves the Search and Rescue Teams of Warren County.

Cover credits

Many thanks to Jerrye & Roy Klotz, MD for permitting use of the Roseberry House image with modification under Creative Commons licensing [CC BY-SA 3.0 (https://creativecommons.org/licenses/by-sa/3.0)].

SOUL SEEK

The 4th book of the

Zackie Story Series

from

Reyna Favis

Follow the Psychopomp to

the next adventure

Author contact information

If you would like to sign up for updates on the latest

Zackie Story, please go to

www.reynafavis.com